THE WARRIOR'S GIFT

THE
WARRIOR'S

A NOVEL BY MACK FAITH

University of Iowa Press

University of Iowa Press, Iowa City 52242

Copyright © by the University of Iowa

All rights reserved

Printed in the United States of America

First edition, 1986

Library of Congress Cataloging-in-Publication Data

Faith, Mack, 1944–

The warrior's gift.

I. Title.

PS3556.A366W3   1986   813'.54   85-24693

ISBN 0-87745-143-5

Jacket and book design by Richard Hendel

Typesetting by G & S Typesetters, Inc., Austin, Texas

Printing and binding by Edwards Brothers, Inc., Ann Arbor, Michigan

*For Upward Bound and for all kids
who still know how to dream*

THE WARRIOR'S GIFT

Chapter 1

Lenny made me do most of the driving. He said that since I had just turned sixteen, I needed the practice a lot more than he did, so he just sat there real straight on his side of the cab, hour after hour, watching out the windows as if he was looking for something. Our little caravan—the pickup and trailer I was driving and the old black Packard and its trailer behind us—had come across Nevada and the Utah desert and into western Colorado. Places like that can affect you. They can make you feel that you're lost when you know right where you're going, and they can make you feel that you're alone when you're with someone else. But it wasn't just the place. It was Lenny. I thought once, *He's got some money buried out here. He's going to find it again by recognizing a rock formation or a little valley way off in the hills.* I liked that idea. It seemed to fit him, especially if you thought maybe he got the money by robbing some little old man too weak and too slow to defend himself. I got to half expecting that he would tell me to pull off on a side road, but he never did. We kept to the pavement all the way into Colorado, and Lenny never seemed to get tired of staring out the window, studying the desert.

"Hard to believe, isn't it, Lou?" he asked.

"Louis," I said. "My name is Louis."

"Don't people get you mixed up with your father?" he asked.

"Louis was my uncle's name," I said. "And he's dead, so there's no problem getting us mixed up."

Lenny drew his thumb and one finger down the length of his nose, tracing the place halfway down where it jumped off to the right and then back again. Then he lifted his hand and spread his thumb and finger out, smoothing down his eyebrows. They were such a pale blond you could barely see them. His little blue eyes, squinted almost shut in the bright sun, shifted from me back to the highway in front of us.

"That's right," he said. "It was your uncle. And it's your father's name I've forgotten."

"What was it you said was hard to believe?" I asked.

He stroked his crooked nose again and stared ahead.

"That this was all under water," he said, after a long pause. "It's hard to believe this was all under water at one time. Don't you think?"

"I've heard of that before," I answered. "It was an ocean or a big lake or something. I guess it's true."

"Well, sure it's true," he said.

Lenny fixed his eyes on me fiercely, the way some guys do when they think you're insulting them and think you might be looking for a fight.

"It's just hard to believe now," he said, "just from looking at all this, that it was once a great body of water."

"Sure is dry now," I said.

I looked down at the temperature gauge. Even pulling a trailer across the desert in the middle of the day, Lenny's truck had been running as cool as if it wasn't working at all. I glanced into the side mirror to check the old Packard and the other trailer. They were just a few car lengths behind us, so I guessed they were doing fine. The mirror was vibrating enough that I couldn't really make out Joy and Dacia back there, much less get any idea of how the car was handling the heat, but I told myself that as long as they were able to stay with us there was probably no problem.

Lenny pointed out details as we rode along, things I admit I probably wouldn't have noticed, like ledges along the mountains that looked as if they might have been a waterline. That would have put us down at the bottom of two hundred, maybe three hundred feet of water. It was strange, trying to imagine us struggling along with all that water up above and it being miles and miles to the next place where we could come up onto the bank and out into the air. And creatures. There would be creatures everywhere. A school of fish, maybe a thousand of them, brilliant blue with colored stripes that looked like the rainbows you see in oil puddles, swam right for the windshield of the truck, then all made a sharp right turn, all at once as if they were turning on one command, their bugged-out eyes looking back at us over their big frowns as we drove past without hitting any of them. There would be all kinds of creatures.

I remembered once, when Washington was with us, we had come up into the same part of Colorado where we were headed now and had gone on a hike. Washington took me way up into the mountains. The road had gotten to be too rough for anything but a Jeep, so we parked the car in a meadow and walked from there. We followed the road for about a mile through aspens with white trunks and bright gold leaves, until we came out on a lake. It was almost perfectly round. The water wasn't moving at all and reflected the trees and sky like a mirror, like you see in pictures or on postcards. Near the water and going into the distance on the other side of the lake were big pines, tall and straight. The reflections of the trees stretched out across the water so that, as we stood near the shore, the tops of the larger ones came right up to our feet. Washington pointed to one of the treetops floating on the surface just yards from us, and we sat down carefully to watch. Fifty or sixty feet above the ground but so close I felt that I could touch it, a chipmunk was dancing through the branches, gathering up the last few bits of seed, knocking loose a pinecone here and there, ones that had lodged in the limbs and stayed there all summer.

"And it don't have a net," Washington whispered close to my ear.

Being able to see the chipmunk working that way was like floating up in the air or maybe like being invisible. It just kept going about what it was doing, not in the way they act when you try to watch them down on the ground—darting quickly, freezing, looking around, darting again. If it wasn't like being invisible—Washington and I looked back and forth at each other several times, talking to each other with our eyebrows and squints and grins—then it was like, somehow, we were not frightening the way people usually are. One thing that has always bothered me is that I have never intentionally harmed any little animal, but they all run from you or fly away if they're birds, just the same as if you had a gun and were trying to get a shot at them. I can't blame them because if I was an animal I don't think I would wait around to figure out which people were friendly and which ones wanted to eat me and which ones would kill me for no reason. But still, I've always wished there was some way I could send out a signal of some kind saying, *I'm not like the others*, and *Don't make me pay for what other people have done.*

Washington and I made our way around the lake to a clearing where half a dozen tiny log cabins were scattered in among the trees. There were four small rowboats tied up to railroad spikes that had been driven into a big log. A sign on a post by the boats said, "50¢," nothing more, and under it, swinging on a nail, a message in pencil on brown paper said, "Be back tomorrow." Three of the boats had water in the bottom and rusty old coffee cans for bailing, but one was dry, so we took that one. Washington rowed us out to the middle of the lake, pulling in low, steady rhythms. When we were as close to the center as we figured we could get, signaling each other with hand gestures and facial expressions, saying as little as possible, he pulled in the oars and let the boat and the water get calm again.

"This lake used to be a volcano," he said, almost in a whisper. "We're up over five thousand feet, and folks say the deepest part is almost down to sea level."

I didn't answer, but sitting quietly in the boat I had a feeling that we were floating in the air thousands of feet above the ocean, the way birds sometimes seem to just float up there.

"Some people come here to fish," Washington said, "but it's no use. Fish in this lake are so big from having all this room and so strong from swimming clear down to the sea and back, you can't land 'em even if you hook 'em."

"You ever try?" I asked.

"Nah," he answered. "I just come here to dream."

We lay there in the boat looking up at the sky and drifting off to sleep and waking up to the brilliant blue sky again for most of the afternoon. We finally switched ends and I rowed us back to shore. After we had the boat tied up, Washington left a dollar bill on the log, weighted with a rock so it wouldn't blow away, and we walked back to the car. On the drive home, he pulled over and stopped several times.

"Got to catch my breath," he said the first time. "You spend a little time where everything that's moving is moving deep and it ruins you for the world."

"Yes," I answered. "I guess it does."

"It takes some adjusting," he said, "to get used to being a fool all over again."

That had been at the first stop.

"You know the fish back there in that lake," Washington told me when he pulled over again, "they don't care about the bait no more."

"They don't?" I asked.

"That's the secret, Louis," he said. "Long as you think you can outfight them, you go looking for bait, and sooner or later they wear you down."

"I guess they do," I said.

"I got plenty of fight left," he said, "but there's this other way. Deeper. Deeper."

I still didn't understand, and Washington paused a third time.

"I been a warrior all my life," he said. "Spain. France. North Africa."

"And here too," I said, "when people bothered us."

"But there's this other way," he answered.

"What way?" I asked.

"I'm just starting to learn," Washington said. "My teacher says we can't win without the deeper powers, but . . . I wish I could teach you to fight, but . . . It's hard to change, once you've known how to grab the bait and get away."

"I understand," I said, because at the moment I thought I did.

That was two years ago, with Washington. Now, for the last

two weeks, we had Lenny. He was new and I was supposed to be patient, but all he had done was give a lot of orders and make me drive while he stared out the window. At least he was quiet, because that was a lot better than when he talked, always having ugly things to say.

Once we got into Colorado, I started having that same feeling I remembered Washington talking about, a feeling that I wanted to stop the truck and catch my breath, that I had been floating on a quiet lake and now I was caught in a current that had started moving faster and faster. But I didn't stop. We went right through all the little towns—Mack, Loma, Fruita—slowing down enough that we wouldn't get stopped by the local police but just passing through. The mountains were closer and closer on both sides. It was still desert, just not as flat. Straight in front of us was a big tabletop, Grand Mesa, where Crater Lake was, where Washington had taken me. The mesa was farther away than it appeared at first, because we drove and drove for a long time and it never seemed to get any closer.

Lenny unbuttoned the cuffs of his blue work shirt, tugged on the sleeves like he was getting the twists and wrinkles out, and buttoned the cuffs again. The shirt was soaked with big swatches of sweat from the heat, but he always kept his sleeves rolled down and his cuffs buttoned. The way his nose was broken and the way the right side of his face wouldn't smile exactly right—because of a scar that ran from the side of his mouth to his ear—I figured he had some marks on his arms that he didn't want people gawking at. But I had never seen his arms, so I didn't really know. He had a brown leather wallet that he carried in his shirt pocket, and he opened that on his lap and took out a metal comb and a pair of small scissors. The rest of the way off the desert he trimmed his fingernails and combed his hair and adjusted his clothes, as if he was going to meet somebody.

When we came to Grand Junction I followed the directions for the truck route. We didn't have to follow the truck routes—a pickup and a car, each one pulling a trailer house—but it was usually easier to get through town that way. Whenever we were in a town, I always felt that everyone was looking at us, would know we didn't belong. We had signs painted on our trailer, not on Lenny's, so I knew for sure everyone could pick us out as carny people. But it was funny because even with the signs, it was that old car that drew most of the attention. They don't make Packards any more, for one thing. And Joy kept it in cherry condition. It was her brother's car before he died—Uncle Louis' car—and she felt special about it. So, it struck me funny. We had put out some pretty good money to get that trailer painted so it looked like three big billboards—one on each side and one in back—advertising Joy's dancing. But even with the signs, every time we stopped in a town, little crowds of four or five people would gather around that old Packard just like our traveling show didn't exist or like old cars was the thing we wanted them to see. We stopped in a town park, along the truck route, to eat our lunch, and I said something to Joy about it— just joking.

"We should get a tent for the car," I said, "so we could sell tickets."

Joy and Lenny had squirmed around on the grass so they could look behind them. Dacia turned her face toward me, letting me know she was interested. Dacia can't see, and lots of times I would describe things for her.

"There's two men over by the car," I said. "One of them looks a lot like Washington—taller than me and thin—only he's white and has shaggy hair like a collie dog. And the other one could be his father. The grandpa is waving his arms and carrying on, telling a story it looks like, something that old Packard brought to his mind, I'd guess, because he started in when they were walking by the car. The old man just leaned on the hood, and now the younger guy is shooing him off, like a fly. He's got his handkerchief out to clean off any dirt the old man might have gotten on the chrome. Now there's a couple of kids on bikes who've stopped to ask him if it's his car. He's nodding toward us and shaking his head."

Dacia turned her face back into the sun and smiled. I don't know if it was because she thought it was funny too, or if she just enjoyed the feeling of the sun on her face, or if she was missing Washington since I had mentioned him. Dacia had a way of smiling sometimes when she was feeling sad. I guessed it was because she couldn't see and so wasn't nearly as aware of what she was doing with her face as the rest of us are, looking at faces all the time, trying to figure out what people mean by what they say.

"He always was the crowd pleaser," Joy said.

She turned back toward me and shook her head and smiled as if she was puzzling over a mystery she enjoyed thinking about.

"Who was?" Lenny asked, still turned toward the two men and the boys. "Who was a crowd pleaser?"

"Louis," Joy answered.

"Her brother," I said. "Not me."

"Everything he did," Joy said. "The clothes he liked . . . his favorite music . . ."

"Billie Holiday," Dacia interrupted. "I never knew a white boy loved Billie the way Louis did."

"Everything he did," Joy said, "seemed to affect other people like there was nothing he could do about it."

"One of the last things I saw worth seeing," Dacia said, "was the way that boy cut loose when we all went down to Denver to hear Billie sing. He was so happy. His face was shining like the sun, and he would hold on to the seat of his chair to keep himself from jumping up and down. She sang 'Strange Fruit' that night, and Louis cried right out loud. Billie come over to our table because of him, the way he cried."

Two more boys had joined the little bunch around the car. I watched them move from window to window and I could almost hear them. People were always amazed by the mohair upholstery and the silver vases inside for holding flowers and by the way we kept the chrome on the dash looking brand-new. Joy led Dacia over to the Packard, and the two of them sat in the front seat. Joy was behind the wheel, and the two men and the boys looked at them like something was wrong. Lenny watched as I got everything ready to leave. When I took the food box over to the car, I put it in the trunk and stopped by Joy's window.

"I want to make a phone call," I said.

"Why?" Joy asked.

"I met a girl here," I answered, "the last time we came through."

"We don't have much time," she said.

"But she's special," I answered.

"When I wrote ahead," she said, "I promised we would get to Delta today, so just make the call, but no plans to meet. And be quick."

"Sometimes the way we live is crazy," I said. "You meet someone special, and then two years later you pass through the town in fifteen minutes, and you don't even meet to say hello."

"If it wasn't for the way we live," Joy answered, "you wouldn't have met her in the first place."

I found a pay phone at the corner and called the number on the card I was still carrying in my wallet. Veronica Rodriguez. I had even written down her father's name, Victor. I thought it would make a good impression if I remembered her father's name. Lenny followed me and stood on the corner nearby, watching the people going by. Veronica answered, but she didn't seem to recognize me from my name.

"My mother is a dancer," I said. "You let me put a poster at the drugstore."

"Joy?" she asked. "Your mother's name is Joy?"

"That's right," I said. "You and your father, Victor, came out to see her dance."

"I remember," she said. "Red hair and blue eyes?"

"My mother?" I asked. "Joy?"

"Yes," she said. "Red hair and blue eyes, very pretty?"

"That's her," I said. "We're in town again. Delta Fairgrounds, actually, but it's not far."

"I know," she said. "My father has talked of nothing else all week but Joy and the fortune-teller."

"Dacia," I said. "But how did he know?"

"The men at work," she said. "Your mother is very pretty. They remember."

"Will you be coming?" I asked.

"At least once," she answered. "He wants me to play flamenco."

"When?" I asked.

"Tonight, maybe," she said. "He is anxious to see her dance."

"My name is Louis," I said. "You made me a belt, a silk belt."

"I remember," she said. "We talked about our dreams."

Lenny was tapping on the window of the phone booth, so I ended the conversation and hurried back to the truck with him. We continued along the truck route, and when we stopped at the traffic lights, Lenny stared openly at the young women who crossed in front of us or walked along the street on my side.

"There," he said, pointing with his crooked nose toward a young woman crossing the street. "There's a nice little ass."

The young woman's bottom and hips and thighs were wrapped in a tight, straight skirt, so tight it looked like she wasn't supposed to move. She took short steps and balanced on heels so high she was almost toe-dancing. Her long black hair swung back and forth just above her waist, covering most of the back of an orange wool jacket with black leather sleeves. Veronica had long black hair like that, but I knew it couldn't be her.

"Watch her, Louis," Lenny said. "She'll stop on the corner when she gets across the street and then she'll look back to see if you're interested . . . Look at that . . . Shake it, baby. Shake it . . . Roll down your window, Louis, so you can wave at her. Come on, Louis."

"I'm looking for someone I knew before," I said and looked up to the traffic light.

"Goddamn," Lenny said. "Ain't she a lovely thing. See there, Louis, just like I said, she's stopping . . ."

The light turned green. I looked straight ahead, eased out the clutch, and pulled forward through the intersection.

"And she's turning," he continued. "Goddamn, Louis. She's looking right at you."

Lenny leaned toward my side of the cab, watching the woman, and jabbed a couple of quick notes on the horn before I could get my arm up to stop him.

"What's the matter?" he asked.

The woman was out of sight behind us and he had settled back down into his side of the cab.

"You prejudiced against Mexican girls?" Lenny asked.

I didn't answer. Veronica's father always told me they weren't

Mexicans. Veronica said there were Utes in the family, but Victor denied it. The family was Spanish, he said, and very proud. I should never call her a Mexican because Mexicans, he said, were different.

"Some guys don't like Mexican girls," Lenny said.

I did everything I could to ignore Lenny and got us out on the next stretch of desert, headed toward Delta, as quickly as I could. I remembered when we had stopped there two years before, when I met Veronica, Washington had taken me and Joy out onto the desert and then back into a deep canyon to a place he knew about, and we had picked up shark teeth until I had about fifty of them. Washington said that it was one of the last places to dry up, so it had gotten more and more crowded with sea creatures until finally the sharks had all killed each other. I asked him how he knew about it, but he wouldn't tell. All he would say was, "You don't have to tell nobody you got them teeth off the desert if you don't want. I got close to a real fine lady telling stories about shark teeth." I kept about a dozen of the teeth, and I had put the best one in a leather pouch to wear around my neck. But after I met Veronica, I gave it to her.

Ignoring Lenny wasn't easy, but I remembered what it was like to travel with Washington, and I just tried to pretend I didn't hear anything Lenny said. I was glad to turn off the main road and glad to see the fairgrounds because it meant getting out of the truck. All I could see at first was a cattle pen with a loading ramp, two old half-dead trees back behind it, and a windmill off to the left a little. I pulled in before the road ended at the loading ramp and followed the circle around far enough that Joy could have room to pull in behind me.

"Jesus Christ," Lenny said. "Where the hell are we?"

"Delta County Fairgrounds," I answered.

"Jesus Christ," he said and pounded on the dash of the truck as if he was playing bongo drums with his fists. "What a dump."

I kept quiet. Lenny's blue shirt was drenched with sweat and his hands left dark, wet prints where he had beat on the dash, but he kept his cuffs buttoned down tight and his shirt closed right up to the top. The scar that ran off from the corner of his mouth didn't tan for some reason, so it was a jumpy white line across his brown face. But the scar turned a pinkish sort of red when he got angry, and when he saw me looking at it, his eyes darted away. He leaned back like he was going to get out of the truck and then smashed down the door handle so hard the door almost exploded open.

"Take care of the truck," he said.

Lenny jumped down and slammed the door shut behind him. I watched him in the side mirror as he marched the length of the trailer, thinking he was going to go back and tell Joy what he thought of the place. But he walked right on past the Packard and the other trailer and out onto the road.

"*Shut off the engine!* Yes, sir," I grumbled out loud in the empty cab. "*Leave the keys in the truck!* As you wish, sire. *Take a walk and cool off!* You are most wise, your majesty."

A three-rail fence looped around into an oval in the middle of the fairgrounds to make a corral. The ground inside was covered two and three deep with tumbleweeds. I walked all the way around the corral, following the fence, and I could see that Lenny was still walking up the road. Joy had gone after him. Dacia was alone in the front seat of the Packard, so I got in behind the wheel and sat down beside her.

"Where are we?" she asked.

"Well, let's see," I began, then paused to think. "Stretch out your arms in front of you like you wanted to touch the dash."

She raised her arms slowly, as if they were filled with gas and she was just letting them float, and she tilted her head back as if she was looking out through the sun visor and the roof. Her face was opened up in a broad smile that showed her teeth and the tip of her tongue. I waited, watching her until her arms rested in the air about shoulder height, and her head slowly came down to the level where she could have seen out over the hood.

"Now lean forward," I said, "until your fingertips touch the dash . . . That's good. Now lean back and relax . . . but keep your arms up floating . . . floating . . . like they are floating on a great sea, and you have just touched the mountains on the shore, and now between your hands and the shore a great long canyon has opened up in the earth and all the water is pouring out. You want to lean forward and close the break and save the sea, but you can't. You can't move. You are in a spell of sadness, and it will not let you move. The water keeps pouring and pouring and you hope the canyon will fill, but it doesn't. It keeps on pouring and pouring and pouring until the sea is gone and only a few little pools are left. And the sun is now five times hotter than it ever was before because there's nothing to cool it, and it bakes the land. You can feel it on your lap and your legs, baking and baking until everything is dried and cracked and burned. And for reasons no one can figure out, some people come along and build a little town right here, just above your knee." I touched her leg gently. "And then for some other reason nobody can figure out either, two cars and two trailers come driving all the way across your lap and down your leg and stop right before they get here where this little town is."

"Where'd you get that story?" Dacia asked, letting her arms float back down.

"A dream," I answered, taking hold of the wheel as if I were about to drive away. "Except for the people building the town and us coming here. I made that up. But the rest was a dream."

"Where's Joy?" Dacia asked.

"Walking up the road after Lenny," I answered. "The road just dead-ends here at the fairgrounds, which is really nothing but a corral and a windmill and a couple of nearly dead trees. Lenny doesn't like it here, and he's gone off up the road, and Joy has gone after him, I guess."

"You got to get us set up, Louis," she said.

"It's pretty bad," I said. "I'm not even sure we have water."

"You got to get us set up," she said. "No matter how it looks."

"I will," I answered.

I leaned over to kiss her on the cheek. She held my face up close to hers and hugged me.

"I wish you could ride with me," I said, "next time, when we move again."

"Joy and me needs to work things out," she answered.

"What things?" I asked.

"Old-time things," she said and let me go. "Now, please, Louis, get us set up best you can, whether Lenny helps or not."

I started up the Packard so I could move the trailer over closer to the windmill. I got Dacia's tent opened up off the side of the trailer, on the side away from the water tank, so she could go out the bedroom door of the trailer right into the tent without going outside and without being seen. I parked Lenny's trailer next to Dacia's and set up the tent for the Wheel of Fortune right by it, but facing away so if you were in the booth, the trailers were behind you and you would be looking out into the desert and not at the corral. The frames for Joy's stage were all aluminum and were stored on top of the trailer she shared with Dacia. It was something Washington had worked out from a setup that was originally made for boats so one man could go off by himself with a boat on top of his trailer and be able to get it down without somebody there to help him. So I got that down and picked a place far enough beyond the Wheel of Fortune that there would be room in between for a cooking fire.

We always carried a little wood to get things started, and I gathered up enough from around the old trees for the first couple of nights. Even in summer, a fire is attractive to people. It helps them gather and get close to each other, so we usually built a good fire and cooked chicken and sausage on it in metal baskets. That had been my job the last couple of years, selling food and keeping the fire up. I liked it because I got to meet most of the people who came out and also because what we made on food was one of the main things that kept us going. I set up the stage with poles holding kerosene lanterns, and built a campfire, and set up lantern poles by the Wheel of Fortune and another one so you could see your way to Dacia's tent if you wanted your fortune told. My idea was to use the fire to burn some of the tumbleweeds so the place didn't look so much like a ghost town.

Just as I got the fire going, I heard an engine and looked up and saw a new-looking Ranchero pickup come bouncing into the fairgrounds and stop right where the Packard had been parked. I didn't recognize the driver right at first, but he must have picked up Lenny and Joy on the road because first Lenny and then Joy got out the passenger side. The driver was wearing a blue hard hat. When he opened his door and it swung toward me, I could see Blue Mesa Construction Company written on it. The man in the blue hard hat stretched both of his arms up above his head as if he was reaching for something way up in the sky, even stood on his tiptoes trying to get it, then came striding across the fairgrounds toward me and the fire. He seemed almost to be racing, as if he had just so much time to get everything done before it would be too late. Lenny was about a pace behind, trotting, trying to keep up and trying to talk to him all at the same time. His hands were clasped together and his shoulders hunched forward the way people do when they're talking to someone they think might fire them or might make them important.

Joy had put on a hard hat too, a white one. She kept her hair red and kept it fairly short, so it hung from the white shell like a little curtain. Standing with one foot on the ground and the other one on the bumper, she leaned on the pickup and watched Lenny and the construction man trot along forgetting all about her, not noticing that she wasn't following. She was posed like she was supposed to look relaxed, but her body was tight, as it would be at the beginning of a dance. The heel of the foot on the ground was raised just a little. Her Levi's were snug, and it was hard to believe they could stand the stress of even a simple movement. But she rocked back and forth and the material held.

Even though she wasn't really doing anything, just leaning against the hood of the pickup, waiting, I was reluctant to look away. She might slowly, effortlessly have risen up from the ground, might have floated, might have defied gravity, stood on one foot on the bumper and swept her other foot over the hood. She might have kicked one foot above her head and spun on the other and gone off in the other direction. She seemed ready for anything, and I didn't want to look away and be sorry I had missed it. And then she moved, gathering herself into a little bundle, and was sitting on the hood with her feet on the bumper and her elbows on her knees and her chin in her hands. And with that she was just my mother, sitting on the hood of a pickup truck, waiting. Her Levi's were a little too tight to look comfortable, and her blue work shirt was a little too frayed and thin.

I could tell by their voices that Lenny and the man in the blue hat were arguing, but they got within a few feet of me before I could hear what they were saying.

"Look," the blue hat said. "The last time these people come down here they were in Grand Junction, not here."

"That's what I mean," Lenny said. "It's a waste."

"And the last time they come," the man said, "it was two niggers, a kid, and the best dancer I've ever seen."

"Then you do see what I mean?" Lenny asked.

"So now you've got it down from two niggers to one," the man said, "and I'd agree that's an improvement."

"There's more we can do," Lenny said.

"It's an improvement," the man said, "so long as it don't distract her from her dancing. I drove down to Grand Junction four nights in a row to watch her with five or six of my crew following right after me, and we all had to be back on site every morning at six. I'd have gone ten nights if she had stuck around that long."

"That's what I mean," Lenny said.

"There's no way you can improve on her dancing," the man said, "so why fuck with it? I don't care where she is. I'll be out here every night she's here to dance, and I suppose half my men will be too."

"I just need a little backing," Lenny said.

"Backing," the man said. "I've already offered her everything I've got. If she wants twenty niggers, bring 'em on, I don't care. So, if that colored gal . . ."

"Dacia," Lenny said.

"So if Dacia," the man said, "reads her cards or coins or whatever, and she says, 'Weather gone ta be good in Delta in June,' and Joy writes me and asks me to get the Delta County Fairgrounds in June, I'm happy because now she's here. Beyond that I don't care."

Lenny didn't answer right away, and I didn't want to listen any more anyway. I turned and walked deliberately toward Joy. She never took her eyes away from me as I came, and I had to glance around because looking right into her eyes was like driving toward somebody at night running their brights. You have to look away.

"How's my boy?" Joy asked when I got close enough to hear her.

"I hate the way they're talking over there," I said. "I wish I believed in killing."

"Don't worry," she said. "Tonight we'll have a fire and we'll dance. Everything will be fine."

"What happened to Washington?" I asked.

"I've told you," she said. "He couldn't come."

"Is that an answer?" I said. "'He couldn't come.' That's it?"

"It's only been two weeks," she said. "It's no big thing. Now go start the chicken. You'll feel better."

I wanted to leave. Even though the Packard was a '41, was nineteen years old, it could still get up and run seventy-five and eighty miles an hour, so I could have made it across the desert to Grand Junction in forty minutes. I would have had no trouble finding the drugstore where Veronica worked because it was right off the bridge when you come into town. I remembered walking in the park afternoons after she had gotten off work. She talked to me about her dreams, wanting to be a dancer, and wanting to go to college, and wanting to be an actress.

But I didn't leave for Grand Junction. I waited. Veronica and her father didn't come. I was ready for them and believed they would. The construction man left and he didn't come back that night either. Joy and Lenny and Dacia and I all roasted chicken together over the fire. Joy sat close to Lenny on the stools I had brought out. She kept teasing him about his collar and his cuffs always being buttoned up, but he wouldn't unbutton them. Finally, the two of them went off to his trailer.

"Tell me about the night," Dacia said when we were alone.

"There's no moon," I said, "and there are no clouds."

"You sound so sad," she said.

"It seems like everything's going wrong," I answered.

"Everything wrong?" she asked.

Dacia held her open hand up next to her face, the way people sometimes hold a hand behind an ear to catch more sound or to tell you that they can't hear, only this was up by her cheek. Her face was naturally long and thin, but it seemed even more so in that moment, as if she had changed it, the way birds can fluff up their feathers or lay them out like slicked-back hair.

"Joy and Lenny go off somewhere?" she asked.

"Lenny's trailer," I answered.

"They been together every night for two weeks," Dacia said, "ever since Washington left and Lenny came."

She moved her hand forward, testing the air.

"Why you bothered now?" she asked.

"I thought there would be people," I answered. "I thought she was going to dance."

"First night," she said. "Lots of times nobody comes the first night."

Dacia reached out further and let her hand float toward me. When her fingers were only a few inches from my skin, her hand paused and hovered as if she was touching my face, feeling it but not touching it. I could feel her hand close like it was electric. Her fingers were long and thin and moved delicately, like smoke. And as her hand moved, her face changed from a thin worried question to delight and changed again when her fingertips passed near my eyes. Her eyes squinted tighter shut and drew her face up into what looked like a smile, mouth open, white teeth showing. But she let out a little moan, which sounded more like sorrow, as if she was right on the edge of tears.

"Louis?" she asked.

"Yes," I answered.

"Do you think I'm a fake?" she asked.

"No," I said. "Of course not. That's silly."

"I'm serious now," she said. "You be truthful with me."

"I don't believe in anybody more than you," I said. "How come you're asking me that? Everything's going crazy."

"Everything's fine," she said, "long as you still trust me."

"Everything's not fine," I answered. "Lenny's evil. I think he's evil."

"Maybe," Dacia answered, "but you're going to be all right."

"And I was expecting somebody," I said.

Dacia's hand settled gently on my cheek.

"She won't come tonight," she said. "But she will come."

As she spoke, Dacia kept her hand on my face and slowly rose from her seat, like a leaf floating on water, barely moving until she was facing me, our faces level with one another, very close together. Her other hand rose to my other cheek, then touched my hair.

"She will come," Dacia said. "The fire in her heart is dim, but she will come."

She lowered herself to her knees and rested her head in my lap, and we were both quiet for several minutes.

"I'm afraid," I said, stroking her head. "Washington's gone and no one will say why. Joy didn't dance, when she said she would. Lenny's with her, and he tries to turn people against you. I'm just afraid."

"It's between your momma and me," she said. "It's a miracle we stayed together this long, but she doesn't believe in me any more."

"We're here now," I said, "because you said it would be good."

"It's down deeper, Louis," Dacia said.

"I don't understand," I answered.

"It doesn't matter," she said.

"Are you afraid too?" I asked.

"A little," she said, "but it's a little thing. Now come on. Tell me about the night, about which stars are where and which ones you feel most strong."

I found Cassiopeia and Perseus and the Big Dipper and drew out the patterns of the stars with my finger in the palm of her hand. And I went back over each one, touched each star with the pressure I felt was right. Dacia told me stories that went with the constellations until the fire was gone and it was clear that Joy and Lenny were not coming back from his trailer.

I walked her back to her tent and turned out the nearest lantern but left the others to burn out on their own. I stayed with her the rest of the night. We both felt strong from the stars and stories, as if we were as big as the characters in them, too big to be afraid of people, almost happy for the trouble we could both feel coming, and joyful, forgetting who people might think we were.

Chapter

2

Lenny came hunting me the next morning, very first thing, a whole lot earlier than I would have expected—if I had been awake to expect anything. I heard him hollering my name while I was still dreaming, while I was still running deeper and deeper into the forest. His voice got louder and louder, closer and closer, like I was running toward him when I was running to get away, and it woke me up. I heard the front door opening, the big clack the latch makes when it lets go, and felt the trailer rock when he came in, but he didn't find me because he didn't look back in the bedroom. The trailer rocked again, and the door slammed shut, and I heard him outside calling for me, but I was dreaming again.

I was looking down on an encampment in a large open place from high in the sky, not from a mountain but from the air, from higher than I would have thought any bird could fly. In fact, the campfires below me didn't look like campfires; they were stars in the night sky, little flickering lights in the darkness where nothing else seemed to be. I was flying so high I was closer to the stars than anywhere else, but I circled lower and lower until the lights became fires, not stars, burning in a great shadow of night, on earth not in space, lighting the faces of an army, most of them in colorful clothes. The brightest fire near the center of the camp drew me closer and closer.

Around the central fire the tents of the knights, not the ordi-

nary soldiers, made a large circle of banners, two on each tent, one black with a white cross, the other white with a black cross. I had seen these knights in dreams before, over and over. That night they were dressed in tunics, all white with a black cross on the chest and on the back, but sometimes in other dreams it was the other way around, with white crosses on black clothing. They were slave catchers camped at the edge of an African forest, waiting for a local tribal leader who would take them to a town, his town, his people. I had dreamed about them lots of times.

I perched on top of one of the tents to watch. The knights were eating large pieces of meat brought to them by servants who were roasting animals over the fire, as if they were preparing for a great celebration. I heard the voice again, calling my name in the camp like they expected me at the fire. I flew away from the tent but the voice came louder and louder.

"Louis! Louis!"

I was awake again. I could hear the groaning sound that heavy canvas makes when it rubs on itself. He was pulling back the flaps of Dacia's tent.

"Louis in here?" he asked.

His voice was inside, yelling, just on the other side of the bedroom door. I rolled my face out of the pillow and looked the other way, over behind me, but Dacia wasn't there. Then I heard her voice from inside the tent too.

"You shouldn't just come in here like that," she said. "You gotta wash first, in the bowl over there."

"Save it for the paying customers," Lenny answered.

"Get on out," Dacia said.

"Louis shows up here," Lenny said, "you tell him I want him."

The canvas groaned again and the metal fasteners tinkled like little bells. After a moment I could hear a low, growling hum. It grew louder and louder until I could tell it was Dacia's voice singing and chanting tones and words I could not understand, something that wasn't English. Her voice grew and grew until it filled the tent and the trailer, and as I lay there only half awake with my mouth open and my head on the pillow, I could feel the tones in my own mouth, and I realized I was singing too. Whatever the words meant, the sound of her singing, and my singing along with her in what became a gentle, swaying rhythm, was very restful, and I drifted back, dreaming about a story Washington had told me from the American slavery days.

Washington was there with me, reminding me of the stories he had told me so many times. It was in the South and we watched from the forest as a tall black magician walked into the slave catchers' camp. It was night and they were sitting around a fire, three of them. The magician was carrying a long curved sword. Washington whispered close to my ear, reminding me that the black man had been a powerful magician in Africa and that he had been taken into slavery. He had escaped himself and lived in the woods, helping slaves escape, using his magic to scare off the slave catchers that came to take them back. As Washington and I looked on, the magician stood quietly in his long black robe, with its beautiful and mysterious designs embroidered in red and green, and offered to let anyone who wasn't afraid strike him with the sword. The bargain, as I knew, was that he could return the blow when one of them had tried. There was a spell he could use to protect himself so his enemies would think they had hurt him when they really hadn't. Washington had told me he had even seen it done once himself. It was a dream the magician would make them dream with his magic. And when they thought they had run him through or thought they had cut his head off, and he woke them, and they saw that he wasn't hurt, they would be terrified and would run away. That is how the spell worked. Washington reminded me of that and reminded me too that the magician was a man from his own family and that that was why we could see him, and be there, and watch.

The magician kneeled on the ground with his head bowed, baring his neck, and a big man in a white robe, one of the slave catchers, stood over him with the magician's sword in both hands. The slave catcher raised the sword up over his head, ready to strike. Dacia had come up into the little bedroom from her tent and sat down on a pillow on the floor by the bed and began rubbing my neck and shoulders to wake me up. In spite of the fact that I was aware of her when she came in, and in spite of the fact that she touched me gently, when I felt her hand on my neck I started awake, afraid that I would see the giant sword falling on me and be unable myself to work the protecting spell, that I was about to die. I struggled to get up. Dacia held me firmly to the bed with her other hand until I was calm, until I knew where I was and what was happening.

Her hair was hidden under a bright orange scarf, and she wore a silver chain and a silver medallion around her head over the scarf, like a headband, so that the medallion hung over her forehead just above the bridge of her nose. I reached up and touched the medal with one finger and pressed it gently but firmly against her forehead. When you did that she could tell how you were feeling and sometimes even what you were thinking. She would ask people, before she would tell the future for them, to touch that medal, and press it against her forehead, and hold it there as long as they felt they should. I knew to do it without her having to ask. As I pressed the medal against her forehead her face squinted up like I was hurting her, but I knew to hold it until it was time. Slowly, her cheeks relaxed into a gentle smile, and then, for me, letting go of the medal was like letting go of a kiss.

"I was dreaming," I said.

"What about?" Dacia asked.

"Washington's great-grandfather," I said. "He was letting the slave catchers cut him with his own sword."

"Were you scared?" she asked.

"Just when I was waking up," I answered. "All of a sudden it seemed like it was me kneeled down. A big Kluxer was coming down on me with the sword, and I didn't know how to do the spell. That part scared me, but not the rest."

"Lenny's been looking for you," she said, still rubbing my shoulders and neck.

"I heard him," I answered.

"And I been reading the coins," she said. "You best come and see."

Dacia got up from the floor carefully and disappeared through the bedroom door into her tent. I sat in bed for a moment. *Even though I was awake, I saw the sword swinging down toward me, but just before it would have struck me it burst into flames. The blade wasn't steel any more but fire, though the man in the white robe continued to swing it down as if it was steel. I held my breath and closed my eyes, and I could feel the fire all around my head. And then it was over.* I wasn't afraid, either. That was one thing Washington had taught me, to finish my dreams so I wouldn't be afraid of them and to trust the dreams too. "That's how magicians learn their power," he used to tell me. "Can't nobody teach you to do something you're afraid to dream for yourself." I remembered him telling me that several times, and I could hear his voice saying it.

My clothes were up in the little closet. I slipped into my pants and a pullover shirt, washed my face and hands, brushed my teeth, and followed Dacia into the tent. She had all the flaps closed, and even though some light came through the rose-colored canvas, it was almost too dark for me to see.

"I need light," I said.

Dacia turned and loosened one of the window flaps behind her and the light danced through the tent, sparkling over the silver and gold and brass. The floor was covered with several rugs, carefully placed so Dacia would always be able to tell right where she was with her feet and wouldn't have to be reaching out with her hands or a cane. The rugs looked as if they might have come from India or Pakistan. They had that kind of design and lots of dark reds and blues. In the middle, so there was room to walk all the way around it easily, sat a low table covered with a large paisley cloth. You couldn't see the table itself at all because it was completely covered. On the floor on two sides, facing each other, were two large cushions. They looked like pillows covered with goatskin, but actually there was a way you could fill them with air and make them float. They went way back, too, to slavery and had been used by runaways to swim the river at night. The catchers would think nobody could get across without a boat, and they wouldn't really be looking to see somebody's head just bobbing along in the water.

Dacia sat down on one of the cushions, and I sat down on the other one facing her. Spread out over the cloth on the table was Dacia's special cloth for telling fortunes. It was a brilliant blue silk, light, the color of blue eyes, and so bright it looked as if it might be a lamp, giving off a glow even in the dim light of the tent. There was a design woven into the silk with gold thread, Dacia said real gold. The gold thread made a wheel with a hub and twelve spokes and a rim. At the hub and at each place where a spoke met the rim was a circle about the size of a quarter. When Dacia read fortunes she laid out coins, special coins, at each of the places along the rim, or sometimes she would have you do that yourself. The circle at the hub of the wheel and at each place along the rim had a five-pointed star in it, and the special coins, silver, the same size as the circles, had the same star on each side. The difference in the coins was that behind the star was either a man or a woman, with one point at the head and one at each hand and one at each foot. You could hardly tell by looking which were men and which were women, partly because the figures were hidden behind the stars, but each coin had a man on one side and a woman on the other. Dacia could tell them by touching. There had been other designs on the cloth outside the wheel, but what Dacia had wasn't all of the original, so the other designs were gone, and you couldn't tell what they had been.

The cloth and the coins came from Washington. He just gave them to her when he found out she could tell fortunes with them, because he said that's what they were for. Washington said they went all the way back to Africa to the magicians, that the cloth had been part of one of the magician's robes that he had somehow kept with him when he was captured. And according to Washington's grandfather, this same African magician had ordered twelve apprentices in twelve cities along the trade routes to Egypt to make the twelve coins from the same design. So they all looked the same, but each one was actually different, and only someone with the power could tell them apart. That was the story Washington had told, and none of us ever questioned it because so much of what Dacia said when she read from the coins was true.

"I've laid 'em out three times," she said when I was settled onto my cushion. "Twice they came out all women and once all men."

"What's that mean?" I asked.

"It's not good," she answered. "It means people going to be torn apart from one another."

"Who?" I asked.

"I don't know," she said. "Maybe us."

"I've been feeling something coming," I said. "I'm not scared, but I don't want it. I want to be with you."

"Hush, now," Dacia said. "It doesn't mean something bad has to happen. It just means you got to be a man. Besides, if your momma dances tonight, it ain't too late to fix it."

"I don't understand," I said.

"Things are happening, Louis," Dacia said. "Nobody knows how it will come out. But you're going to have to use the powers you got. You understand? Won't help to wish you had more or wish things were different. That'll only make you weak. You understand?"

"I think so," I answered. "I'll try not to be afraid."

"Just remember," she said, "when you think you're going to be afraid, there's nothing anybody could do to make me curse you. Nothing! As long as you know I've never cursed you, you're going to have the power."

"I don't understand," I said. "Why would you curse me?"

"It's a spell," Dacia said. "Wanting to tear us apart, all of us— you, me, your momma, Washington. But it can't work so long as you always know Dacia loves you, boy. Then you can be a man and do whatever you've got to do."

"I won't forget," I said.

I wanted to kiss her, but I could feel it wasn't the right time.

"Now go find Lenny," she said. "Don't make him find you."

"Is Lenny behind this?" I asked.

"He's part of it," she answered. "But don't ever let yourself be afraid of him. No matter what."

Even though I did not really feel that I was cleaned up and ready for the day, I got up slowly and left the tent by the door that went outside. I didn't go straight to Lenny's trailer. I didn't want to have to find him and Joy together inside, so I took the long way around, following the corral fence. There were trails wandering off in every direction. I walked all the way around the corral slowly, looking out into the open spaces to see if any of those trails went anywhere, but they didn't seem to, except out to the end of the water and the grazing. The corral was like a hub, except that the trails spoked off from it into nothing, into confusion. It was a wheel with no rim. Even just standing there looking, I had this feeling of wandering that seemed to be part of the desert.

All your experience with highways and roads tells you that following them should get you somewhere, but out there the desert seemed to be saying something different. It seemed to say that one direction is just as good as another, that the little pool of shade on your left would be as restful as the one on the right. You hear stories about people going around in circles in the desert and never finding their way out. I had thought before that something must happen to their minds because of the heat, but standing there looking off into the distance, I began to think that it might not have to do with losing directions. I kind of wished I could follow one of those trails and wander off into the mountains the way the cows do, eating and going to where there's more to eat or there's a nice place to lie down with the others and enjoy the day.

I began to think that there might be a kind of getting lost that felt as good as or maybe even better than knowing where you were, sort of the way people say you feel warm before you freeze to death, and it feels better than being so cold. Maybe people got lost out in the desert because it seemed that going one direction was just as good as going another. Maybe there was something restful, something peaceful in it, and that's why they didn't just look at the shadows to see which way they were headed. I kept following the fence all the way around until I saw Lenny, sitting on the steps of his trailer, his elbows on his knees and his head propped up in his hands.

At first I thought he was just sitting there thinking about something, but as I got closer to him I realized that he was sleeping. He had changed his clothes from the day before but he had that same covered-up look, everything buttoned up as tight as he could get it, even when he was sleeping. When I was ten or eleven years old I went through a thing of wanting to be just like Washington, wanting to be a soldier because he had been one when he was barely out of his teens. I used to button my collar and cuffs like that and imagine I was in uniform. But it came and went, didn't last very long. Someone took my picture and I was anxious to see it because I thought I'd look grown-up and handsome. I just looked like a strange little boy with a tight collar. Besides, I found out that all the time Washington was a soldier he almost never had a uniform, and that a lot of what he did was secret. I think that's what ended it.

"Lenny," I said.

I was close enough for him to hear me and several feet away in case he reacted to being awakened. But he didn't move the first time I called his name.

"Lenny," I said again.

He twitched, and was awake, and then raised his head real slow with his eyes open and his forehead wrinkled as if he had a big question to ask about something. I laughed.

"What's funny?" he asked.

"I never saw anyone wake up like that," I answered.

"I was thinking," he said.

"You were sound asleep," I said. "I called you five times, standing right here."

I wanted to see if he could catch me in the lie, but he just stared at me. The scar at the side of his mouth tugged at his face so it looked like a cover carelessly put on, like a bed made up in too big a hurry, with folds and wrinkles still there that weren't supposed to be.

"You were looking for me?" I asked. "Earlier?"

"It's your mother!" he almost shouted. "Come on!"

He did jump then, as if he had finally awakened, and he stood up and turned to go inside.

"What's wrong?" I asked, not moving.

"Come on," he answered.

"Why?" I asked, standing my ground.

"She keeps asking for you," he answered. "She tosses around

and says strange things, but I can't wake her up. Now, come on, damn it."

Lenny stepped up into the trailer, into the dark.

"Come on!" he hollered again, but by then I couldn't see him at all because he was inside the shadows.

I followed Lenny into his trailer, down the hall past the bathroom, past where I'd ever gone. I had used the kitchen and the bathroom, but I hadn't gone any further back. There was a little bedroom, and there was Lenny's room at the end of the hall. When he slid the door open, I couldn't see anything at all until he switched on the lights. The back window was covered with heavy red curtains that might have been velvet, and the walls were covered with flocked paper that had a fancy French design in fuzzy red stuff. The wall lamp was brass with a frosted glass shade that was supposed to look like an old-time lamp from a mansion. I could see the closets on the left, with mirror doors, but I couldn't see the rest of the room because there was a heavy red curtain on the right, hanging from the ceiling, running the length of the room, hiding the bed. Lenny paused inside the doorway, then turned back to me again.

"Come on," he said.

Most of the room was filled with a bed surrounded by the red curtain. The wall behind me as I stepped into the room was almost completely taken up by a huge felt painting of a naked Caribbean woman with a bright head scarf, dark skin, gold earrings, large breasts, and a cloth tied at her waist. The painting was so big and the room was so small that you couldn't get the effect of it. You just saw paint strokes on black velvet and had the idea of what the picture was about. But, really, you kind of had to guess at it. Lenny pulled back the curtain on one side of the bed, tried to cover Joy with a sheet, but had to give up because she twisted and kicked it away every time he put it over her.

"Louis," Joy said and kicked the sheet away.

She did that several times.

"Louis," she would say and kick. "Louis."

"She's been doing that all night," Lenny said.

"She's just dreaming," I answered.

Joy's skin did not tan easily, and the dark red curtain made her look even more pale than usual. She was pretty, auburn hair, red lips and fingernails and toenails, dark eyebrows, and the little tuft of dark curly hair where her legs and tummy all came together. She had a small butterfly tattoo on her leg near there. Her cheeks still had a faint pink blush from her makeup, about the same color as the little circles on her breasts. I wondered about the tattoo. I had seen her naked at different times, sometimes when she was dancing, and I'd never seen that before.

There was a large mirror over the bed, hanging from brass chains, up close to the ceiling. Most of Joy's body, except for her feet and part of her head, was reflected back in it when I turned enough upside down to look.

"Why don't you answer her?" Lenny asked.

"It's not me," I said. "It's her brother."

"How do you know that?" he asked.

"I've been living with her all my life," I said. "She dreams about him."

I looked back up at the mirror. Joy twisted and muttered something. She didn't look real in the reflection for some reason, and I looked foolish, like somebody who goes to have his picture taken at the fun house and looks completely foolish, different from when you do something for fun but you're still yourself.

"Just let her dream," I said. "It's a good morning for it."

"What if she stays like that?" he asked.

"Why should she?" I answered.

"Well, last night," he began and then hesitated. "I don't think you'd understand."

"Maybe," I answered. "Maybe not."

"We were experimenting," he said. "Imagining different people. I was thinking about my old girlfriend, and I didn't tell her who I was thinking about, but she talked to me like she *was* Darlene, my old girl. It was incredible."

"Wire walking," I said.

"What?" he asked.

"That's what she calls it," I answered. "Being someone else, as long as you can keep your balance."

"And what if she falls?" Lenny asked.

"Is that what happened to your old girlfriend?" I asked. "Maybe you pushed her?"

"You're kind of a smart-assed kid," Lenny said. "I thought you'd be worried."

He tried to cover her with the sheet again, but she kicked it off.

"Let her dream," I said, turning away from the bed. "That's my advice."

"Your own mother," Lenny said. "I'd think you'd want to take care of her."

"Guys come out and see her dance," I said, "and stay with her, sometimes all night, and then go. Lots of times she dreams afterward. You just happen to still be around."

"Don't try to fuck with me, kid," he said.

"I don't know what you're talking about," I said.

"I'm supposed to feel bad, right?" he said. "Well, I don't. Last night was great. But it wasn't 'wire walking' or anything else she's ever done before. And it's been like that for two weeks. She'd do anything I say."

"Except wake up," I said.

I was about to throw up, and I didn't want Lenny to see me, so I left him there in the trailer with Joy. I didn't see him or hear him until real late in the afternoon. I didn't see anything of Joy or Dacia either, so it was a quiet time for me to take care of things, get things ready, and think.

We needed fresh water in our tanks, and I needed to be sure the tents would stand a strong wind if one came along. I walked over the whole fairgrounds slowly and carefully, just to be a little more familiar with where we were. At the bottom of the windmill there was a waist-high metal tank maybe eight feet across with a foot of water in the bottom. It was big enough that if it had been full you could have stretched out in it and floated. Up on top of the tower a big round fan barely turned in the quiet air, but it was turning, sipping water from some place deep, deep down. Just under the hub of the big fan there were different gears and a shaft that came down and went through a mechanism with a long, smooth metal handle and vanished

· 32 ·

into the earth. I pulled the handle and the gears up on top moved. The shaft began moving, slowly. There was a pipe that ran up the outside of the tank and over the edge. Little spits and gulps of water started jumping out of the pipe, not much but a little.

I thought how much fun it would be, if the tank was full, to take all my clothes off and get in that tank at night, out there on the desert when it was hot, under the stars, and float in three or four feet of cool water, how much fun it would be to bring a girl there and look at the stars and be naked in the water, but be covered by the water so it would be relaxed and exciting all at the same time. Maybe some young lady from the town would come out to see the show and want to come back out and float in the water and dream. Maybe Veronica. Maybe Joy. I didn't know what to do about Joy.

Further back behind the corral, beyond the windmill and the water tank, two trees stood at the edge of what turned out to be a ravine. From even a little way off I hadn't noticed anything but the trees, both of them nearly dead, almost leafless, giving practically no shade at all. But when I got up closer I could see it, maybe fifteen feet deep, walls straight up and down except where the cattle had made their trails. That ravine had probably been cut out by flash floods, but it looked as if something even wilder had happened that had maybe even caused the earth to crack. That's how Washington would have thought of it. He liked to talk about how people thought they were so powerful, but how they weren't much next to real power that could make oceans turn into deserts and deserts turn into forests. I kept thinking about him and knew there had to be a good reason why he wasn't here. And I kept thinking about Lenny, about how what I really wanted to do was to hurt him, to kill him. But I also kept remembering Dacia telling me not to be afraid of him, and I knew the reason I wanted to kill him was mainly because I was scared.

I built another fire and kept it going for several hours, walking around picking up odd bits of trash that would burn and bringing tumbleweeds that had piled up in the corral. And I dragged over a couple more dead branches that had fallen off the trees and cut them for wood for the evening. Those two trees were about the same size and age, as if someone had planted both of them together when they decided to call the place a fairgrounds, but there weren't any younger ones. It kind of made me want to figure out a way to run the water over to them, but I guess you can't water a whole desert.

I put fuel in all the lanterns so the stage would be well lit, if Joy danced, and strung banners around to help people see where to go and to help them see things they might bump into or fall over. I even changed the oil in the Packard, but I was careful to keep the fire going, listening for it all the time and interrupting whatever I was doing to build it up again when it needed it.

By late afternoon I had a nice cooking fire and had chickens roasting. That's about when Joy came out. She was wearing Levi's as she had the day before, and she was still buttoning a blue work shirt and tucking in the tail as she came, so I could see she had a black leotard on underneath. She came and stood behind me while I sat on my stool and turned the chickens on their metal rod over the fire. She didn't say anything, just stood behind me real close with her legs against my back and rested her hands on my shoulders. We stayed like that for quite a while, looking out over the desert. Nothing seemed to be alive out there, nothing you could see except for the low bushes, but I wondered how far the smell of the water and the roasting meat would carry. Some people don't like to cook over fires because of that, but I like to find out what kinds of creatures are around, so I invite them.

"Chicken's almost done," I said.

"I'll go tell Dacia," Joy said.

"What about Lenny?" I asked. "Is he sleeping?"

"Poor Lenny," she answered and shook her head. "But, he'll be all right. He'll come when he's hungry."

She walked off toward Dacia's tent without saying any more and disappeared beneath the door flap. *Poor Lenny*, I thought. *The son of a bitch*. I didn't see how she could feel sorry for him.

While the others stirred themselves for supper, I kept thinking about those two trees. In a way, I couldn't help it because there I was burning their dead limbs, wondering why they were dead. It was water. They planted the trees so the fairgrounds could be a nicer place to be than just being out on the desert, and then they wouldn't give them any water. I had known a fair number of farmers from our traveling around, and lots of them were like that, stingy for the sake of being stingy. Other guys, like construction workers, lots of times would spend as if they were rich just so they'd get a reputation for being big spenders. But the farmers wanted everyone to think they were real hard to get money out of, and they would do things like start a little park and then not water it. I had learned, though, that if you didn't try to sell them, they'd come after it like everyone else.

Joy and Dacia and, finally, Lenny brought their plates and fruit, and we ate chicken, not talking very much. Joy had trouble just sitting still and paced back and forth slowly with her food, trying different rhythms in her steps and different ways of turning. One move I really liked was where she would take the last step, stretching her leg out for a long stride, but wouldn't bring that foot all the way down, wouldn't shift her weight onto it. Instead, she would pivot slowly on the ball of her other foot and roll her whole body so her extended leg would stay right where it was, only it would work out so that that leg was extended out behind her, not in front. It was real smooth and easy but with that feeling you like of watching things that seem impossible when you know they aren't. I watched her and wondered why it was that a dancer could make walking look like the most amazing thing, which I guess it is.

Joy was the first one finished, didn't eat very much, and went to the little stage I had made and began her warm-ups. Dacia was much slower with her food, pausing regularly to hold one hand over it, palm down, as if she was praying. It wasn't exactly prayer. I had asked her about it several times. She said it was just what she had to do to have respect. I didn't do that myself, hold my hand over my food, but I always liked it when I ate with her, and I would think about the chicken that probably never got a chance to get out of the cage in its whole life, or the orange growing up on a tree out in the sun with bees and butterflies and then suddenly going inside a dark box and a cold truck and bouncing along for a couple of thousand miles to get eaten by some hungry kid who might gobble it down without even thinking.

I watched Dacia and tried it myself, holding my hand over the chicken to respect it. Lenny saw me do it, and he smiled, a crooked smile because of that scar. He tossed a bone into the fire and came back for another piece.

"You take up religion?" he asked.

"Just respecting my food," I answered.

"The chickens?" Lenny asked and laughed.

"Yes," I said. "The chickens."

"Respect the greedy bastard that raised 'em and killed 'em," he said. "It's greed that feeds you, kid."

"The Indians say you can love the animals you hunt," I said. "I believe that. I don't think it's funny."

"Indians," Lenny said. "If one of these ranchers out here loves his cattle, loves their big brown eyes, and feels sorry for them because they are so dumb they can't protect themselves, can't do anything but eat and get fat and wait, then he can't bring himself to sell them because he knows what will happen to them. But if he's greedy, instead of big eyes and dumb looks, you get big juicy steaks and barbecued ribs."

"And he'd rather kill them himself," I said. "More money that way, right?"

"It's not just money, Louis," he said. "It's control. He starts out nobody. He gets the cow to eat the desert, and he sells the cow. When he does, he has changed nothing into something, a ranch, a kingdom. And if he's a man, it changes him from a slob with cowshit on his boots into somebody people have to deal with, have to respect."

"I think I'm going to throw up," I said.

"Maybe you need to lie down," Lenny said. "Use the trailer. Use my room. I'll wake you up when Joy and I need the bed."

"Son of a bitch," I said and stood up, holding one of the long, hot steel rods.

Dacia turned her ear toward me, and Joy stopped and looked.

"Louis!" Joy shouted. "Let's get started."

I dug into the trunk of the Packard and brought out the drums.

We had several different kinds, because of the different dances but also because people who came liked to try them out, the congos and the bongos and the tom-tom—and a small log drum. It was only about the size of a fireplace log, not a tree trunk, but it was hollowed out and then cut so that on top there were several slots that made wooden fingers. You'd tap those wooden bars with the beaters and they would make different tones over the hollowed-out space. It was really a lot like a voice singing. Dacia knew different dances she could play on it and you'd recognize them when you heard them over again, but quite a bit of the time when she played it she'd just start in and go wherever it took her.

I just about had the drums set up when I heard and then saw an old blue Ford, a '49 or a '50, bouncing and lurching up the dirt road toward us. Other than the construction man, it was the first sign of human beings we had seen since we stopped there, and I glanced around to see how we looked. Tents and banners always look a little better after it's dark and you have the lights on, but other than that—because it was still at least an hour before dusk—we looked ready, like the place belonged to us.

Most people when they come to a sideshow or a carnival will try to park out on the road where there is no chance of getting blocked in, so they can leave anytime, and so they always know they can leave. Even the first car, when it looks like no one else is around, will usually do that. I've seen it over and over. But this Ford pulled in off the road and followed the corral around, moving slowly past our trailers and our tents. All the windows on the car were tinted dark so I couldn't see who was inside, but they drove all the way through, out onto the road again, and back around again. The Ford stopped, backed in as close to the stage as it could get without disturbing the banners I had strung around, and then sounded one of those trick air horns that plays a little melody.

La Cucaracha
La Cucaracha

The door handles had been shaved off, along with most of the original chrome trim, and had been replaced with electric latches, so the door popped when it opened.

The man who got out was short, and he was round in the tummy, not real short and not fat, but it was something you noticed. He was wearing black boots with high square heels and narrow, almost pointed toes, Spanish style. His pants were also black and so tight that he had to tug at them so the fly wouldn't pull and let the zipper show. The waistband was high and wide, up above where the waist was on Levi's, and was partly covered by a bright red vest with black buttons and black trim. He had a gold chain running across the front of the vest from one pocket to the other with gold coins hanging from it. Under the vest he wore a ruffled white silk shirt with white pearl buttons. His black hair was combed straight back and shone like the Packard when it was washed and waxed. I should have recognized him, but he was wearing black wraparound sunglasses that hid his eyes and cheeks and brows.

"Victor Rodriguez," the man announced when we were all turned toward him. He lifted the glasses from his face slowly, like a lover might reveal a bunch of flowers he had been hiding behind his back. "Everything is okay now."

Chapter

3

Victor moved around our little group like he was a doctor and we were there because of a disaster of some kind. It was as if we were huddled near a fire in the desert in the bright and warmth of the early evening because we had survived a horrible event, whatever it was, and were afraid not to build a fire, not to eat, not to stay together. Victor was going to be our comforter. He walked like that, keeping his body as straight as possible, though he had to hunch a little so his vest wouldn't ride up the curve of his tummy. He circled the fire once with long, relaxed strides, as relaxed as his tight pants would allow. He was showing himself to us. If we were still troubled, or fearful, or anxious, he was letting us see him, see that he was calm and everything was okay.

Once he had circled the fire, he stopped by Dacia, squatted down without a stool, said something quiet, up close to her face, something I couldn't hear, and touched her easily on the shoulder. It was not as if they were old friends but as if it was perfectly natural for him to be familiar with her, the way a doctor might move through a group and reassure people by touching them. Victor and Dacia both laughed at whatever he had said. She held out her chicken to him, offering to share it. He tore off a tiny piece, not even enough for a bite, slipped it into his mouth, touched her shoulder, said something quietly to her again, and stood up. Lenny was watching him as carefully as I was, but sideways, not just looking right at him the way I did. Over on the little stage Joy was stretching and warming up and gave no sign that she had noticed anything.

Victor's clothes were all out of adjustment from sitting, and he had to tug at his pants legs to get everything in order again. Nothing had happened to his shoes, but he shined them anyway, balancing on one foot, lifting the other, pointing it sideways so he could rub the toe of the boot on the back of his other leg, a couple of quick strokes, then he shifted to the other foot to polish the toe of the other boot. All of this happened quickly, back and forth, back and forth, from foot to foot until he seemed satisfied that his appearance was restored and he could circle the fire again. In all of this his wraparound sunglasses never moved. The curved lenses covered his eyes both from the front and from the sides and never slipped, as if they were the only part of his costume that really fit.

Watching the way Victor moved, the way he held himself and the way he took his strides, kept making me think about a time in Florida when we were hooked up with a little circus. It surprised me to be remembering it, but there had been an accident. Something wasn't right with the rigging, so when the highwire walker went up to go through his routine, he complained, and they sent up a rube, with a big wrench, half the size of his body, to tighten things up. But the rube fell. He held the big wrench tight in both hands all the way down, like he couldn't remember he was supposed to holler a warning and was supposed to throw it. He never screamed. He hit on his back still holding the wrench, and it smashed his head, and he was dead without a whimper. And then the ringmaster appeared. That's what Victor was reminding me of. The ringmaster appeared, it seemed from nowhere, and while people came to take care of the dead man, the ringmaster walked around and around the outside of the ring with great long strides, holding his arms stretched out, commanding everyone's attention. Victor had that same way of moving that insisted that everybody look at him, but for a reason, not just because he liked to be noticed.

The thing was I had no idea why he felt he needed to do that.

Lenny was trying to pretend there was nothing to notice. Joy was not about to be distracted from her exercises. Dacia couldn't watch him, so it was just me. There wasn't any other crowd, and I wondered if Victor was in some strange place in his mind where he thought there was a crowd. So I watched him carefully as he circled the fire, two, three times, and then came and sat beside me.

"Hey, Louis," he said and put his arm around me. "Where'd you get your red hair?"

I did not want to answer, so I looked into the fire as if I hadn't heard anything. My mother always kept her hair auburn, so it might seem like a funny question, "Where'd you get your red hair," but it was really dark brown. She dyed it. He knew that from sleeping with her, I guess. I knew what I was supposed to answer. I was supposed to say, "From the iceman," and then he was supposed to laugh. It was a routine. I had learned years before that people thought it was funny to see a kid say that in front of his mom. I had picked it up and given that answer for a long time before I understood what it meant. I had just liked getting the laughs. But I was tired of it now. I remember once I told Washington I was tired of people asking me that and he told me to tell them I'd got my red hair from him. Washington actually had a brother who was black like him and had red hair, but most people couldn't imagine that. I laughed out loud remembering.

"What's funny?" Victor asked.

"Nothing," I said. "I was just thinking it's been a long time since anyone asked me that."

"For me," he answered, "it has been two years."

"Two years what?" I asked.

"Two years since I have seen you," he said, "and your beautiful mother. A very long time."

His voice trailed off into his thoughts and he was quiet for a moment, staring into the fire with me.

"But all that is changing now," he said with a start. "The past is gone now, and we must celebrate. Yes?"

"Celebrate what?" I asked. "What do you mean?"

"I have come for the job," he answered. "We will be brothers."

"What job?" I asked.

"The driver," he said. "Mr. Leonard, he told my boss he needs a driver, a strong man, to put up tents, to travel one year without quitting."

"Lenny has big ideas," I said.

"Yes," Victor said proudly. "He knows there is no woman like her."

"Like Joy?" I asked.

"Yes," he said. "I have only heard of one woman who can dance as she dances, and that woman is in Spain, a very long way away. And I have only heard of her, but I have seen your mother. It is not right this way that so few should know her. Everyone must see her. Everyone."

"Everyone?" I asked.

"Yes," he answered. "Big plans. Mr. Leonard was wonderful, big plans. But, you are here. You know these things already. We must celebrate. Veronica!"

He turned his head toward the car and yelled again.

"Veronica!"

"She's here?" I asked, standing up.

"In the car," he said. "A shy little bird, waiting for you to come and bring her out."

As I walked toward Victor's Ford I glanced back to see him straightening his clothes and approaching Lenny. The two men shook hands, though Lenny never got up from his stool.

Victor had left the driver's door slightly ajar, and I probably could have gotten in from that side, but I walked around the front of the car to the passenger door—glancing quickly at the tinted windshield as I passed and then into the tinted side windows, seeing only my reflection. There was no handle on the passenger door either, just smooth metal and the expensive-looking blue paint. I searched for the little button I knew was there somewhere to trigger the electric latch. I never did find it, but the door popped open. Veronica looked amused. I guess from the inside I must have looked pretty foolish, trying to figure out how to open a car door, unable to do it.

Inside the blue Ford everything that could be upholstered was upholstered—white—and that was everything except the dark blue carpet and a few highlights painted blue here and there, like the steering wheel and the metal frames around the windows and the gauges. Even Veronica's dress was white, with big puffy sleeves and a full skirt. She had a turquoise and lavender sash tied around her waist, and even that went with the blue. Her dress had a V neck that made a sharp point that just touched the top of the sash. I tried not to stare. It was July and the girls wore summer dresses and you were supposed to act like there was no big thing to it, but it wasn't always easy.

Veronica's eyes were as bright and sharp as I remembered them, and I immediately felt the effect of being watched by her. We read something in correspondence school once about whether or not a tree makes a sound when it falls if there's no one in the forest to hear it. And that came back to me as I looked down into her black eyes, wondering, as I had before, whether or not there weren't some things about me that were visible only because she was there to look. It was a little embarrassing, and I felt I blushed—whether I did or not—because I felt she was changing me just by seeing me. It was embarrassing because I would have liked to think that I was myself and that other people would have to come on with something pretty strong to change me, even though there was no doubt at all that when I let myself feel that I really was the person she created out of her eyes, I liked that person better than the usual me.

"There's no button on this side," she said.

"No wonder I couldn't find it," I answered.

"Want to sit down?" she asked.

Her hands were folded in her lap, but one of them held a pinch of material, so when she let go to use her hands to scoot across the seat a fold in the material fell away and revealed a mended tear in the dress. Once she was behind the wheel, her right hand tucked quickly under the skirt, under her right knee, lifted it and carried it over close to her other knee so her legs were together again, and then caught the fold of material, all in one motion, and concealed the rip again.

I sat down on the passenger side, closing the door behind me. With the door shut and the tinted windows I could see, but it was darker than I had expected.

"I was going to say, 'It's good to see you again,'" I said, "but I can't see you very well."

"How's this?" she asked.

An interior light came on, bright, slowly dimmed, and came back up so I could see without there being a glare.

"This car's got everything," I said.

In the middle of the dash, under the rearview mirror, standing waist deep in white nylon fur, a cream-colored plastic statue of the Virgin Mary seemed to be glowing. I reached out and stroked the nylon hair and ran my fingers through the fur until they touched the statue, gently.

"Something else, isn't it?" Veronica asked.

"Yes," I answered.

"Watch," she said.

The light in the statue brightened and then dimmed.

"Is it because he believes," I asked, "or because he doesn't?"

"I don't know," she answered. "Everyone else had stuffed animals in the rear window with turn signal eyes. I think he just wanted something different."

She sounded amused and I couldn't help chuckling as she brightened and dimmed the Virgin two or three more times.

"I'm glad you're still here," she said, turning out the light in the statue.

"Shouldn't I be?" I asked.

"We heard there was trouble here yesterday," she said. "That's why we didn't come last night."

"What kind of trouble?" I asked.

I was looking directly at her, deliberately—her hands tugging the folds of her skirt into position, adjusting the neckline of her dress to reveal and then hide the hint of a suntanned breast, brushing her hair back over her ear—trying to see her as she saw me. Her hair was even more deep and brilliantly black than I had remembered. And her lips, bright red with lipstick, were more full and womanly than I recalled. She seemed to know that I was feeling foolish because she pushed her lips into a pout and melted my stare. I should have realized that in two years the last traces of the girl would have disappeared. But I hadn't thought about it until I was there, looking at her, and there was no girl for my eyes to change. I was still staring, and she waited, didn't answer, just stared back.

Outside, Dacia had begun a rhythm on the drums, and we sat looking at each other, listening and not saying anything for some time. I was familiar with all the dances Dacia regularly played. Part of the dance she had just started up was to say people's names, people special to you. Once I saw a whole audience whispering out so many names, following the lead as Joy drew name after name from her own lips and freed them to the wind with a sweep of her arm, that the whispering sounded like a wind, an actual wind. Two or three times, moving with the music, I opened my lips to say her name—Veronica, Veronica— but no sound came out. And I raised my hand to touch her— her chin, her cheek, her ear—but didn't. Finally, I looked back at the dash.

"What kind of trouble?" I asked again.

"We heard that Lenny and Victor's boss had an argument," she answered, "and that Lenny wasn't going to let Joy dance until it was settled."

"Nobody owns Joy," I said. "Nobody tells her when she can and cannot dance."

"Then, they called today," she said, "and told us everything was worked out, that Joy would dance after all."

As she spoke, Veronica tucked her right leg up even tighter against her other leg, folding and refolding her skirt.

"Who called?" I asked.

"Men from work," she said. "From where Victor works."

"Would you have come anyway?" I asked. "Would Victor have come?"

"These men influence him," she said. "They call him a Mexican, and they don't like to hire Mexicans to work on the dams. He is proud, but he worries about his job."

"He was just talking to me like we were old friends. He called me his brother," I said. "But he thought we were having trouble, and he wouldn't come because of the other men on his job?"

"My father is a good man," Veronica said. "He has much love in his heart. But he is not brave, not courageous."

Dacia's song with the drum was concluding.

"But when he got out of the car tonight?" I asked.

"Victor Rodriguez," she imitated his voice. "Everything is okay now."

"Yes," I said.

"He meant the job," she said, "driving the truck."

"Jesus Christ," I said.

"They don't let Mexicans drive company trucks," Veronica said. "The boss picked him. He's proud."

"What job?" I asked. "What truck? Why haven't I heard anything about any of this? What the hell is going on?"

"She's finished the dance," Veronica said, turning her head toward the tiny stage. "We've missed it."

"There will be more," I said.

"You see her all the time," she said, looking back at me. "For me it's still special, something to remember."

"You still want to be a dancer?" I asked timidly, barely saying the words.

"An actress," she answered.

"But, Veronica," I whispered, "I remember you dancing, with Joy, and swearing that if she'd teach you . . ."

"Well, it's over," she said and touched her leg. "I can walk, with a cane, but that's all. I'm going to school this fall to study acting."

"What happened?" I asked.

"This is hard, Louis," she said and paused. "When I knew you two years ago, I was beautiful."

"You still are," I said, but she stopped me with her eyes.

"I have a boyfriend," she said. "Danny. He's like you, not Spanish. He likes to drive fast, to race, so he made them chase us in his car."

"Who?" I asked.

"The same men," she answered. "The ones where Victor

works. They don't think Danny and I should go together to certain places. But Danny is stubborn and he likes to take me to nice places, to eat. They said something to him and he said something to them. He didn't tell me what, but it made them mad, and they chased us. Danny wanted them to because he knew they couldn't catch us. His car is very fast, and he is not afraid. We went off the road and went over and over. Someone finally came. Danny had to stay in jail, but he's okay now. I have to walk with a cane."

"Always?" I asked.

"Maybe," she said. "Maybe not."

"Do you still go out with him?" I asked.

"He says he wants to marry me," she said. "And he wants me to finish school in whatever I want."

"But you can't just say, 'Oh, well, he almost killed me,'" I said.

"I'll tell you something that matters," she said. "You should appreciate what you have."

She paused and drew a deep breath.

"When you came," Veronica said, "all of you, two years ago, I was beautiful, and I was on fire. I saw Joy dance and something happened when I watched her. I saw what happened to my father after he saw her and after he stayed with her, and I knew what I was going to do with my life. I met you and I felt like I had my first real friend. It was wonderful. I was so happy."

She paused again, this time for several breaths.

"And the other thing that happened," she said, "was that Dacia laid out the coins. She saw two men, and she said I would fall in love with the dangerous one. She saw this coming. She warned me, and she told me what to do, but when you were gone, and I was by myself, I didn't believe her."

She turned toward me, and I thought she was going to cry and I was going to hold her. Her eyes were moist, but she didn't cry.

"I came to tell you I am ashamed," Veronica said, "and to ask you to forgive me."

"You don't have to do that," I said.

"I still have this," she said.

She pulled a small leather pouch from her purse, opened it,

showed me the shark tooth, put it back, and took out a coin.

"Dacia said a magician, a powerful magician gave it to you," she said, "for protection."

"Washington," I answered, but stopped myself from saying more.

"She told me how to use it," Veronica said. "But I didn't believe her. Not until it was too late. So, I came to ask you to forgive me, and to return your coin."

"Keep it," I said.

"Are you sure?" she asked.

"Yes," I answered. "Dacia gave it to you."

"I wanted you to know," she said and slipped the pouch back into her purse, "that Dacia knew it was coming. She told me to be careful, and I didn't listen. But I wanted you to know that the power she has is real and that I know it's real."

"Thank you," I whispered. "You're still beautiful. I'm still your friend."

"I'm sorry, Louis," she said. "I know it wasn't fair."

"Fair?" I asked.

"I'm sorry," she said again. "But it's done. I need to see her now. Will you help me out of the car?"

"Of course," I said.

I opened my door and walked quickly around to the other door to support her while she stood.

"My cane is under the seat," she said.

I leaned in past the wheel, fumbled under the seat until I found the cane, and brought it out for her. She made her way over to the fire and stood next to where Dacia still sat. Once she was moving, her walk was smooth and graceful. The cane seemed mainly to help her start and stop and change direction. Victor and Lenny sat near the fire, roasting chickens and talking in low tones.

I found Joy in her trailer. She was sitting on the edge of the bed, staring into the mirror on the built-in dressing table. I had thought she would be changing into a costume, but she wasn't. She was just sitting there, not moving except to draw a deep breath and go on looking at herself. I stood quietly in the doorway watching her, until she finally looked up at me and smiled.

"I'm supposed to be dressing," she said, still not moving. "I'm glad you're here. You can help."

"We have to talk," I said.

"Now?" she asked.

She turned her face toward me with a puzzled look. Seeing that confusion in her face scared me, just for a moment, the way you sometimes feel a rush of panic when you wake up from a dream and don't know where you are for sure.

"We have to talk now," I said.

"But I have to dance," she said.

"It's only Lenny and Victor," I said, "and Veronica. They're eating. Veronica's talking to Dacia. We have time."

"I've never had trouble like this before," Joy said, looking back into the mirror.

"Like what?" I asked.

"Waking up," she answered. "Dreaming and waking up."

"What do you mean?" I asked.

I sat on the floor, leaning against the doorframe.

"Sleeping and dreaming and waking up," she answered. "Dancing and dreaming and waking up."

She paused and glanced at me quickly. I wanted to hold her and rock her and tell her she didn't have to talk, but I also felt that nothing was really wrong, that we were just afraid.

"Do you think I'm a whore?" she asked.

"No," I answered.

"Some people do," she said. "You know that some people do and that they have reasons to."

"I don't care what people think," I said, "and neither should you. You've always said you don't."

"Dancing and dreaming and waking up," she said slowly, carefully pronouncing each word. "And making love and dreaming and waking up. I've never had trouble coming out of it before now."

Joy took a deep breath, straightened her back, lifted her head high on her neck. The blue jeans and the work shirt suddenly looked ridiculous on her. They were for the wrong world, and I could see why she needed the costume because she was in the dance already.

"But you didn't come to talk about my dreams," she said. "You wanted to talk about something else."

"Yes," I answered.

I had wanted to be angry and insist that she tell me what I wanted to know, and she had made that seem impossible now. She was so sad and afraid.

"Victor and Veronica," I said, "both say that Lenny wants to hire someone to drive for us."

"That's right," she said. "Didn't he tell you?"

"No," I answered.

"Well, he should have," she said.

"Why do we need a driver?" I asked.

"We're getting a truck," she answered and paused and gathered her posture again, "and another trailer."

"Where do we get the money for all that?" I asked.

"Lenny signed a contract," she said, "for a year."

"To do what?" I asked.

"To dance, with a circus," she said.

"Just to dance?" I asked. "What about the rest of the show?"

"That's why we need the other trailer," she said. "We'll all travel together, but the rest of you will have to set up separately, as usual."

"And when does all of this begin?" I asked.

I wasn't angry. I was astonished, as if someone had just told me the sun wouldn't come up or a river was on fire or something like that.

"Soon," she said.

"How soon?" I asked.

"The truck comes tonight," she said.

"The trailer?" I asked. "When does Mr. Leonard buy that?"

"The trailer is already mine," she said, looking down into her hands. "Like the Packard. It was Louis' and it's been mine all these years—since we lost him."

"So where is this invisible trailer?" I asked, standing up. "I mean, if we've got to have a driver and we've got to have a truck and we've got to have them tonight, this trailer must be here, and I just can't see it."

I pulled at the curtain as if I was looking out the window.

"I see Lenny's trailer," I said, "and I'm standing in your trailer, yours and Dacia's, but I just can't see the other one."

"The truck is for this trailer, Louis!" Joy shouted. "Now stop treating me like I'm crazy. I don't like that. Even if you're just angry, I don't like it."

"Then say something that makes some sense," I said and sat back down against the doorframe.

"Lenny should have told you all this," she said.

"Well, he didn't," I answered.

"The truck isn't really ours," she said.

She brushed her hair back over her shoulders with her hands.

"It belongs to a construction company here," she said. "Lenny's known the owner for years. He was out here yesterday. He was against it, but Lenny talked him into it. We get the truck for a year. If it works out, if we make good money, they get a percentage for the use of the truck, and we have a home base here."

"Delta, Colorado?" I asked. "Home base?"

"It's business, Louis," she answered. "It's hard to get these contracts without an address. That's one reason we've never gotten them before."

"We never wanted them before," I said.

"This will be Dacia's trailer," she said, as if I had not said anything at all. "The truck is for this trailer. Victor will drive that and work for the circus, setting up tents and so on, and that money will cover the cost of having Victor drive and take care of Dacia and maybe Veronica, if we can talk her into coming along, so Dacia has another woman to be with. And you and I, Louis . . ." She paused and looked me in the eyes and waited until she could go on without looking away. "You and I are going to take the Packard and drive to my father's farm in Kansas and get Louis' trailer, my trailer, and visit my father for a few days, and meet up with the others in Wichita. That's the plan."

"Mr. Leonard's big plan!" I yelled. "Jesus Christ. I can't believe you're going along with that. I can't, cannot believe that you let that son of a bitch sell you to the highest bidder."

"Like a whore?" she asked.

"That's not what I mean," I said. "You and Dacia have been together all my life."

"She was there when you were conceived," Joy said. "Don't try to act like I don't know something important is happening, because I do know it."

"Have you talked to Dacia about all this?" I asked.

"She thinks it's a mistake," Joy answered.

"And you're going ahead anyway?" I asked.

"I thought you would understand," she said. "I have to think about Dacia, but I have to think about other people too."

"Like who?" I asked.

"Like my father," she said. "I really thought you would understand."

"Well, I don't understand," I answered. "For years I begged you, 'Tell me about my daddy.' 'Can't we go see Grandpa?' 'Why not? Why not?' And you had all kinds of answers, but they all added up to 'This is your family. Carny people. Free people.' Now I'm sixteen, and I'm beginning to think for myself that I'm the lucky one, not the kids with their 'real' families who are too scared to live, and you think I'm going to understand why we're leaving Dacia and going against what our guidance tells us we should do. Something's happening to your head. Something bad."

"Don't talk to me about guidance," she said.

"Somebody needs to," I answered quickly.

"My father needs me," she said.

"How do you know that?" I asked.

"Lenny told me," she answered. "And I've called him since then."

"You never told me that," I said.

"I'm your mother," she said. "I don't have to tell you everything."

"You don't *have to*, but you could have," I said. "I've got other things I could be doing with my life. So, what's *have to* got to do with anything?"

"It's the dreaming, Louis," she answered. "I sleep and I dream. I dance and I dream. I make love and I dream. What else is my life? Making dreams. And for years they were about everything and everyone you can think of. But now they are always the same. I see my father standing by a fire, crying. I saw him tonight while I was dancing, just now. I call to him and call to him, but the only time he hears me is when I promise him we'll come. And it's the only way to come out of the dream. To promise I'll come. Tonight when I was dancing—and last night with Lenny too—I tried to come out without making the promise, but I couldn't. I just couldn't." She hugged herself and shuddered as if she had a chill.

"Maybe I understand more than you think," I said, standing up again.

"I have to get ready now," she said and straightened herself before the mirror. "I have to dance."

"Maybe if you trusted me more," I said. "Maybe if you treated me more like a man instead of just your son."

"You are my son, Louis," she answered. "I have to get ready."

"Dacia thinks it's a spell," I said quickly, "and so do I. And I think it's a mistake to split up. And I think you won't listen because I'm your son."

"And you think you could take me into that dream," she asked, "and bring me out without giving in to him? Without promising him?"

"Maybe," I answered.

I was scared and my voice quivered.

"It's not a game," she said. "I'll tell you for sure, Louis, if you can take me in and bring me back out free, I don't care who you are. Son, father, mother, brother. I'm serious. It doesn't matter to me who you are. Somehow my life got stolen, and I can't go on much longer without it."

"I dream too," I said. "Maybe I could do it. Maybe I could."

One button at a time she began to open her shirt, all the way down to where it tucked into her jeans. She paused and looked at me. I didn't look away, and I didn't move either. She unbuttoned the cuffs and pulled the shirttail out of her pants and slipped the shirt off her shoulders. What had become familiar to me from our life together—her dance costumes, the contours of her body—was new to me then, as if I had never seen

her breasts pressing through a leotard. She ran a finger back and
forth along the scooped neckline, watching to see that my eyes
were following, and touched the zipper that would have opened
the suit to her waist. Her face was a question.

"Please, Joy," I whispered. "Let's just go to Wichita with the
others."

"I have to get ready," she said.

She stood up, turning her back to me, stepped out of her
jeans, and dropped them on the bed. She held herself straight in
the leotard, like a diver before the plunge. I heard the zipper and
watched as she slipped the black material off each shoulder,
baring her back to the waist.

"I guess you were right," I said.

"About what?" she asked and froze.

"I guess I am just your son after all," I said.

"Oh, I don't think it's that," she answered.

Joy slid the leotard far enough down her legs that she could
step out of it and drop it on the bed with her Levi's. She was
naked, pale, untanned.

"If it was that," she said and turned to face me, standing
straight, unembarrassed and unashamed, giving no sign of awk-
wardness that I could see, "if it was just that, we could erase the
doubts, if there are any. I know I'm a woman, Louis. I know
you're a man."

"Then what is it?" I asked. "Why not just give up this plan?
We've changed before, at the last minute."

"It's because you and I both know," she said.

Joy stepped close to me and slipped into my arms.

"We both know," she said, "that the dream is stronger than
either of us."

I held her for a few moments, and she cried quietly and
briefly, just a few little sobs that heaved her body against my
chest.

"I can't go on this way," she said, pulling back matter-of-
factly, as if I had performed some routine service, washed her
windshield or something. "Someday I'll go into that dream and
never come out if I don't do something about it."

"I think I understand," I said. "I hope I do."

"I have to dance now, Louis," she said.

"I'll go wait with the others," I answered.

I left as quickly as I could without running. As I stepped down from the trailer, I saw that the construction man had arrived with the truck. Victor and Lenny were following as he led them around it, pointing out its features. I couldn't even make myself pretend I was interested, so I walked to where Dacia and Veronica sat talking by the fire and sat with them.

"How is she?" Veronica asked.

"She's getting ready," I answered. "You'll see her dance, I'm sure."

I wanted to stay there with them, with Dacia and Veronica. I wanted them to have a vision and see that what had seemed to be a little fire somewhere, just a puff of smoke, no big thing, had exploded, that my whole city was burning like Chicago had or San Francisco, that there was nothing to do now but search for cool air to breathe, a place to be quietly thankful that I wasn't dead in my sleep. I wanted them to understand without my having to explain. But I was afraid to stay there with them, afraid they would ask more questions and would want to talk. Just as I stood up again to move I heard the trailer door and saw Joy coming.

She had knotted two corners of a large red scarf behind her neck and connected the other two corners behind her back. I couldn't tell how they were connected at first, but as she passed I saw a short gold chain with a clasp at each end. Her back was bare as I had seen it a few moments before. I wanted to touch her and stop her, but I didn't move. She had wrapped a full skirt around her waist, full of color, also scarves. She had a dance she sometimes did, when we could have a tent so she was indoors, that was a dance of veils, and that skirt was part of the costume. The scarves tucked into a belt so she could pull them free as she danced and do whatever she felt. I had seen her dance until she was absolutely naked, and I had seen her dance with that skirt and not even pull one scarf, so most people wouldn't have known that she could have. It all depended on what happened when she was into it, and she said herself that she had no way of knowing ahead of time and couldn't explain it afterward either.

Joy stopped at the edge of the stage, turned slowly toward where Dacia and Veronica sat side by side, walked carefully toward them, and squatted down between them. She looked each of them fully in the face and then kissed them, first Dacia and then Veronica.

"Help me as much as you can," she said. "Please."

She stood and walked to the center of the tiny platform. Victor and Lenny and the construction man had come out from behind the truck and were moving awkwardly as a little group, as if they were linked together and didn't know how to unhook. I was scared for her and scared for me, but I couldn't make myself watch because I knew I wasn't the one who could break the spell. And if no one could, I didn't want to see it. I wanted to be blind or be somewhere else. The best thing I could think of was Dacia's tent. I took off my shoes at the door and stretched out on the floor, listening as the drums began, hoping suddenly that if I wasn't watching, maybe I could dream the dream myself, dream it for her.

I never did see her father or his tears, but I did dream, most of the night, long after the drums stopped, and long after Dacia and Veronica had come to the tent to wait. I was aware of these things, but they did not break my dreaming.

I was a bird again, flying high over a large, clear body of water. As I looked down I could see Joy swimming beneath the surface, never seeming to need air. After we had traveled for some time together—her under the water and me high in the air, but together as if we could touch—she dove and I dove. When I entered the water I was no longer a bird. I was myself, a man, and we went deeper and deeper and saw all kinds of beautiful creatures and jewels and were absolutely free and happy. She was always in front of me, searching for something, beckoning for me to follow, and I did until we came upon a beautiful pearl, almost too large to hide in your fist. She held it out to me, and I took it, and she kissed me, long and passionately. And then, suddenly, after what seemed hours under the

water with no concern for breathing, she shot toward the sur-
face and, with an almost unbearable sense of joy, I followed.
I broke the surface at the same moment she did, and was a
bird again, and shot straight up until I was so high there was
almost no sound. I turned to glide in a circle and looked down
and saw a column of fire burning on the water. Joy had burst
into flames when she came into the air, and I was alone.

When I woke up, Dacia and Veronica were sitting on the floor
of the tent, Veronica with her cane across her lap, looking at the
coins laid out on the cloth.

"He's awake now," Veronica said.

"He's finished the dream," Dacia said. "Washington taught
him to do that."

I fell back asleep almost at once, and when I woke again,
Veronica was gone and Dacia was sleeping quietly on the
cushions. I stepped outside the tent. The new truck was backed
into place, ready to hitch up to the trailer. Victor was asleep in
the cab. The blue Ford was gone. The construction man had
driven Veronica home—that was my guess. Except for the tent
where Dacia and I had been sleeping, everything else had been
taken down and put away. Even the Packard was loaded with
things for Joy and me. We were really going to do it.

When it came time to go, I left with hardly a word to anyone. It was hard to know what to say, so I tried to say good-bye as if Joy and I were just going into town for groceries, not as if it was anything important. But with Dacia it didn't work so well.

"We won't be long," I said.

"Longer than you think," she answered.

"Just a few days," I insisted, "three or four. Then we'll meet up with you again in Wichita. It won't be long."

"It's in the coins," Dacia said. She was quiet but firm. "A dangerous journey. Much suffering. Long searching before happiness."

I just looked at my shoes and walked away.

"We won't be long," I said again, but nobody could have heard me say it.

We formed a caravan and drove east. Joy and I took the lead in the Packard, followed by Victor and Dacia in the new truck, pulling Dacia's trailer. Lenny came last. The easiest route would have been for all of us to have stayed together all through the mountains and down into Pueblo. We could have spent the night together there. They would have gone on east to Dodge City and Wichita the next day, and we could have turned north to Colorado Springs and then northeast onto the prairie and into Kansas. But Joy insisted that she and I had to go through

Denver, even if it was longer and even if it meant splitting off from the others sooner. So we struggled up two passes and glided down, all together, into Gunnison, gassed up, made the long climb to the top of Monarch Pass, still together, and worked our way carefully down the other side, going slow because of the trailers. Then, as if it was nothing, Joy and I took a left-hand fork near Salida without even stopping. I honked and tried to wave good-bye, but they had gone on east, down the mountain, and we were headed north across the plateau, through South Park.

By the time we had gone only a few miles I had realized that we really had separated from Dacia and the others, and I had also figured out that it was a waste of breath to ask Joy for explanations. Either she didn't answer, or the answers she gave didn't make sense, so I just kept quiet and drove. But as we got close enough to Denver that we began seeing signs of the city, she changed and wanted to talk.

"With all the hundreds of places we've been," she said, "I haven't been here since I was your age."

"Why's that?" I asked.

"Your Uncle Louis," she answered, "and Mark, Dacia's brother . . ."

"I didn't know Dacia had a brother," I interrupted.

"She used to," Joy said, "but he's gone now."

"Like Uncle Louis?" I asked.

"Yes," she answered.

"So, he's dead," I said, "like Uncle Louis."

"Don't be cruel," she said. "The world is too cruel as it is."

"I'm not being cruel," I said. "It just irritates me when you say that."

"Say what?" she asked.

"That somebody's gone," I answered. "When someone is dead, what's wrong with saying they're dead?"

"Nothing, I guess," she said. "It just sounds so harsh when you're talking about certain people."

We rode along in silence for a mile or so, staring out the windshield at the road and the mountains. I realized that I was the one who had interrupted her, so I started up the conversation again.

"So, why haven't we come to Denver in all this time?" I asked. "You were about to tell me."

"Louis and Mark graduated from high school in the same class," she began, "1943. They were best friends, and the four of us—Mark, Louis, Dacia, and me—wanted to go to the graduation dance together."

Her voice trailed off, and I knew I would have to prod her if I was going to keep her talking, but I wanted to hear the story.

"So, did you go?" I asked.

"It would have meant Louis would have been taking his sister to the dance," she answered, "and it would have meant Mark taking his sister too, and Mark especially felt that would have been humiliating."

"Well, why didn't Mark take you?" I asked. "And Louis take Dacia?"

"That would cause trouble now," Joy answered, "but in 1943 in Kansas . . . We thought about it, and that's what we wanted to do, but everyone was against it, a black boy and a white girl, and a white boy and a black girl. We didn't have one person who was in favor of it, so we got the idea of driving to Denver, the four of us, to see Billie Holiday."

"Billie Holiday?" I asked. "Live?"

"She only died last year," Joy answered.

"I know," I said. "I just meant, 'You saw her live?'"

"That's right," she answered. "Lester Young was still with her then too. Louis told Daddy he was taking me to the dance, so he could get his '40 Ford sedan. That was as new a car as you could get then. Mark got everything arranged to be sure we'd be able to get in when we got there. His father was a porter on the trains in and out of Denver. That's how we knew Billie was going to be there and how Mark got everything fixed up."

Joy and I were actually getting into the city by then. She gave me directions and pointed out landmarks. I was amazed that she remembered it as well as she did, considering how long it had been since she had been there. We got through downtown and onto the east side, and she had me circle a couple of blocks.

"There it is," she almost shouted, "right at the end of the block!"

I stopped at the curb in front of the Blue Palace. It was blue, sky blue, and large enough to have been a gymnasium.

"It's gigantic," I said. "I was thinking it would be some small little nightclub."

"It was going to be a bowling alley," Joy said, "but the guy who started it ran out of money. So, they made a dance hall and nightclub out of it."

"It's huge," I said again.

"And it was packed," she said proudly. "We had to park five blocks away and walk. Everyone was going to the same place, so we all talked about Billie with people we'd never seen before. I loved it."

Joy directed me through a couple more turns and on east about half a mile to what was now just a vacant lot with a cement foundation.

"It looks like it burned down," she said. "But there used to be an all-night diner here. We had breakfast there in the middle of the night. We needed to go straight back, and we were out of gas, so we told the man who ran the place, and he talked to one of the customers. That man led us in his old pickup truck to a junky-looking little one-car garage where he sold us gasoline out of a steel drum. We didn't even have to use our ration coupons."

"Ration coupons?" I asked.

"The war was already on by then," she said. "Gas was rationed, but the guy with the gasoline liked us for coming all the way to Denver to see Billie Holiday, so he didn't take the coupons."

From the burned-down cafe, Joy directed me on out of Denver. We drove southeast, following the same route the four of them had taken that night years ago.

"Did your father ever find out?" I asked when we were actually out of sight of the city, and I was certain we had the right route.

"Everybody found out," she answered.

"How?" I asked.

"Louis was mad about the town," she answered, "about the

four of us not being able to go to the dance. He drove us right through the middle of town, all dressed-up, before we left for Denver, knowing people would think we were coming to the dance together in spite of what they all thought. It was like a dare. Mark didn't like it that Louis had done that. Louis could be very stubborn when he was mad, and so could Mark. But when we were finally away from Hemmings and out on the road, headed for Denver, we all began to joke about it, kind of nervously at first, about how there was probably an ugly bunch that would be hanging around the dance all night with their clubs and knives and guns all ready, waiting to make trouble, waiting and waiting and waiting for nothing."

It sounded like a good joke to me too, but Joy's voice was heavy and grim, so I decided not to say so.

"How did they all find out?" I asked.

"Mark was right," Joy said. "We shouldn't have been laughing because the trouble came, one night later, when we were coming back in from Denver."

That's where she stopped talking. We didn't say much all the way into Kansas. There wasn't any north-south highway, and we had to go north and east to get to Hemmings, so we fumbled around at times, taking country roads, not really sure where we were. Ahead of us and behind us, out the window on her side and mine, no matter which way we were pointed, the wheat fields stretched off in every direction. At times it was spooky because it seemed as if there were just the two of us on the whole earth, and I thought that even with the four of them together, they must have been scared too, being out there all alone. Joy seemed frightened and far away.

I saw something up on the horizon, and I began hoping for a town. We drove toward it, without saying a word for a long time, until it was clear that it was a grain elevator. When we finally reached it, that's all it was—no little cafe or movie theater or roadside stand. And up on the horizon was another one.

"What happened?" I finally asked.

"There was trouble," she answered.

"What kind of trouble?" I asked.

"It's hard to talk about," she answered. "I don't know if I can."

"We should be in Wichita with the others," I said. "I should be helping set up. You should be rehearsing. . . ."

"We've been through that, Louis," she interrupted.

"We haven't been through the part where you tell me what really happened," I said and waited for her to talk.

"When we got close to Hemmings," she began after several minutes of silence, "a car passed us going the other way with four guys in it, just out drinking and driving fast, it looked like. But they spotted us and turned around and came back and caught up with us. The car with the four guys followed us real close, honking and driving in the lane beside us, weaving back and forth, almost hitting us, getting in front of us and slowing way down. Mark was driving. Suddenly, they drove off from us real fast. Mark went faster, as fast as the Ford would go, trying to get us home before something bad happened, but . . ."

"But what?" I insisted, after a long silence.

"It's hard to talk about," she answered.

"I don't care," I said. "Either you tell me, or I'm going to take the next road south and forget all this stuff with your father."

"One of them was Lenny's older brother," she said.

"Jesus Christ!" I almost shouted. "Have you lost your mind?"

"Lenny's not like them!" she shouted back. "He's different. That's why he found us. That's why he wants to help."

"Different?" I asked. "Different than what?"

"Different than the others," she said and stopped.

"Goddamn it!" I shouted again and started to slow the Packard. "Tell me what happened or I'm going to park until you do."

"When we got close to town," Joy began again, "a car came off a side road and got behind us. About a mile up the road, two other cars had the road blocked. There were twelve men, and they had clubs and guns and bandannas over their faces, but you could tell who some of them were anyway because they didn't care."

"And then what happened?" I asked.

She hesitated, so I pulled over to the shoulder and turned off the engine.

"They killed him," Joy said.

"Who?" I asked.

"Mark," she said. "They held guns on us and guns on him and made us watch. They chained him to a highway sign and shot him, over and over and over."

"Jesus Christ," I muttered.

"They held guns right up to our heads and said they would shoot us if we didn't watch."

"Jesus Christ."

"I watched, and Louis watched," she said.

"And Dacia?" I asked. "Didn't they know she's blind?"

"She wasn't blind before that," Joy answered. "She looked right at it, but she didn't see anything. That's what she says. And she hasn't seen anything since."

"We can't stay here," I said, starting the car again.

"They should have killed all of us," Joy said, "if they were going to kill him and make us watch. But they didn't. Dacia went blind, and I was wild crazy for two or three weeks. Louis took care of us. He took us back to Denver, and he did everything he could think of until I was okay, and I could take care of Dacia. Then he went into the army, right from there, without going back, and went to the war."

My mind almost wouldn't work, but I got the Packard back onto the road and got moving again. It was too much all at once. She should have told me years ago. She shouldn't have told me at all. I wasn't sure. So I just kept driving, concentrating on the road. It was cruel not to kill them. It was cruel not to let them come to the dance. My mind couldn't think right.

"That's why I have to come back now," she said, "to help him understand."

"Who?" I asked.

"Daddy," she answered. "He's never understood."

I just kept driving. There were so many things to think about. Too many. I needed more time. We kept driving.

"You're about to come to a curve, to the right," Joy said, after a long silence.

"Okay," I answered.

"Just after that," she said, "there will be a little crossroad. Turn left."

I slowed the Packard as we went through the turn and pulled

it to a stop just short of the unmarked intersection. The one-and-a-half-lane road was just three worn tire tracks running between the fences. Beyond that it was like an ocean, nothing but wheat.

"Are you sure?" I asked.

"Louis," Joy said, "I grew up here. I rode a bus up and down this highway five days a week for all the years I was in school."

"I mean," I said, "are you sure we should go? Dacia's with Lenny. Shouldn't we go to Wichita now?"

"Turn, Louis," she said.

I eased out the clutch, swung wide, and turned off the pavement. It was amazing. Even bouncing around in the car, Joy was able to set her compact on the open glove box door and draw a fine dark line across each of her eyelids, just as she would have done at her dressing table. It helped me think to see her doing something like that, drawing on her eye makeup. If we had been in Wichita, that is what she would have been doing. She would have been dressing and putting on her makeup, and in an hour or so I would have been watching her rehearse, letting two or three of the local boys slip in with me to see what they would be too young to see tomorrow when the barkers started selling tickets. It was an experience to be with her when she danced. I loved it every time, but the local boys, they would be in a trance.

If we had been in Wichita, I would have been going downtown on the bus, finding places to put up the posters advertising her dancing, meeting guys my age and maybe even one of the local girls. I'd be wearing a silk shirt, probably the purple one with billowing sleeves and long, three-button cuffs, and my black boots, the ones from Spain. And I'd be wearing satin pants like the ones the acrobats wear, black ones or something else very dark, and my scarf belt. I had a long scarf that Veronica had given me when I first met her. She had made it from her favorite blouse so I'd remember her. I thought about the cane and the story she told me. It was hard to understand. Everything was hard to understand, but it helped to remember things that I did understand.

Joy wasn't in her dressing room, of course, and I wasn't downtown. Instead, we were bumping along a narrow country road, driving into nothing, it seemed to me. The smell of lilacs filled the car from the perfumed powder in her compact, but she didn't daub the powder on her nose and forehead the way she usually did. She only wanted the mirror. Joy's lower lip pouted naturally, and she drew it as accurately as always, but with a pale pink lipstick barely darker than her natural color. I had never seen her wear anything but a bright red. It was a trademark. In fact, the poster we used was a drawing of her shoulders and neck and face done in black and white except for her bright red lips. Sometimes we printed it so it was black lines on a white background and other times white on black, but the lips were always brilliant red. She must have bought the pink just for going to see her father.

"When did you switch to pink?" I asked.

"What?" she asked.

"The lipstick," I said. "When did you switch to pink?"

"I won't be onstage," she answered. "I don't need to be made up for dancing all the time."

"It never bothered you before," I said.

"It doesn't bother me now," she answered.

When she had finished with her makeup, she pointed each ear, first left and then right, toward the little mirror, lifted her hair, and unfastened her pearl earrings, one after the other. Next to bright red lips she loved pearls. What money we'd saved over the years she put into lengthening the strings or starting new ones. "It's safe," she used to say. "No one can believe they're real." She unsnapped the chrome jaws of her coin purse and dropped the two pearl studs in among the nickels and dimes and a couple of strands she wore for necklaces. She was beautiful with her auburn hair and blue eyes. She knew she was beautiful, and she knew she was special. We rode along watching the little speck coming toward us become a barn and then watching a house appear on one side. The wheat grew right up next to the buildings, and there was nothing that looked like a lawn or a garden.

"It looks deserted," I said, pulling the Packard to a stop beside the mailbox.

The flag was up as if someone was sending out a letter, but it wasn't red any more, it was tarnished and rusted to a dark maroon, almost black. The faded letters on the box said Bradley, our family name.

"One of the neighbors rents the fields," she answered. "He must have planted the yard too. There used to be a row of trees along the road and in back of the house."

Pushing against my own feeling that I was making a mistake, the way you push against the building drifts when you drive in heavy snow, I drove past the mailbox, through the open gate, and stopped the car between the house and the barn.

"It looks deserted," I said again, "like a ghost town or a haunted house."

The house was deserted. Its windows had been boarded over. The metal chimney pipe lay bent and broken on the roof. The stairway to the cellar was partially filled with dirt, and there were sunflowers growing everywhere—out of the hole and right up next to the house itself. I eased the car along, looking for some sign of Joy's father. When I spotted him, he was behind the house in what had been the backyard, standing in wheat nearly up to his waist, but he seemed almost unaware that he was in a field. His white hair curled over the collar of his plaid shirt, longer hair than I was used to on farmers. Spread over the surface of green stalks was a full-sized American flag, the kind you see at a school or a post office. The old man tugged at one corner, waded through the wheat partway around, as if he was walking in mud, and pulled at an edge, trying to get the wrinkles out—like a bachelor straightening the covers on his bed.

"How come he's got such a big flag?" I asked.

"It was Louis' casket flag," Joy said.

"What's a casket flag?" I asked.

"The army gives them out to cover the coffin," she said. "You put the car in the barn. I'll go talk to him."

"Aren't you scared?" I asked. "What's he doing out there?"

"It's the Fourth of July, Louis," Joy answered. "You're supposed to fly the flag and decorate the graves of the soldiers. He's just a little mixed up, that's all."

"But aren't you scared?" I asked again.

She was already getting out of the car and did not answer. I sat behind the wheel with the motor running and watched as Joy waded into the wheat and stood at the bottom of the flag. Her father looked up, combed back his hair with the fingers of both hands, and nodded to her as if she had been there all along. He gave no sign that he was seeing his daughter for the first time in over fifteen years. Together they pulled out the last of the wrinkles and then stood there staring at the stripes and the stars as if they were looking through the surface of a pool and could see something in the deep water.

I put the Packard in reverse, backed to the front of the barn, and parked. The big double doors were barely parted, just enough that I could slip through without disturbing them. The inside of the barn was dark, and I paused for a moment to let my eyes adjust. As far as I could tell there were no windows or other openings. I could not see walls or a ceiling, though I knew they must be there somewhere since it was bright daylight outside. It was like being in a big tent before they've set up the lighting. If you don't concentrate on something, you can get dizzy and scared. The only thing to put my attention on was a bright wedge of light on the ground in front of me. It was five or six feet long, a narrow strip where the sunlight squeezed in through the space between the doors, and that appeared only when I stepped to the side so I wasn't blocking it. I moved back and forth, turning the light on and off with my body, wanting to know what I would be able to see if I pulled the doors shut. Dust swirled in the air where the light came through, and I whistled soundlessly to watch the little particles whirl and dance like water, then settle down to their quiet drifting until I blew again.

When I blocked the light I could see a pair of dim, pale yellow rectangles floating in black space, ghosts of light coming from nowhere. I wanted to see them, but my eyes wanted the sun and made my body jump to the side so the wedge and the dancing dust appeared again. Deliberately, I stepped back, blocking the light again, and waited for my eyes to accept the darkness. One of the lights was close to square, maybe three or four feet each way, but square, and the other was nearly twice as wide but not very high. They seemed to be moving, and I let my body sway with them. Daylight jumped past me onto the floor and my eyes riveted to it. The other lights were lost. I stepped backward, pulled the big doors together, held them until I knew they would stay put, then turned around again and concentrated. As I walked toward them, carefully, one step at a time, the rectangles seemed to be moving, but as I got closer I could see that they were not. Slowly I realized that the two shapes were windows, that there was a rounded, curving corner between them, locking them together. The bad feeling I had had out by the mailbox before I drove in through the gate was even stronger here in the barn, so as I began to understand that what I was approaching was the trailer that Joy had said we were coming for, I did not feel relieved. When I opened the trailer door, even that dim light was a shock to my eyes, but I stepped up inside anyway and closed the door behind me.

It wasn't a bad little trailer, out of style by several years, but it had a bedroom in the back and a sleeper couch in the living room, with a kitchen and a bathroom in between. Everything looked new, as if no one had ever lived there: there were no scratches on the woodwork and no water stains below the windows. All around the walls in the living room were pictures of Joy and her brother. There was one picture of her in a little cheerleading uniform and another in a fancy evening dress, ready for some big event. My mother had always been pretty, even back then when she was sixteen or so. The dress looked almost identical to one of her dance costumes. There was another picture on the wall, a funny one of the two of them together, dressed up in costumes for a party or a play, looking like royalty from the French court. The photograph had been pasted onto a black background. Two balloon-shaped pieces of paper had been glued on to make the photo look like a cartoon. My uncle was saying, "I AM Kansas," and Joy was saying, "Let them eat wheat." Even without the quotes, I would have gotten the French idea.

I had no trouble recognizing the pictures of my uncle. Joy had pictures of him, and she liked to show them to people and to tell stories about how much they had loved each other and how happy they had been together before he died. She would never say how he had died. Even though I knew my uncle was dead, the pictures and the trailer and the farm all made me feel that I might meet him at any moment, alive and ready to go into town for the carnival and the fun. Joy liked to tell stories, too, about how it was really Uncle Louis who taught her how to enjoy life. "I haven't met anybody since," she liked to say, "who loves life as much as he did." He did look happy in the pictures.

Over the couch there was a built-in bookcase with no books. I stood on my tiptoes to look. There was a hunting rifle lying up there, and there was a framed picture of a man and a boy standing by a dead deer. The man was holding the head up by the antlers and the boy was staring at the ground.

I was about to go look for Joy and her father when I heard the barn doors creak and knew they were coming. Joy stepped up into the trailer, looked at me quickly, and looked away without saying anything. She had buttoned her blouse all the way up and had folded her arms across her chest as if she was cold. Her eyes looked glazed, glassy. The old man followed her in, cradling the flag, neatly folded in a triangle. He turned with the flag, carefully, and walked down the hall to the bedroom in the back, and we both followed. There was an open trunk in front of the closet, a green army footlocker with army uniforms folded neatly side by side. The old man kneeled in front of the locker and laid the flag in as if he was lowering the injured body of a child into bed. Joy closed the lid carefully, and we all stared at the trunk like a family gathered around a coffin. I wanted to run, to get outside for fresh air.

"Did you see that black sedan out there?" the old man said and looked up at me.

"I drove it here," I answered. "What about it?"

"It's a 1941," he said. "I went to town and bought it the day I heard on the radio that the war was over in Europe. Louis loved Packards. It was a surprise."

The glee drained away from the old man's face.

"But he never came back," he said.

"He died in the war?" I asked.

"He never came back," the old man said.

"There's no need to be cruel," Joy said.

"What are you talking about?" I asked. "I just asked if my uncle—my uncle—died in the war."

"Why are you talking like this?" Joy asked.

She stepped between me and her father and started backing me down the hall, away from the bedroom.

"Maybe I should be proud of him," I said. "Maybe he was a hero."

"Calm down," she said.

She forced me all the way back into the living room.

"Why won't he answer me?" I asked.

"He did answer you," she said.

"'He never came back,'" I mocked the old man's dreamy voice. "That's not an answer. Uncle Louis is dead. Isn't that where you were with that flag? That's his grave, isn't it, out in back of the house under the wheat?"

"Death is hard," Joy said.

"Why is he buried there?" I asked. "Why doesn't he have a real grave?"

"Louis was his son," she said. "He never got over it, so just leave it alone."

"We should get out of here," I said. "He's crazy. And besides, Dacia . . ."

Hearing myself say Dacia's name, I saw her face in my mind and I was suddenly scared.

"I'm going to go get her," I said. "She's out there somewhere with Lenny."

"I'm not going to argue with you any more," Joy said. "If you have to go, go. Bring her back—if she'll come."

"Why wouldn't she come?" I asked.

"Because it's hard," she said, "too hard."

"Come with me," I said. "We can just leave."

"Go ahead," she said. "Come back when you're ready. I'm not going anywhere."

"Don't stay here," I said. "He's crazy."

"We have to talk it out," she said. "I've avoided it all these years. Louis faced it. I have to stop hiding."

"Faced what?" I asked.

"It's something I have to do because he's my father," she said. "It's too much to talk out now, Louis. Just go."

I opened the trailer door and stepped down. Ten feet in front of me I could now see a wall with a ladder leading up to a loft. I turned to the right, walked through the barn and outside to the car. Joy stayed right with me, holding my arm. The old man followed and reached the car just as I was starting the engine.

"This here's a 1941 Packard," he said. "It was a surprise for my son. He loved Packards."

"I'll be back in two days," I said.

I put the car in gear. Joy's purse was lying on the seat beside me, and I handed it out the window to her.

"Keep it," she said, "in case you have to buy things."

"Joy's here now," the old man said. "Louis will be here soon, to get his trailer. Everything is ready."

"I'll be back," I said to Joy. "Unless you want to go with me now?"

"Go on," she said. "The sooner you go . . ."

I couldn't stand it any more. It was like being under water. I was starting to have trouble thinking, and I pulled away so I wouldn't drown. But I had not driven much more than a mile past the gate and the mailbox and up the road when I heard the first shot.

Crack!

It came from behind me and hung in the air until the sound had reached out in front, way over the next horizon, and then, all of a sudden, it was gone and the prairie was quiet again.

"Oh, please, Joy!" I yelled. "Be okay, please!"

I stopped the car, turned left as sharp as I could, and pulled forward.

Crack!

"I'm coming, Joy!" I yelled. "Oh, please!"

When the front bumper touched the fence running along beside the road, I stopped, cut the wheel the other way as hard as I could, put the Packard in reverse, and began to back toward the fence on the other side.

Crack! Crack!

Two more shots, close together. Back and forth. Back and forth. It took me three times up to the fence on each side before I could finally pull forward and drive back toward the farm.

Crack!

The last shot had come after a long pause and there were no more after that. When I reached the barn I left the motor running, put the car in neutral, set the emergency brake, flung the big doors open, and ran into the barn. The building smelled like smoke and gunpowder. It was flooded with light now. I could see smoke drifting down from the loft and out the open trailer door, and I ran there first.

Joy was kneeling on the kitchen floor with her back against the cupboard doors. She was clutching a small wooden cross in her right hand. Her head was tilted back as if it was the ceiling fixture she had looked to for mercy. Her mouth was open, and her face was frozen in surprise. Her eyes were fixed and staring, but there was no light in them. Her arms hung limp; her legs were folded beneath her. There were four large powder burns on her white blouse, all close to her heart. He must have made her kneel on the kitchen floor and pray, with the rifle barrel pressed to her chest. I stood on my tiptoes and turned far enough to see that the rifle was missing from the shelf above the couch. He must have held her at gunpoint and forced her to pray, shot her while she was doing it, and then again and again and again, each time with the gun barrel right to her heart. I kneeled in front of her and tried to take the cross out of her hand, but her grip was too tight. There were no tears on her cheeks. Perhaps she had not had time for suffering, only surprise.

My mother was dead. I wondered when I would begin to feel it.

I stood up and walked to the bedroom. It was empty. I turned back the covers, returned to the kitchen, lifted her as carefully as I could, and carried her to the back. It was awkward. She could not help. I tucked her into the bed, covered her, and drew the bedspread up over her face. That is what they do, I knew, cover the face. The look of surprise is too much for the rest of us. I felt very tired.

Joy was dead. I knew I would have to tell people. How do you do that? My mother is dead. I could not make the words sound real in my mind.

I did not know what to do next, but when I turned to go I saw the green army footlocker. "Louis Bradley." It was my uncle's, but now it was mine. He was Louis Bradley, but so was I. The box would help me remember things, even my name perhaps. I looked back at the bed, at Joy's body under the covers, and tried to remember what it had been like when she was alive, but I couldn't. I was afraid for the first time since I had seen the body. Already I knew far less, remembered less, than I had an hour before. Soon there might be nothing left. The box would help, I decided, at least until I had told people that Joy was dead. I lifted the locker and carried it into the living room. The pictures would help too. I got the cheerleader picture, and the evening dress picture, and the French one, and put them in the green footlocker, and got the locker up on my shoulder, and carried it out of the trailer and out of the barn to the car. The engine was still running. I shut off the motor, got the keys, opened the trunk, put the locker in it, and went back into the barn.

Joy's father was in the loft, leaning against the rail. I walked slowly to the ladder near the trailer door and climbed. It was like a little apartment up there with a small refrigerator, a cot, a dresser, a camp stove, a washbasin, and a car seat for a couch. The old man was sitting on the car seat with the hunting rifle tucked between his legs and both hands gripping the barrel. His head was rolled back, but the gun barrel was still caught in his mouth. I approached him slowly and tried to take the rifle away from him, but his hands were frozen on the gun. I thought about hurting him. He had killed my mother and killed himself, all very quick. I tried to think what it would be like to really want to hurt him, but I couldn't. It seemed so far away, years and years ago, when my mother had been alive and when I had worried about her and wanted to protect her, a long, long time ago. I pulled a blanket from the cot and covered him, rifle and all.

It was hard to know what to do next, but we had come for the trailer. I remembered that. I stood in the loft looking down. It wouldn't be stealing. It was Louis' trailer. He was dead, so it was Joy's trailer. Joy was dead, so . . . Joy was dead. I would close the trailer door and make sure it was latched. I wouldn't go back in. There was no need for that. But it was mine now. I would bring in the Packard and hitch it to the trailer and let down the jacks and make sure the hitch was tight. I would unplug the electricity and store the cord, then I'd disconnect the water hose and pull loose the drainpipe. Then I'd be ready to travel, always ready to travel, but this time I would be alone. I stood in the loft looking down at the trailer.

This time I was alone.

Chapter

5

There were times when I lost time, lots and lots of hours, sometimes whole days, and even a month or two. But there are things that I know for certain did happen. I did drive into Hemmings, and I did have the trailer hooked on behind the Packard. I knew we were going to need a funeral, and I had gotten the idea somewhere that town people went to churches about weddings, births, and deaths. So I drove into Hemmings and followed the main street along until I came up in front of a big building with stained glass windows and large wooden doors, and I pulled to a stop. People in suits and nice summer dresses were coming up the sidewalk from both directions in groups of four and five and were coming across the street right where I was parked. One woman with short brown hair and a white straw hat stopped and smiled at me and tapped on my window with her white leather Bible. I thought she had seen that I didn't know exactly who to talk to and was going to offer to help, so I rolled down the window.

"Young man," she said, "you're blocking the crosswalk."

"What?" I asked.

"You're parked right in the crosswalk," she said. "If you don't move, you'll get a ticket."

"Thank you," I said and smiled.

The woman smiled back and stood up straight, but she did not go into the church. She just stood beside the car as if she was going to stand there until I pulled away. But I didn't want to leave. I knew someone in the church could help me if they would, and I did not know where else to go. I had not told anyone yet what had happened out there in the barn, and I did not know what I would be like when I did. I had thought about it the best I could before coming into town. I had one feeling that I might start crying and not be able to stop, maybe not ever. I was kind of afraid of that. And I had also thought I might suddenly start tearing things up, smashing things. I could even drive the car into a store with a big window. That wasn't as frightening because I knew that if I started smashing things, people would stop me one way or another, so it wouldn't go on forever. Since I didn't know what I would do, I thought it would be best if I didn't talk to the woman any more. I rolled up the window.

The woman had a young girl with her who looked a little younger than me, but not much. She had black hair, longer and wavy, and sparkly eyes. She was pretty in that frightened way that church girls are sometimes pretty. She stood behind the woman where she could see me, and I could see her, and winked at me and made funny faces behind the woman's back, making fun of the way the woman was trying to boss me around. Looking at her made me feel lonesome in the Packard all by myself, but I knew she would be trouble if I stayed, so I put the Packard in gear and pulled away from the curb real slow. I watched them out the side window and then in the mirror. The woman looked very satisfied, but the girl was pouting. I decided to keep driving around the block until the crowd had all gone inside.

Working in carnivals, I had met a lot of church girls. They liked to get you to come after them just enough so they wouldn't feel it was too late to have fun. The other thing I had learned about church girls was that a lot more than other girls they liked to see guys fight because of them. So I kept the Packard moving around and around the block. That girl was standing out in front of the church the first time I came back, and she tried to walk along the sidewalk beside me and duck down so she could look inside, but I kept moving and she gave up at the corner. She was looking almost as scared as I was, but I couldn't see what she had to be afraid of. All she had to do was go inside and she'd be safe.

I kept moving around and around real slow until the bells had rung and the people, even the girl with black hair, were inside, and then I pulled up in front again where I had been before. After I sat there for a while, it came to me that I could get some help if I honked the horn. And at exactly the same time that idea came to me, I got a strong wave of the feeling that I was going to drown, that same feeling that had made me drive away from the farm and leave Joy there. It was real strong, and I thought I better act quick before it made me do something wrong again, so I punched the horn. Everything that was inside me started pouring out on the beautiful sound of that horn, and it felt wonderful, like I had been inhaling all day and finally I could let it out. I honked and honked and honked. And that's one of the places where I lost some time. I don't know how much, but I do know for certain that after a while I was in jail.

I felt better after honking, less afraid I would start something I couldn't stop, but I was very tired, so I didn't mind being locked in. I wanted to sleep. What does it matter whether you're free or not if all you're going to do is sleep? They tried to keep me awake to ask me questions. They came in the cell and talked in loud voices and soft voices, but I couldn't stay with it, and they didn't understand my answers anyway. They kept telling me that horrible things were going to happen to me because of what I had done. I tried to tell them that the horrible things had already happened. The things they said would be horrible didn't sound so bad compared to what had already happened. It made them mad when I said that, but I honestly couldn't understand why. No one had hurt them, and they didn't even pretend that they were sad about finding out Joy was dead. Besides, once I had told them that Joy was dead, I didn't have much else to say. There was no one in the little jail but me, and that made it good for sleeping, so I slept and slept, even when they wanted to ask me questions.

One thing I remember is that a policeman came into the cell, and I decided to look at his face. I'm not sure why. I hadn't looked at any of the others, but I had this feeling that I should look at his face, so I did.

"Lenny," I said.

I was going to go on and ask about Dacia, but he started laughing the minute I called him that, and I started laughing too. It felt so good, even better than honking the horn. For a little while it was like I wasn't even in the cell, like I was way up in the stars, but just for a little.

"Now what made you think I was Lenny?" he asked, after we had worn out laughing.

"You look just like him," I answered, still trying to catch my breath.

"Do I, now?" he asked, suddenly grim.

"Yes," I answered. "You must be brothers."

"Did he send you here?" he asked.

"Not exactly," I answered.

"To hear him tell it," the policeman said, "he set the whole thing up."

"You've talked to him?" I whispered.

I was so afraid he was going to tell me that something had happened to Dacia, I couldn't speak any louder than a whisper.

"We're family, me and Lenny," the policeman said. "Close, real close. I ought to take you out back tonight and let you escape and blow your damn head off. That's what I ought to do, but Lenny, he says no. He says to let you go. He says we'll get more use out of you that way, and I got to do what he says because my pa put him in charge right before he died. But it's a shame, boy, because I sure enough would like to be the one blows you away."

"Why?" I asked. "What did I do?"

"You got born," he answered.

He began to laugh again, but this time I couldn't laugh with him. I wanted to even more than before, wanted to get out of there any way I could, but I couldn't let go. Suddenly, the policeman shut off his laughing.

"It don't have nothing to do with you," he said. "It's between your family and mine—if you call that scum of yours family.

You just got born into the wrong bunch. Me and Lenny's all that's left of mine, so we got to think and work careful. But I want you to know that if it wasn't for Lenny, I might shoot you right here in this cell, might not even take you outside. So you owe him whatever time you got left."

The policeman left me alone in the cell. There wasn't time to ask him any more questions, and I couldn't have anyway. Horrible things were happening, and he and Lenny were glad, and they wanted me to make more horrible things. I was scared. What if I did help, not meaning to, of course? But what if I did anyway? I couldn't understand, but I thought it would be best if I didn't do the things I wanted to do the most. Like I wanted to find out that Dacia was okay, and I wanted to go away with her somewhere where we would both be safe. But maybe they wanted to hurt Dacia. Maybe if I tried to go to her or find out about her, I would help them do that. Wasn't that a way they could use me by keeping me alive?

But Dacia was supposed to be with Lenny. It was too hard to figure out, so I went to sleep. In my dream, I forgot who I was and all about my life and everyone I had ever known. I didn't hurt anyone. People liked me. It was as if I was a little bird, and they were always trying to sneak up on me the way children do. I woke up and wondered if I could really do that, forget who I was, but my mind started screaming, "Louis, Louis, Louis," and making songs out of my name and the names of people I knew—Dacia and Veronica and Washington and Victor. The forgetting wasn't going to happen right then, I could tell that.

This thing about losing blocks of time was bothering me. I had the idea that the longer I was there, the more and more danger Dacia would be in. That could be true if my getting out and finding her would make her more safe. But if Lenny and his brother wanted to use me by letting me out, that might mean that Dacia had gotten away from Lenny somehow, and if that was true, the more time lost between now and when I found her, the safer she would be. Some people say that being in jail will affect your mind, but I thought I was doing pretty well, being able to think this through. It could be that if I was losing blocks of time, that might mean I was losing the rest of my mind too. But if I was giving blocks of time away, especially if it helped a friend in danger, that would be different, very different. I wouldn't mind that so much. So, I decided that I needed a way to keep more careful track of time while I was in jail. That way, I could deliberately take up more time before I left.

The jail was the upstairs part of a brick building with wooden floors. It was one large open area that had high ceilings and tall, thin windows on all sides. It could have been a dance hall or a roller-skating rink. They had bolted the steel right through the floor to make the walls for the cells. There were flat pieces running along the floor and along the top of the bars and halfway between the bottom and the top. The ceiling of the cell was made out of bars too, held together by the same long, flat plates, bolted to the top of the walls. It was funny how in town they built things so they would never move and in the carnival we were always trying to figure out how to build things that would be easy to move.

There were three cells in a row, just one row, each cell a little longer and a little wider than I am tall, and there was an open space about the same width all the way around between the cell walls and the brick walls. Each cell had a bunk and a hole in the floor that went to a sewer. I could tell from the smell. With all those shadows running every which way from the bars, it wasn't hard to figure out a clock by how the shadows moved. It was good in the daytime anyway. I'm glad I was working on this system for telling time because it made it easier for me to know for sure what things I dreamed and what things happened.

One of the policemen, a different one, not Lenny's brother, came up the stairs, and he had a girl with him. It was the same girl I had seen at the church, only her dress was a lot simpler and showed a lot more of her body. The policeman stayed in the corner with a big smile on his face, watching her walk toward my cell and watching me. She moved her hips a lot while she came toward me and held her hand against her stomach, making the dress show the lines of her body even more. She was pretty, but she was still a girl and even the dress and the sexy walk didn't change my mind about that. She was one, maybe two years younger than me. It made me feel kind of creepy to see how much the policeman was enjoying watching her, but I couldn't help staring too. If we had been out on the street, just a couple of kids, I would have looked at her for sure, and enjoyed it, and decided she was too young, but I wouldn't have felt bad about it.

She smiled when she saw that I was staring. Her hair was either black or dark brown, I couldn't tell for sure in the jail light, and hung down past her shoulders. Her eyes were steady as if she was trying to catch something, the way they would be if she was slipping up on a butterfly, except more bold, the kind of eyes you have to have to walk up to animals, such as deer, without their running away. It was as if the something she was trying to catch wasn't me, but I was where it was, like maybe it was inside me and she could see it in there. And I could sort of feel it, like a creature knowing human beings are dangerous but wanting to let this one touch me. And for a minute my mind made a picture of her walking up to me, and I was a deer, and the picture seemed just as real as what I was seeing in the cell, until she spoke. Then I was me, and it was a jail again.

"Do you remember me?" she asked, up close to the bars.

"At the church," I answered. "With your mother."

The policeman chuckled when I said that.

"She's not my mother," the girl said. "She's more like my employer."

"She wanted me to move my car," I said.

"Yes, she did," the girl said.

She looked steadily into my eyes. I looked right back. It made me feel stronger, as if I was having a good meal, and I realized I couldn't remember having eaten anything for a long time.

"I moved because of you," I said.

"You did?" she asked.

"Only you seemed different then," I said.

"How?" she asked.

She shifted her weight to make her body move and pressed herself closer to the bars.

"I thought your hair was black," I answered, "but it has other colors in it. And I didn't think you would come to a place like this."

"My name's Kelly," she said, extending her hand through the bars to shake.

"Mine's Louis," I answered.

I stepped toward her to take her hand. She squeezed it and drew me closer to her. The policeman chuckled.

"Come up closer," she said, "I want to whisper something secret."

I did what she asked me to, and she spoke close to my ear.

"The pig gets his jollies watching me do this," she said, "but don't worry. Just trust me. Trust me."

"I can't," I said out loud.

"Of course you can," she said, loud so the policeman could hear.

She looked over her shoulder at him. He was smiling so big his teeth were showing. Then she put her free hand up behind my neck and pulled my head down close to her face, where she could whisper real soft and I would hear her.

"They're going to let you go," she said. "The bastards have known for a week that you didn't do it. Don't be afraid. I'm going to help you. I'm going to help you."

"How can you do that?" I asked, still talking too loud.

The policeman chuckled over in the corner. She looked over her shoulder at him again and smiled. She let go of my head, slipped her hand into the neckline of her dress, and got a little piece of paper out of her bra. I knew it was folded paper because she sort of scratched it across my chin, and I could feel it. She ran her hand down my back and slipped it into the hip pocket of my jeans. While her hand was still in my pocket, she pulled me up closer against the bars and let go of my hand so she could pull my head right up against her face. She kissed me real lightly. It wasn't sexy like I thought it was going to be. At the same time she drew her hand carefully out of my pocket and put her lips up close to my ear, on the side away from the policeman.

"Don't say anything to anyone," she whispered, "nothing, until we're out of town. Do you understand?"

I nodded the best I could. She had a pretty tight hold on my head.

"Trust me," she whispered again. "Don't say anything to anyone."

While she was talking she patted my pocket gently. I drew back and smiled and nodded, hoping she would understand that I knew she had left the paper in my pocket and knew she had made the policeman think she was doing something else.

"I'll be back to see you later," she said.

Her voice sounded as if it was deliberately loud enough for the policeman to hear, and she smiled in a way that made her look like she really was my age and I really could trust her. She walked back over to the man in the corner. He put his arm around her waist and patted her bottom and then they were gone.

"Kelly," I said to myself. "Kelly. Kelly."

I wanted to be sure I would remember her name. I slid my hand down into my hip pocket slowly and carefully, afraid there wouldn't be anything there, and I would find out I was dreaming. But the piece of paper was there, folded up to about the size of a postage stamp. I decided I would wait to read it until I saw if the things she said would happen really did.

"Dacia and Washington," I said to myself. "Victor and Veronica. Louis. And Kelly."

I repeated the names over and over in every order and combination I could think of, trying to make myself remember which ways I had put them together and which ones I hadn't said yet. When I had done that, I started practicing how I would tell people what had happened. I started with Dacia.

"Joy is dead," I said. "Joy is dead, Dacia."

I went through each one—Dacia and Washington and Veronica and Victor and Kelly and myself too—repeating the message until I could hear how I would say it a little differently to each of them. By the time I finished with that, the smiling policeman had come back by himself.

"I've got some bad news for you, kid," he said, up close to my cell.

I didn't answer at all. *Don't say anything to anyone until we're out of town.* That's what Kelly had said, and since her visit I had somehow come to the decision that I was going to trust her.

"No more free rent," the policeman said and unlocked the door. "Come on out."

I walked carefully out of the cell.

"The old man left a suicide note in the mailbox," he said. "Said right there on paper he was going to kill her when she came. It looks like that's what he done."

When I was outside the cell, he closed the door and locked it. I guess he was afraid I would want to turn around and run back in.

"There wasn't no witness, of course," the policeman said. "We had the FBI check out the handwriting. Can't be too careful. You might have forged the note."

I looked at him, but I didn't answer.

"Besides," he said, "we thought we had us one could be a big story in all the papers all across the country and on TV too. A kid kills two people for no reason at all and makes it look like suicide. I'd like to get on the TV, just once, wouldn't you?"

I looked at him and shook my head. I knew that wasn't exactly the truth, but I had made up my mind not to talk, and I couldn't remember right then what it was I had thought I could do to get on TV.

"Well, come on," the policeman said. "We got people down on the street to watch us let you go."

I didn't move, and I know my face was full of the question why, even though I didn't say it.

"Don't look so shocked," he said. "It's standard practice, kid. When something happens to you, we don't want nobody to say we done it. And something sure will if you hang around here."

We started toward the stairs, and he put his arm around my shoulder.

"It's too bad about the girl," he said. "She's got the hots for you. All she's ever let me do was feel her up a little, but she'd have come back tonight after the town was in bed and given you a time worth dying for. Would have been something to see too."

It made me mad, but I didn't answer him when he said that either. Kelly had said not to talk, and I had decided to trust her, so I just walked down the stairs with him behind me and signed the papers they told me to sign to get the envelope with my wallet and keys and other stuff in it. When I had signed everything, the policeman opened the front door for me, and I walked out onto the sidewalk. The Packard was parked right in front. "We're keeping the trailer for evidence," the policeman said.

I still didn't answer. There were fifteen or twenty people standing around watching, like he had said there would be. Kelly wasn't there, and neither was the woman she had been with at the church, and neither was Lenny's brother, so there wasn't anybody there that I knew. The car started right up. It even had gas. The way it looked to me, there was about an hour of sunlight left, and I thought I would rather drive west and watch the sunset. So I did. I drove west out of Hemmings onto the prairie and had my first grain elevator in sight up on the horizon before I let myself dig down in my hip pocket and pull out the little folded-up piece of paper and read it.

"I'm in the trunk," the note said. "Be sure you're away from town and no one is following, then stop and let me out. Kelly."

I kept driving until I had passed the first grain elevator, and it was dark, and the next thing off in the distance was a tiny red light, winking off and on slowly like it could go on forever. I hadn't even seen another car or truck for miles, but I pulled off on one of the narrow little farm roads anyway and followed that for about a mile in the dark, until I didn't think anyone could see me even if they did go by on the highway. I opened the glove box to read the note again by the light in there and saw Joy's purse. I was surprised because when they told me they were keeping the trailer, I figured they would keep her purse too. But when I opened it and checked, even the pearls were there—the earrings and two strands long enough for necklaces—along with fifty dollars in cash. I sat there for a while holding the purse and trying to remember Joy, but I couldn't very well. I read the note again.

"I'm in the trunk. Be sure you're away from town and no one is following, then stop and let me out. Kelly."

There was also a flashlight in the glove box, because Joy always wanted to have a light in case of trouble. That was true. I remembered her opening the glove box and flicking on the flashlight to check the batteries before she closed the door on her side and was ready to go. I turned on the flashlight. It worked fine. I closed the glove box, folded up the note, put it back in my pocket, walked around to the back of the Packard, and opened the trunk. Kelly was curled up in the back of the trunk, face down, half behind and half on top of an army duffel bag, as if she was wrestling a giant pillow almost as big as she was.

"Get that thing out of my face," she said.

Her voice was muffled by the duffel bag.

"What?" I asked.

It hadn't been all that long since I had talked, but I was startled to hear myself.

"The light, goddamn it," she said. "Point that thing somewhere else."

The only way I had been able to tell that it was her in the trunk was to shine the light on her face. The rest of her was covered up with a dark-colored blanket, black or dark blue.

"Where are we?" Kelly asked.

"Away from town," I answered.

"No shit," she said. "I thought I was going to be looking at California by the time you let me out of here."

She rolled over the top of the duffel bag and crawled out of the trunk.

"'Be sure you're away from town,'" I said, trying to imitate her voice. "That's what your note said. 'Be sure no one is following.'"

"You did a hell of a job," she said and stretched.

"Thank you," I answered.

I ran the light over the inside of the trunk. There was nothing else in there but the duffel bag.

"You worried about your stuff?" she said.

"What stuff?" I asked.

"It's all here in the bag," she said. "Don't worry. I got it all."

"All?" I asked.

"The flag," she answered. "The army clothes. The book. The pictures. The letters. All the stuff in the footlocker. Everything."

I was only half sure I understood what she was talking about, but I knew from her voice that she was proud of herself for doing it, and I thought she would probably make it all clear to me later.

"Thank you," I said.

"I even got the purse and the money," she said. "They were going to hold it, 'evidence,' but I didn't think you'd have much cash, so I took it too."

"I don't," I said, touching all of my pockets, one after the other. "Just this."

I held up the little note and put the light on it.

"Thank God you can read," Kelly said. "I could have died in there."

"You look fine to me," I said.

"Yeah, just great," she answered. "Can we get in the car and go?"

"Go?" I asked. "How do you know we're going the same way?"

"Where were you going?" she asked.

She was challenging me. I didn't have an answer. Even though it wasn't like being in jail, I still felt trapped, and I wanted to shine the light at her and make her go away. It would have been okay with me to have just stayed out there in the night, by myself, forever, or until something happened, like the policeman said it would. At the same time, I wanted to do something to know for sure that she was really there, that I wasn't imagining it. I thought I might put my arms around her, but that was kind of scary to think about. The idea of holding on to her had a lot of that same feeling that I had about crying, that if I started, I might not be able to stop, ever. So I didn't move.

"Where were you going, Louis?" she asked again.

"To the mountains," I answered. "To the water."

"Good," she said. "Let's go."

"Who said you could come?" I asked.

"You'll never get off this goddamn prairie without my help," she answered.

"What makes you so sure of that?" I asked. "All I have to do is drive."

"Like you drove into Hemmings?" she asked. "With a trailer with a dead body in it? Like you parked in front of the church

· 88 ·

and honked your goddamn horn? You don't exactly have your shit together, you know."

"I needed help," I said.

"That's my point," she said. "You want me to drive?"

"No," I answered. "I feel better when I'm driving."

Kelly insisted on having the duffel up front, in the back seat, not in the trunk. I didn't get a very good look at her, just a glimpse when the door was open and the inside light was on and she was struggling with the bag. She wouldn't let me carry it. She had on the same dress she had worn when she came to the jail, and it made me want to look at her body. Her legs and arms looked strong. I could see the muscles. She was small, a lot smaller than me, but her legs and arms showed that she had worked a lot. I had been right earlier when I thought that she wasn't really a woman yet, that she was even younger than me. But I felt a little bit ashamed of myself because I kept looking at her body and trying to tell myself that she thought she was a woman, so it shouldn't matter to me if she was too young. I was kind of relieved when we were both in the car, in the front seat together, and I had the Packard turned around and headed back toward the highway. That way I could be close to her but would have to pay attention to driving and not worry so much about wanting to hold her.

"Jesus, it was funny," she said after a while.

"What was?" I asked.

"They were passing the plate," she said, "for money."

"Who was?" I asked.

"In the church," she answered.

"I've never been," I said.

"You should go sometime," she said. "They have this part where they pass the plate around for you to put money in."

"We do that sometimes," I said, "at an outdoor show where you can't sell tickets."

"Show?" Kelly asked.

"Joy was a dancer," I answered. "We traveled around with carnivals and circuses and on our own. But Joy is dead."

We were quiet for a moment.

"Joy was my mother," I said.

"My mother's in an institution," Kelly said.

We were quiet again.

"Well, anyway," she said, "they were passing the plate for the money. It's a very, very serious thing. They have special music and everything. The basic idea is that Jesus isn't going to like you if you don't put in any money. The people sitting close to you can see whether you do or not. I guess they're helping Jesus know who to cut off. Some people even put their money in an envelope with their name on it, so Jesus won't get confused. It's the big moment in the whole thing. As soon as they've got the money you know it won't be long, even if you don't have a watch. Anyway, they were passing the plate, and, oh, shit . . ."

She started laughing, but I was driving so I didn't let myself.

"They were passing the plate," she said, "and here comes beep, beep, beep. God, Louis, you should have seen them."

She began laughing really hard this time. We were out on the highway by then, and there was no one in sight anywhere, so I began honking the horn, just like I had in front of the church. Kelly laughed and laughed until she cried, and I just kept honking as long as she thought it was funny. Then it was over, and we were quiet again.

We both had a lot of questions and a lot of things to say to each other, but for quite a while we rode along without saying much. I'd look over at her once in a while. She sat up straight and watched the highway, then she slumped down in the seat and tried to sleep, and then she slouched way down so her knees were up against the dash and she was staring almost straight up into the night sky.

"You know what I'm going to do?" she asked. "When we finally get up in the mountains?"

"No, what?" I asked.

"I'm going to go where there are no lights," she said, "and lie under the stars all night long."

"And watch for shooting stars?" I asked.

"Sure," she answered. "Why not?"

"I used to do that," I said. "I can remember looking at the stars and looking and looking and looking. I remember feeling that if I watched long enough, I would see something that would tell me a secret."

"You like secrets?" she asked.

"Yeah," I answered. "I guess I do."

"I got lots of secrets," she said. "Too many. You ever want to know secrets, just ask me. I'll tell you all the goddamn secrets you want."

"If you want to," I said. It was suddenly in my mind to say, *I love you, Kelly*, but I didn't want to say it.

"If it would help," I said, "go ahead. I won't tell."

"How could you tell?" she said. "Jesus. They screwed up your head so bad you hardly know your name. Nobody would believe you anyway."

I didn't answer, and we were both quiet again for quite a while.

"You know what I really should do?" Kelly asked. "After we really do get up into the mountains?"

"What?" I said.

"I should go where there are no people," she said. "Where I don't have to listen to people run all their crummy shit out on me, and where I don't have to talk to nobody. God, I get sick of the way I sound when I talk."

"We could do that," I said. "We could go where there are no lights and no clouds and no other people. And we could lie under the stars all night long and never say anything. We could agree not to talk through the whole night, just watch the sky for shooting stars."

"I sound like a fifty-year-old whore when I talk," she said. "Jesus, I hate it."

"I like to listen to you," I said.

"I sound like my mother," she said.

I didn't answer or say anything.

"Was that really your mother back there?" Kelly asked, after a while.

"Where?" I asked.

"That got killed," she said. "In the trailer."

"Yes," I answered.

"The bastards," she said. "They could at least have let you out for the funeral."

"Joy's dead," I said.

"Yes, she is," Kelly answered. "Yes, she is."

We rode along again for a long time without talking.

"I know a place where we can go," Kelly said, after the long silence.

"Where there aren't any people?" I asked.

"That doesn't make sense, Louis," she said.

"Why?" I asked. "It would be nice."

"If you and I went there," she said, "there would be people. You can't get away from that."

"I meant other people," I said.

"What difference would it make?" she asked.

I didn't try to answer.

"Besides," she said, "you need to have people around to make it."

I still didn't answer. I wanted to say, *We're not the same as them*, but I didn't want her to tell me I was wrong.

"But I know this place," Kelly said, "up in the mountains. The Indians used to go there to heal themselves. They thought it was magic or something."

I didn't say anything, but she paused as if I was answering or was asking her to tell me more about the place. I kept quiet and waited for her to quit listening to whatever she was hearing. It was still in my mind to say, *I love you, Kelly. I'm glad you're here*, but it seemed like it would be bad to change the subject.

"Anyway," she said, "there's a natural hot springs there. The Indians went there to heal themselves, and then thirty or forty years ago a rich doctor from Chicago built a lodge there for his rich patients. It's way up in the mountains, but there are lots of rich people around. It'll be perfect."

"We'll go there," I said. "And we don't have to talk if you don't want to."

We didn't talk for a long time after that. Kelly went to sleep, and I kept driving. After she had been asleep for a while, she wiggled all around in the seat and put her head on my leg and slept that way. With her close to me like that, I began to smell lilacs, faintly at first, but then stronger and stronger. She slept that way for a long time, until the smell of the lilacs was so strong and so sweet I was afraid it was making me drift away from what I was doing. I felt her stir and then turn, so she was looking up at me, rubbing her eyes.

"Are you sleepy?" she asked.

"You smell pretty," I said.

"I used some of the powder," she said, "from the compact in the purse. I hope you don't mind."

"It smells pretty," I said.

"Are you sleepy?" she asked and sat up.

I was tired, so I pulled over. We traded places so she could drive and I could rest.

"This is a big car," she said, when she was settled behind the wheel.

"Do you know how to drive it?" I asked.

I was suddenly aware that she was too young to have a license and might not have much experience, might get us in a wreck.

"Don't worry," she laughed. "Right now I could fly an airplane if it would get us off this goddamn prairie."

I believed her and was asleep almost as soon as I leaned over against the window. When I woke up, we were parked behind a gas station in a little town, not off the prairie yet. Kelly was asleep with her head on my leg again, and the sun was coming up over the horizon behind us. I didn't disturb her until the old man came to open up the station.

"We made Colorado," she said. "I could have made the mountains if we'd had enough gas."

Chapter

6

Kelly was fourteen, and it was her first time off the prairie. So, from Denver on, I had to do the driving, up into the mountains to the top of Monarch Pass. That's a place so high no trees grow up there, at least not if you hike up a little way, like we did, to where you can see the continental divide. At the lookout site, they had a big map, cast in metal, showing the rivers and explaining where we were. A trickle of water going around one side of a rock would flow into the Arkansas and the Mississippi and on to the Gulf of Mexico at New Orleans. But if that same little bit of water went around the other side of the same rock, it could run down the Colorado to the Gulf of California and be on the Pacific side. I had been through New Orleans several times and in California too. Even though all of these places were new to Kelly, standing up there on the divide, it seemed like we could go anywhere.

"Where do we go now?" I asked.

"Down Monarch," Kelly said, pointing west, "toward Gunnison."

"How do you know how to find this place?" I asked.

"From the letters," she answered. "I'm just following directions."

"You know somebody there?" I asked. "Somebody that wrote to you?"

"No," she answered. "They're Louis' letters."

"What Louis?" I asked.

"Joy's brother," she said. "Your uncle."

"How could he have written to you?" I asked. "He died in the war, before you were ever born."

"That's bullshit," Kelly said.

"What is?" I asked.

"That your uncle died in the war," she answered.

"How do you know that?" I asked.

"From the letters," she said.

"Where are these letters?" I asked. "How did you get them?"

"In the duffel bag," she answered. "Right down in the car."

"How could he have written to you?" I asked. "He never wrote to me. He's dead."

"He didn't write to me," Kelly said. "The letters are from Louis to Joy."

"And you read them?" I asked. "Do you go around reading other people's mail?"

"The cops in Hemmings read everything," she said. "So I read them too."

"You must have been in good with them," I said.

"Don't go acting pissed off," she said. "I got you and me out of there. And besides, I paid the price."

I knew what she meant, and I had a flash of feeling that I should drive back down there, on the Arkansas side, and kill somebody to even things up. I looked out over the mountains again. Everything can change so fast. A moment before I felt like a bird, like I could open my wings, and lift, and go anywhere the wind could go. But now I felt that I either had to go with Kelly to this place she wanted to go to, or I had to go back down to Hemmings and find those cops and even things up. It was one or the other.

"Maybe we should go back," I said.

"You're not ready for that," Kelly said. "Besides, that's what they want. They'll be waiting. They'll kill you."

I looked out over the mountains. I didn't care so much about dying, but I remembered the faces of the policemen who had talked to me when I was in jail. They looked so happy telling me all the terrible things that were going to happen to me, what it was like for a young guy like me in a prison full of men. I could even picture myself lying on the street dead, all shot full of holes, and it didn't bother me that much. But seeing their faces, how happy they'd be if I had done what they wanted, that did bother me.

"Uncle Louis wrote to Joy," I asked, "about some place we can go?"

"The lodge," Kelly said. "It's just on this side of Gunnison."

"She never told me about it," I said. "I think I would remember."

"She never got the letters," Kelly said.

"We always traveled a lot," I said.

"It wasn't that," she said. "I don't understand the whole thing, but Lenny's father had them, for years, and he never delivered them. They were written way back in the war, and he was supposed to get them to Joy, but he didn't. He kept them all this time, and then, not long ago, Lenny gave some of them to Joy's father. The ones in your footlocker, in the trunk of your car, are the ones Lenny gave to her father. You've read those, haven't you?"

I didn't answer right away. I saw Joy kneeling in the kitchen, holding the little wooden cross, and I saw her father up in the loft with the gun still in his mouth. I remembered how tight both of them were holding on, how I had covered up Joy in the bed and had put the blanket over her father, with him still holding his rifle.

"You've read the ones in your footlocker, haven't you?" Kelly asked.

I shook my head, but I didn't say anything.

"It doesn't matter," she said. "The letters are all down in the car."

"Are you sure Uncle Louis didn't die in the war?" I asked.

"Positive," she answered.

"Good," I said. "I'm glad he didn't. I'm glad he came back."

We looked at the mountains a little while longer before we hiked down to the car. It was a powerful place to be, up there on that lookout point, seeing how the shape of a small rock could influence a river and feeling the wind blowing out of the west.

The wind had to come all the way up, almost two miles straight up from the ocean, to get over the top, and I felt up there that the wind blowing on my body wasn't just ordinary wind, that it was special, that it could heal. The short hike up had made me tired, and it wasn't just the altitude. I almost felt that I had never been in shape, had never done physical work, had never trained to walk the high wire. But the wind was powerful, and it made me want to go there again and again until I got my strength back.

We drove on west, down the mountain onto a high plateau. I had been through there before because there are only two real highways east and west through Colorado, so it wasn't as if I was seeing it for the first time. Still, it was a disappointment. Down on the prairie the mountains look impressive. All I could think about when I was in Kansas, after Joy was dead, was that it would be good to go to the mountains, that it would even be good just to look at them. But when we were actually up in them, they lost some of that impressiveness. The plateau just looked like a little prairie, a little Kansas. I could feel the difference. I had to close my eyes, but I could tell we were in the mountains. Of course, I could only do that for a second or two at a time, driving the car, but it felt so good to be up in a higher place that it was worth it even just for a real short moment.

On the west side of the flatland, Kelly directed us up a two-lane dirt road north into a large valley. The lodge was just a few miles off the main highway, but it looked completely alone. It looked like it might be the only large building in the world, like the feeling I imagined I would have if I went way up in the mountains in China or was going up toward Everest and came on a temple. It was just a feeling, though. It wasn't because of the design of the lodge. That was kind of ordinary. It sat on the last bit of level ground before the rock rose sharply upward into a glacier. It was a large building, white with green shutters, but it looked small against the mountains. There was a middle section with a high peaked roof and a huge stone fireplace. Judging by the windows, it was two stories with an attic above that. The paint was peeling, and the shutters were closed over all the windows. Back behind the lodge there was another building, but as we approached on the road all we could see of it was a roof that looked like an unusually big barn.

"We drove right to it," I said.

The tall weeds rattled and brushed the underside of the Packard as I pulled into the lot and parked in front.

"I guess this is it," Kelly said.

"Sure it is," I said. "There's no other places around."

"But there's nobody here, Louis," she said. "This can't be it."

"Maybe you should look at the letter," I said.

"I should burn the goddamn letter," she said. "Your uncle was full of shit. There's nobody here."

I didn't want to talk to her, so I got out and looked around. The first door I tried was open. Behind it was a hallway that ran the length of the wing. Most of the plaster on the ceiling of the hall had come down, so it was either hanging there waiting to fall or was piled on the floor where it had already fallen. The light fixtures were loose, and one was dangling by a wire. There were three rooms on each side of the hall, and the doors to all of them were open. All the light was coming from the back side of the lodge, because for some reason the shutters on the front were closed, and the ones on the back were open.

There was almost no trash on the stairs, so I went up. It was hard to believe right at first that it was the same building up there. It was dusty, as if no one had been there to clean it up for quite a while, but the ceiling was smooth white plaster, and the round, frosted glass light fixtures were all in a row the way they should be, so there was a hall light above each door to each room. The doors were open up there too.

I walked down the hall to the end, checking each room as I went. The last one on the front side was dark, like all the others on the front, but there was enough light coming through from the back that I could see there was a small fireplace just inside the door. It wasn't so dark that I had to feel my way, but I kept one hand on the wall anyway as I moved toward the shuttered window. The bricks were cool, even though it was upstairs and was a warm day. Crouching a little, I touched the bed with my other hand. There was a big chair backed into the corner, and when I got between the foot of the bed and the chair and then followed the footboard a few feet, I was right in front of the window. The curtains were dusty, but the window was unlocked and slid up easily. I felt the shutters until I found the catch, unlatched it, and pushed them open. The sunlight was blinding for a moment, but when I got used to it I was looking right down on the parking lot.

"Kelly!" I hollered.

I could see her through the windshield of the car.

"Come up and see this one!" I yelled. "It's got a fireplace."

She didn't move, and she didn't answer.

"Kelly!" I yelled again. "Hey, Kelly, a fireplace."

She still didn't move. I had never lived anywhere with a fireplace in my whole life, but I sure did know how to build a fire. That would be good later on when it got cold. I liked that. The room had a double bed, rumpled but still made, with a nightstand on each side. On the other side of the window there was another overstuffed chair backed into the other corner. They both had the same deep purple material, heavy like on the seats of the Packard, and with the shutters open I could see that the curtains and the bedspread were a light lavender, like lilacs it seemed to me. On the wall on the side of the bed away from the fireplace there was a wide dresser with six drawers, painted white with gold trim. It had a frame going up the wall, but the mirror was missing. There was a closet just past the dresser, in the corner. It was a big closet, big enough to dress in.

I sat down on the bed with my back up against the metal headboard. It was cold too. I could see out the window across the plateau to where the mountains rose up on the other side. The valley was wide and flat and open, but it had been fenced to make fields and pastureland. The grass was long and brown, light brown, kind of blond-looking. The mountains went up sharply on the other side. I studied the shapes for a while. I probably couldn't really see all the way to the continental divide, but I liked sitting there for a few moments thinking that I could. Continental divide or not, I knew right away that it would be possible to someday know all the places formed by the shapes of the mountains and be able to tell where I was. That was so different from the prairie, where it all seemed to be the same thing forever.

I was about to get lost tracing out the lines of the mountains, so I got up and went back down the hall and down the stairs to the first floor and back outside to get Kelly.

"Come on, Kelly," I said through the window on her side. "I found a room with its own fireplace."

"We can't stay here," she answered.

"Why not?" I asked and opened her door.

"Because we can't afford it," she answered. "And there's no way to make any money."

"We won't have to pay," I said. "Half of the place is a wreck. Nobody would pay to stay here, and there's nobody to charge us anyway."

"I shouldn't have come," she said.

"Bullshit," I said. "Back there on the mountain, up on top of the pass, you said you 'paid the price' to get us out of Kansas. It's bullshit to say you should have stayed there, with them."

"The sons a bitches," she whispered.

"Come on," I said. "I found a room with a fireplace."

"It's July," she said. "What the hell do we want with a fireplace?"

"It won't be July for long," I answered. "Besides, it's got a bed. You can get some rest."

Kelly followed me back into the lodge and up to the room I had picked. After we got the dust off of things and got the duffel bag upstairs, and Kelly changed into Levi's and a blue work shirt, we decided to make our first trip toward town before sleeping. We didn't go all the way into Gunnison but stopped at the first little store with gas pumps and filled the car before we spent anything on food. We were down to thirty-five dollars and the pearls. Since we weren't really sure we would have any way to cook, at least not right away, we bought mostly stuff we could eat right out of the can, like beans and tuna and peanut butter, and we got bread and milk and crackers. On the way back to the lodge, we drank a whole quart of milk between us and ate half a package of crackers with peanut butter. I parked the Packard in back, out of sight from the road, between our wing and the big barn, and Kelly went up for a nap.

There was a closed-in walkway two stories high between the middle section of the lodge and the back building. It wasn't a barn. There were windows, large bay windows, each standing out like its own little glassed-in balcony, all around the second-story level. There were large flat windows around a third story. No one ever built a barn with windows like that. I walked all the way around outside, looking for a way in, but the only entrance was inside the lodge through the walkway. I checked the doors on the rest of the lodge. Nothing was locked. Everywhere things looked pretty much the same. Downstairs was a mess. Upstairs, not too bad. It made me nervous that the place wasn't locked up, made me feel that the owner might show up at any minute, but so much was in such bad shape it was hard to believe that there was an owner.

Everything has an owner, I know. You can't go anywhere without trespassing. But I figured we would just have to wait and see what would happen when the owner showed up, if he ever did.

Kelly was asleep when I got back from looking over the lodge. She was tucked in under one sheet, still in her Levi's and work shirt, on the side of the bed away from the fireplace. She had taken off her tennis shoes and set them neatly side by side, under the dresser. It seemed warm enough that I didn't think we would need a fire. Maybe it would have been good just for the light, until we got lanterns or candles, but I hadn't thought about that soon enough to get the wood together or to find matches. So, I slouched down into one of the chairs at the foot of the bed and waited to get sleepy.

Kelly was pretty, curled up on her side all soft and quiet. I wanted to touch her hair and be closer to her, but I couldn't tell, yet, what kind of friends we were going to be, so I thought the best thing to do would be to sleep in the chair and show her I wouldn't try to take advantage of her. It wasn't all that easy, though. She looked real comfortable, and the chair wasn't that great a place to sleep. I woke up several times during the night and even got a little chilly before sunrise. I pulled the covers up over Kelly, so she wouldn't get cold, and then walked up and down the hall to get warm until the sun was all the way up and I could walk around outside.

The mountains went up on every side. We were in the northwest corner of the valley, but there were even mountains on the south between the lodge and the highway. I kept looking off toward the east, partly because of the sun rising and warming things, but also because I was thinking about what we had seen from the top of the pass. The winds coming out of the west had to come up over the mountains behind us and then pass over the valley, still climbing for the divide. That's how it seemed, and I felt, as I had felt in my dreams lots of times, that I could spread myself on the wind and just rise and rise until I was in the full power of it. I stood in front of the lodge with my eyes closed, swaying for a few moments, arms spread, feeling free and powerful, rising on the wind, glad there was no one around to remind me that people can't fly.

Even as I moved and began walking again, I seemed to be seeing the lodge from high in the air, and I could tell from up there that if I went out in back of the lodge, I would find a large hole, away from everything else. When I walked out back, I did find a hole, and I began figuring out a system for sorting out stuff like plaster and wallpaper and glass from wood. I gathered up wastebaskets and buckets and made several trips out to the big hole with plaster and other trash and kept doing that until the wood I was saving out of it made a whole armload, and then I carried it upstairs for the fireplace. I knew that if I just kept doing that I would eventually get the whole place cleaned up, and we would have wood to burn to stay warm. I also knew that if there had been people around and I had said I was going to clean the place up with wastebaskets and buckets, they would have said it couldn't be done. I felt good about being there alone for a while and not having that much to do with people.

Kelly slept until a couple of hours after the sun was up, and by then I had a pretty good stack of wood in the room. Most of it was narrow stuff, about an inch wide and real thin, the strips they put on the walls before they put on the plaster. I knew it would burn pretty fast, but it was a start. And I had discovered that the big barn was a cover for a naturally heated swimming pool, where the patients were supposed to be soaking, I guessed. I was hoping Kelly would be impressed by the wood and excited about the pool and would want to go soak, but she wouldn't even look at it. She was more concerned about the fact that we didn't have much money and that we weren't very well prepared to take care of ourselves. So, after we had eaten more crackers and peanut butter, we got in the Packard, went down to the highway, and drove west toward Gunnison, looking for any sign we could see of a job that needed doing, things that people didn't want to do for themselves.

We saw lots of things—weeds that needed pulling and trash that needed to be picked up and lumber that needed to be stacked or hauled off to be burned—but most of the people were happy to leave things the way they were rather than pay us to do something about them. We did find one woman, in a farmhouse near the highway, whose husband had bought her a new gas stove, and she let us fill up the trunk with firewood because she said she hoped she'd live the rest of her life and never build another fire. After we got the wood, we went on down the road about another half mile and pulled into a little roadside diner to have coffee and donuts.

The only other car at the diner was a light blue 1956 Ford. It had almost no chrome and had a big decal on the door, showing mountains and saying Gunnison County Department of Health.

"Remember this car," Kelly said.

"Why?" I asked.

"It's the health inspector," she said.

"Who's that?" I asked.

"He can close a place," she said, "if he says it isn't clean."

"And we do the cleaning," I said.

"Unless he bribes cheaper than we work," Kelly answered.

We did get a job there. The inspector was leaving just as we came in. The cook was mad. He rumbled back and forth behind the counter, spilled our coffee when he finally waited on us, and cursed under his breath because we weren't having a meal. I was for leaving and coming back when he was in a better mood, but Kelly asked him questions about what came with the different meals on the menu and how much extra he charged for extra portions of things. She got him talking and worked the conversation around to the inspection. His name was Art. He had been running the diner for almost ten years, since he got out of the army. He had learned to cook in the army, and he had also learned to hate being told what to do and to hate cleaning. The health inspector had made him mad on both counts. Art was just over six feet tall and weighed close to three hundred pounds. He barely had room to move back and forth between the counter and the grill.

"Hell," he said, confidentially, "even if one of those cute young gals from the college come in here and wanted to go out with me if I'd just get down and clean under that grill, it wouldn't do no good because I'd never get back up."

He laughed and looked sad all at the same time, but he wasn't as mad as when we first came in. Kelly struck a bargain with him that we would clean up the things the inspector didn't like, and Art would pay us in meals or in food we could take home, whichever he liked best. There was a pillar of grease behind the grill because the grill and the trays for catching the grease didn't fit together right, never had, and it had built up to where it was maybe two feet wide at the bottom.

"Used to be," Art said, "I'd give him liver and onions, no charge, and he'd be happy. But no more. He's moving up."

"Up?" I asked.

"City council," he said. "He's running for city council."

"To clean up government?" Kelly asked.

Art laughed and laughed. It was a nasty job, and he knew it. We settled on breakfast for both of us every morning for a week, two eggs, hashbrowns, choice of meat, and coffee.

"And I get to tell him I done it myself," Art said.

"Deal," Kelly said. "He'll wish he had taken the liver."

Art laughed again and told us stories about some of the pranks they played when he was in the army. We went back to the lodge, unloaded the wood, and rested up before we went back. He closed at ten at night. It took us most of one night, but we had the place shining by 5:30 when Art had to start getting ready to open. He was happy with what we had done, and he had been celebrating the joke he was going to have. Art gave us two extra days of breakfast. We were tired, but we felt good too.

When we weren't cruising around looking for the health inspector's blue Ford and weren't staying up all night getting the spoiled meat out of a meat saw or digging broken bags of french fries out of a freezer, when we had time to be at home, little by little we got our room fixed up. I had found a room on the main floor, back behind the desk in the lobby, that looked like it might have been the janitor's shop, with tools and ladders and things for making repairs. It had lanterns and lantern fuel and boxes of candles and matches, so we could have light at night. There was a little trash burner stove in there too. Kelly and I got the stove up the stairs, and I got the chimney pipe worked out so it went into the fireplace and up. I even cut some tin to go around the pipe so a gust of wind wouldn't blow all the smoke back down through the fireplace into the room.

I hauled out the double bed and brought in two singles from other rooms. We put them almost right next to each other because there wasn't room any other way, so it was almost the same as a double. But I thought it was important for Kelly to know I wasn't trying to take advantage of her, so I insisted on the two single beds. There was just enough space that you could sit on either side of either bed. It crowded the room more than it had been, and I even suggested we might want a room for each of us. Kelly didn't think we could keep two rooms warm in the winter, and I agreed with that.

I thought we were doing pretty good. The jobs we were getting were nothing big, but they kept us in food and gasoline, and that was what we needed the most. Kelly was fine about not having extra money or fancy things, but she didn't like not knowing what was going on. It wasn't just coming up there thinking the lodge was going to be a nice place and its turning out to be in such bad shape. And it wasn't just having big dreams about how there would be rich people everywhere, eager to pay a couple of kids like us to do whatever they needed to have taken care of. It was all the other things that people did that had probably gone on for a long time, long before the lodge was even built, things that were still going on now that the lodge was closed. It was all the things we wished we had known about before we came. We had never been through the changes in the valley, so we found out about everything that happened after it happened.

One morning we heard a tractor engine roaring and roaring, pulling a big piece of machinery up the road, creeping along. By noon a truck had brought in a small crew, and they were out in the fields following the machine and the tractor, standing bales of hay on end in pairs, leaning them against each other to dry. By the time I saw the crew was there and had watched to see that it was a simple job I could have done real easy, they were close to finished, and it was too late to get in on any of the work.

All kinds of things like that happened. They herded cattle down out of the mountains into the pastures, and loaded the hay onto big trucks, and then later loaded the cattle and hauled them away too. That was about the time the first snow came up high in the mountains, when they took the cattle away. It was also the time when the hunters came, but they were already there before Kelly and I even knew about it. We had gone into Gunnison to price warm clothes and figure out how much cash we were going to need. We went into a restaurant for pie, and there were three or four booths full of people dressed in college sweat suits, wearing bright orange ribbons tied all over their bodies.

"What's that?" Kelly asked.

"The college ski team," the waitress answered.

"Why the ribbons?" Kelly asked.

"Where are you from?" the waitress asked.

"Kansas," Kelly answered. "Why?"

"That explains it," the waitress said.

"Explains what?" Kelly asked.

"They run up and down W Mountain," the waitress said, "to get in shape for ski season."

She laughed.

"They look pretty shapely to me," she said and laughed again.

"Why the ribbons?" Kelly asked.

"So they won't get shot," the waitress answered.

"Who the hell wants to shoot a ski team?" Kelly asked.

"Hunters," the waitress said. "Texans. Most people around here just stay out of the hills while the Texans are here. They kill one or two people a day, mostly each other, but not always."

"You're kidding," Kelly said.

"Don't find out the hard way, dearie," the waitress said. "Stay home or wear bright clothes."

There was a newspaper on the counter, a Denver paper, saying there were a hundred thousand out-of-state hunters on the western side of the mountains in Colorado for the out-of-state season. It was an army. We had been invaded, and Kelly and I found out about it from a waitress in the town cafe.

We went across the street to price long underwear and hats and gloves. It came to almost a hundred dollars for both of us, and we didn't have anywhere near that much, but we saw the rolls of bright orange ribbon. They had a stack of it right by the cash register. Someone had drawn a poster with two men who looked exactly alike, except one had ribbon tied all over him. One was labeled "A" and the other one "B." Under the picture was the question, "Which is the deer: A or B?" We bought a roll and drove on back to the lodge.

At first I felt funny about wearing the ribbon, but we tied it on us the way we had seen the ski team do when we went out for a walk, even if it was just on the road. And we were glad we did because we started hearing stories, like how the year before a hunter had shot two kids off of motorbikes up in the mountains, two brothers, and had gotten away with it, swearing he thought he was shooting at an elk. A game warden in a place we were going to clean told me that some of the hunting accidents were murders, two guys going for the same promotion in the same company, but they just couldn't prove it in court, so one guy could shoot the other one and say it was a hunting accident and get off with a fine. We started having our own experiences with them too, because they would come to the lodge.

Most of the hunters we saw had come a long way, California or Nevada or, more than anywhere, Texas. We didn't have any liquor or ammunition to sell them, and that's what most of them wanted. Neither of us was old enough to buy booze, and we didn't have the money. One morning, real early, a man woke us up, pounding on the door. It was about four o'clock, and he was drunk.

"We're full," Kelly told him, just like we were a big hotel.

"I don't see nobody's trucks," the hunter said.

He had on an orange cap with the earmuffs turned down, and an orange hunter's vest, and so many layers of warm clothes that his arms wouldn't hang straight down at his sides.

"My pa's out with a party now," Kelly said, "hunting for elk."

"We just want permission to hunt," the man said.

"You'll have to pay for that," Kelly said, "and you'll have to wait until Pa comes back."

She started to close the door.

"We got to be out there at sunup to get anything," the man said.

He was swaying on his feet and almost fell.

"How much would your pa charge," he asked, "if he was here?"

"A hundred dollars," Kelly said.

"That's a lot of money," the man said.

"It's only fifty each for the both of you," she answered.

I was standing behind her and could see that there were two others in the truck, so I knew Kelly should have been able to see them too. But I didn't say anything.

"How's your pa gonna know we paid?" the man asked, digging the money out of his layers of clothing. "We might run across him out there. Wouldn't want to get shot."

He laughed.

"Sure wouldn't want to get shot," he said again.

"Wear these," Kelly answered and traded the hunter orange ribbons for the five twenties. "On both arms."

We went back up to our room and waited in the dark until we couldn't hear their truck any more. Both of us were scared they would get up into the hills, sober up and figure out what had happened, and then come back and make trouble. Still, I admired her for being able to think so quickly.

"I never would have tried it," Kelly said, "if he hadn't been drunk."

"Didn't you see the other one?" I asked. "There were three of them. Maybe you could have got a hundred and fifty."

"I saw them all," she answered. "He thought he was cheating me. That's why he didn't put up much fuss about paying. The son of a bitch thought he was cheating us out of fifty dollars."

"You were great," I said. "You think so fast."

"I was scared, Louis," she said. "Did you see their license plate?"

"Texas?" I guessed.

"Kansas," she said. "I didn't know them from Hemmings, but they could have been. They were drunk, and they had guns, and we don't even have a ball bat by the door. I was scared."

"I've never even shot a gun," I said, "except in the shooting gallery at a circus where it was easy. Nothing was going to get hurt."

"I wasn't thinking about a gun," she said. "It's you, Louis. I don't even know if you're really here half the time."

"What did you want me to do?" I asked. "Beat him up? You wanted to answer the door. You always want to answer the door or talk to people about jobs. So what is it I'm supposed to do? You're better at that than me."

"Don't you care that I'm scared?" she asked. "Did it ever cross your mind they might think I'm pretty? Don't you think they might want to come back here because they thought I was pretty?"

"Sure," I said. "I thought about it lots of times. I wouldn't let them hurt you."

"Louis?" she asked.

"What?" I said.

"Could we have the one bed back?" she asked.

"Sure," I said. "If you want."

"I get scared at night, sometimes," she said. "And I get afraid that you don't care, because you're way over there, and you never read the letters."

"The letters?" I asked.

"To Joy," she said. "The letters from Louis to Joy. I saved them so you could have them. They'll know I took them, and they'll know about this place too. I'm scared, Louis, and I worry you don't care."

"I'll change the beds back," I said. "I just did it so you wouldn't think I was going to try to take advantage of you or something."

"And the letters?" she asked.

"I'll change the beds around," I said, "and then you can explain to me what's in the letters."

"Can I come over with you now?" she asked.

We cuddled in my narrow little bed until she fell asleep, then I got up and walked through the whole lodge, in and out of every room, looking to see if there was a gun anywhere I hadn't seen before, but there wasn't. The hunters never came back after Kelly or their money. It started snowing that afternoon and kept on snowing for three days. Kelly and I didn't try to go anywhere and didn't hear any news. We stayed in the lodge, and took out the twin beds, and put in the double, and concentrated on moving all the wood we could up to the room right across the hall from us. Kelly was happy about everything but the letters.

"Why don't you just read them?" she asked. "They're right there on the dresser all the time."

"I'm not very good at that," I said.

"You can read fine," she said. "I've seen you lots of times."

"No," I said. "It's like math. Did you ever take math?"

"Sure," she said.

"Well, it's like that," I said. "Sometimes they would send problems, and if I couldn't get them, I would look at the answers."

"Who sent you problems?" she asked.

"The school," I said. "I forget the address. But sometimes, if I looked at the answer, I would understand how they worked the problem, and how they came up with what they did. But sometimes, even looking at the answers, I couldn't figure it out, because I'm not very good at that."

"I'm lost," Kelly said.

"I don't think I'm going to understand the letters," I said. "I know the answer. 'Joy is dead.' But I'm not very good at figuring out why it happened, and I can't even remember lots of things."

"But the letters would help," she said. "It's not that big a thing, just to read them."

"I could dream about it," I said.

"What do you mean?" she asked.

"You could read them aloud while I'm asleep," I said, "and I'll dream about it. I can do pretty good that way."

"One of these days," Kelly said, "Lenny or Larry or both is going to . . ."

"Who's Larry?" I asked.

"Lenny's brother," she answered. "His slimy brother."

"How do you know them?" I asked.

"I know all the people you're mixed up with," she said, "from my mother and from the letters."

"You never tell me about your mother," I said. "Why should I read the letters?"

"They fixed my mother so she's never going to hurt anybody," Kelly said. "But those letters are going to kill us both if we don't get smart soon."

I didn't have any answer for her, but I still couldn't make myself read. We didn't talk about it any more that day or for several days, until one morning Kelly was counting the money, had it laid out on the dresser in piles, the twenties together and the tens and the ones. She was stacking the coins, and she held one up, about the size of a quarter.

"You ever see one of these before?" she asked.

I turned the coin over in the palm of my hand. There was a five-pointed star on each side. On one side there was a figure of a man behind the star so one point was at his head, and one was at each hand, and one was at each foot. On the other side was the figure of a woman behind that same star. You could hardly tell which was the man and which was the woman, but they were different. It looked like one of Dacia's coins.

"Where'd you get this?" I asked.

"Lenny," she answered. "He gave it to Larry. He told him to show it to you, and you'd tell them anything to get it back. So I took it."

"It's Dacia's," I said. "She traveled with us everywhere, until we split up."

"I know," Kelly said. "I know all about your people."

"Will you help me if I read them?" I asked and picked up the letters from the dresser.

"I'd be pretty stupid not to," Kelly answered.

I started that same afternoon.

Some parts of the letters gave me no trouble at all, but it took me a lot longer to read through them than I let Kelly know. She thought I read them all, but the thing was, when she showed me the letters all piled up on the dresser, she didn't tell me there were pictures in there too. If it hadn't been for the pictures, I might have gotten farther through. There were three bundles, two of them had photographs, and the other one was just letters. I didn't pay much attention to the photograph in the first bundle until I had read the letter tied up with it. It was a posed black-and-white studio portrait, in a gold-colored metal frame. It looked like most of the other pictures of young soldiers I had seen, but the letter was so different from the face in the frame that it was hard to make myself stop staring at the picture.

The young soldier was Uncle Louis in a dress uniform with a knotted tie and a cloth overseas cap. The Kansas prairie was still there in his face, all the lines of it blending into each other with nothing sharp or jagged or startling. His eyes looked out to somewhere far away, not at the camera, not at me. His hair lay close to his head, even and modest as if it was wheat. He was smiling, but his smile barely shaped his mouth. I had seen that face over and over at the carnivals, a farm boy not used to socializing, content to share his life with his sister and a few close friends. There was no meanness in it, and it was hard to imagine him hurting anyone. I read the letter over again, slowly, to be sure I hadn't made a mistake.

Germany. February 1945. Dear Sis: Bob Hardy died in the war today. We have been together from the time we buddied up to go onto the beach at Normandy. Just when we were both beginning to think we would escape this war alive, a German kid—you couldn't call him a soldier—a boy with a rifle, stumbled on to our foxhole. He was barely bigger than his gun, maybe fourteen or fifteen years old, lost and scared and probably certain he was going to die, like most of us are. He looked surprised and stood there looking down into the foxhole at us. For a long moment I thought he would not shoot, so I hesitated. I guess it's because of the way we had been talking about coming home. I don't think I really believed the kid was there. I thought it was just my imagination testing me to see if I believed the things we had been saying. Then suddenly the boy fired without aiming, and Bobbie was dead. I didn't even think. I killed the kid. I shot him point-blank, looking right into his eyes while he was still too stunned by what he had just done to react to anything. It's horrible. I started to say I wish you were here with me, but I don't. I wish no one was here. I have killed a boy who killed my closest friend. Tomorrow will be more. I just hope it is over soon. I love you, Louis.

I stared at the photograph for a long time, trying to get the picture and the letter to fit together in my mind. I had had the idea that Uncle Louis didn't really want to go to the war but that he had gone, and had been killed, probably because he was too reluctant to be a soldier, because he loved life too much to kill anybody. The boy in the picture looked like that, as if the uniform wasn't really his, as if it had been picked out for him by someone else. It looked almost as strange as the pictures they sometimes take in carnivals, where you put your head through a hole so it will be on the body of something they have painted there. It was odd, though, because I couldn't really remember people having told me things about Uncle Louis. I knew people had, but right then, I couldn't picture even one scene in my mind where someone was describing him to me. That didn't mean that it had never happened.

Ever since Joy died, I had had trouble with my memory. Sometimes I would remember something as clearly as if I was dreaming it. Other times I couldn't recall what had happened, even though I knew it had happened, as I knew we had decided to split off from Dacia and go see Joy's father, but I couldn't remember how we had decided or whether I had argued against it. There were times when I would try to remember Joy, and I couldn't. It was as if all I could see in my mind was photographs of her, but not her, dancing. It used to be that I would see something and that would remind me of one of Joy's dances, and I would see her dancing in my mind, like I was dreaming. It would be real clear, so I could tell where we were, what part of the country, and could pick out the faces of people we knew who were there in the crowd. Since she died, it seemed as if all the dances were gone too, as if no one would be able to remember them without her at least there watching. I worried sometimes that I was losing my memory and that someday I would lose it all, and they would lock me up. When I tried hard, though, there were lots of things I could remember clearly, so I felt pretty sure I wasn't going to lose everything. I just needed some rest.

Kelly had been sitting in one of the chairs by the window, in her blue jeans and a plaid wool shirt. Most of the time her hair looked jet black, but with the sun coming through the window behind her, I could see little streaks of brown. She was looking out the window, writing, and looking again, making a list of warm clothes we could buy with the money she got from the hunters. She saw me staring and looked right into my eyes.

"Are you all right?" she asked.

"Sure," I said.

"I'll be back in a few minutes," she said.

She bent forward in her chair to put on her tennis shoes. Her hair was long enough that her head seemed to just disappear when she did that.

"I was just noticing the brown in your hair," I said.

"I'll be right back," she said.

I watched her leave the room and wondered if she had ever told me why she came with me. I couldn't remember whether I had ever asked. We were just together, and I hadn't thought to question it. She had to have her own reasons, and maybe she wouldn't stay forever. But she had said she would be back, so there would be time to find out.

I stared at the photograph and went over the letter again, trying to make the face in the picture change into someone dirty and tired, living in a hole, someone who watched people die and who killed people, but I couldn't make it change. All that happened was that everything would go dark, and lights would flash, and everything would go dark again, so I looked at the other picture. It was an unframed shot of Joy in a cardigan, Uncle Louis in a plaid civilian shirt, and a baby in almost nothing, sitting on his arm. Joy's hair was very curly, and her breasts were large and firm-looking, probably full of milk. She looked right into the camera, not off into the distance, and it was like even then she had been able to see the people who someday would be looking at the picture. I looked at her eyes, and I could remember thinking how she was so strong that there was nothing anyone could say or do that would make her act ashamed. She could make you feel that too, could make you feel that you didn't ever have to be ashamed either.

Uncle Louis held the baby high, like a race car driver with a trophy, proud like a father. He and Joy both looked happy and pleased and eager for what might be coming next. On the back of the picture it said, *Joy, Louis, and Louis, Jr. Summer 1945.* Joy had always told me Uncle Louis was killed in the war, and Kelly had said that it wasn't true. If he was killed in the war, he couldn't have been in Kansas in the summer of 1945, after the war was over. The inscription might be a mistake. There were two letters bundled together with that picture, and I guessed they would tell, because Kelly had seemed awfully certain, and she had read all the letters.

Germany. February 1945. Dear Sis: The only day in my life harder than yesterday was the night Mark was killed. That was the worst, but yesterday was next. They came and took away the bodies—Bobbie's and the German kid's—and I felt like I was dead too, like they had forgotten to take my body or would come back for it. This war is terrible. It has changed me. I hope not forever. All that keeps me alive now is the thought of you and my boy, of coming home and being like we were, taking care of Dacia. That's all I think about now, living our lives quietly and peacefully together, forgetting I was ever gone, forgetting all the killing. I love you and I always will, Louis.

The letters weren't all in order by when they had been written, and I knew there were things I wouldn't understand without reading them all. But there was another one written after Bobbie was killed, and that was all the letter reading I could take at one time.

Germany. February 1945. Dear Sis: It's so hard losing Bobbie. He understood about everything, about you and me, about everything. He made me feel like I could live my own life, not bothering other people, and everything would be fine. Most of the men here have families or girlfriends. They all carry pictures of their kids or their sweethearts. I've never seen Louis or his picture, but I know he's beautiful, like his mother. I just know he is. I want to see you and see him. That's what keeps me living. It's so easy to die here. I could just crawl out of my hole and go for a walk at sunup or sundown. But I want to see you again. Take care. I love you and I will for as long as I live, Louis.

I looked at the picture again, the one with the three of us together. I couldn't remember ever having seen a picture of myself as a baby before. Uncle Louis' shirt had short sleeves, and I wasn't wearing anything but a diaper. It had to be summer. Joy was wearing a sweater, but it was too big for her, drooped over the shoulders, and had a letter on it that someone had probably won playing a sport. So she could have been wearing it, even if it was too hot, if it was Uncle Louis' sweater, and if she wanted to show she was proud of him. The name on the shoulder was Bradley, and there was a metal badge pinned on the letter, but I couldn't make out what it was. On the back of the picture it said, *Summer 1945*, and there was also a stamp I hadn't seen before of the place that developed the picture. I couldn't read all of it because it was too faint, but it was in Denver and it was 1945.

If he had been killed in the war like Joy said, he would have been dead by the summer of 1945. If the picture really was taken in the summer, the way it looked, it couldn't have been the summer before, in 1944, because Uncle Louis went onto the beach at Normandy that summer. I knew that from correspondence school, and, besides, I wasn't born until June 1944. He said in the letter he had never seen me, and if it was me in the picture, I looked at least a year old. Joy had one arm around Uncle Louis' waist, and her breast was pressed up tight against him. I looked at the two of them standing together, so close to one another, and read the inscription on the back one more time. When Kelly came back, I was still looking at the picture, trying to see any other details I had missed.

"You were right," I said.

"About what?" she asked.

"About my Uncle Louis," I answered. "Joy lied to me."

"You really didn't know before?" she asked.

"No," I answered. "She told me he died in the war. I just believed what she told me."

"But, didn't you ever wonder who . . . ?" she asked.

She didn't finish the question. It was like she was waiting for me to say something. It was like she was checking to see if I understood.

"Who killed him?" I asked. "I just thought it was the war. People don't usually know in a war who they killed and who they didn't."

"No, Louis," Kelly said. "Your father. Didn't you ever wonder?"

"You said it was bullshit," I said.

She looked puzzled.

"Up on the divide," I said, "damn it. I told you that Louis died in the war, and you said that was bullshit."

"He didn't die in the war," she said. "But that's not what I'm talking about."

"You were right," I said. "Okay?"

"Okay," she answered.

"I'm just trying to tell you," I said, "that you were right and I was wrong. That's all."

"That's not all," she said, "but we can talk about it later."

"Jesus Christ," I said. "What's the big mystery?"

"I haven't ever known who my father was either," Kelly said. "So I understand. It's not easy to talk about. We'll discuss it later."

"I need to go for a walk," I said. "You can come if you want."

"Let's go out to the pool," she said.

"It'll be dark in there before long," I said.

"We can take a lantern," she said, "and go out back to the pool."

I built up the fire in the stove so the room would be warm when we came back, then followed her out toward the pool. In the back of the room across the hall from ours there was a door that led into a tiled room with changing areas and showers, and that connected by another door to another hallway. Once we were through the locker room and into the hall, we went through a set of double doors onto the walkway to the pool. The walkway was carpeted and plastered just like the halls in the rest of the building and had the same kind of lights and the same radiators under the windows along the walls. The shutters on the windows were all open. They had been like that since the day we arrived.

When Kelly and I went through the doors at the end of the walkway, we were standing on the second-story balcony of a three-story building. Below us was the pool. It was big enough to have been the town swimming pool in a city park, at least big enough for a small town. The water was hot. I could see the vapor coming off the surface, and I could smell the minerals. The sun was setting, and the light down on the pool level was already dim. Kelly stepped up beside me at the rail, put her arm up around my shoulders, and pulled my face close to hers.

"Look," she whispered.

She pointed toward the center of the pool.

"Isn't he beautiful?" she said.

Floating on his back in the middle of the water, in the mist, with his arms and legs spread out wide, naked, his eyes closed as if he was asleep, was a man, twenty, maybe twenty-five years old. He had long blond hair, almost long enough to touch his shoulders. I stood quietly watching him, waiting for him to move, and I slipped my arm around Kelly's waist to keep her close.

"Isn't he beautiful?" she said again.

The floating man was slowly turning in the water, like a clock with four hands, keeping the time.

"Are you okay?" I shouted, leaning over the rail.

The blond man opened his eyes, looked at me for a long fiery moment, and closed them again without moving or speaking.

"Are you okay?" I shouted again.

He didn't answer or open his eyes this time but slowly raised his arms out of the water, and pressed his palms together in front of his face, like he was praying or like he was bowing to us, and began to sink. Just as slowly, his face disappeared under the surface. I couldn't see any sign of panic from him. Kelly almost jumped forward and leaned way out over the rail. Slowly, as if it was important to be graceful, as if it was a special ritual, he extended his arms back out, like they had been, and his face reappeared. He was smiling. Kelly stepped back but stayed close enough to me to talk in a hushed voice.

"Do you think he's real?" she asked.

"He's real," I said. "What makes you think he isn't real?"

"I've seen him three times in the last week," she said. "In the pool. I never see him come or go, and I never hear him moving around. He's just there, like he came from nowhere."

"Just because he's quiet," I asked, "that means he isn't real?"

"He can float like that for an hour," she said.

She stepped back close to the rail, and looked over, and waited for a moment.

"And he knows a lot about you," Kelly said.

"You've talked to him?" I asked.

"Yes," she said.

"Why didn't you tell me about this?" I asked. "When you first saw him?"

"I thought maybe it was my imagination," she said. "And . . ."

"And what?" I asked.

"He told me you should read the letters," she said.

"He knew about the letters?" I asked.

"Yes," she said. "And I didn't tell him either. He just knew about them."

"Jesus Christ," I said. "How could he know about private letters nobody's read in fifteen years?"

"He told me you should read the letters," she said. "Then I should bring you."

"Jesus Christ," I said.

"His name is Joseph," Kelly said. "He knows everything about you, Louis."

"Everything?" I asked.

"More than you know yourself," she said. "Lots more."

Kelly sat down on the floor of the balcony, at the edge, with her legs hanging over. She folded her arms on the lower rail and rested her head on her hands without ever looking away from the man in the pool. We couldn't both stare at him, and, anyway, I hadn't come out there thinking I was going to meet someone new. I came out there to try to relax and understand the questions the letters had put in my head. So, I walked a few feet away, toward the corner, and lay down on the balcony, on my side with my head propped up on one hand, where I could watch Kelly watching.

Kelly's legs swung slowly back and forth from the knees, but other than that she didn't move for quite a while. I turned onto my back with my hands folded behind my head, able to see her only at a sharp angle out of the side of my eyes. The sky was turning yellow, and I had a very good view of that, looking almost straight up to the windows above. There was a balcony all the way around the third story, but there wasn't much up there, and I guessed that it was there just so the windows could be opened and closed and cleaned. The second-story balcony went all the way around too, but there were stalls with doors on all four walls, six stalls on each wall.

Kelly still wasn't moving, and I got up to look behind the door at my feet. Inside it was like a booth for changing clothes, except there was a large window and an easy chair instead of a bench, and there were no hooks for hanging clothes. But it was nice. Even though it was a cold day, the walls and the floor were still warm from where the sun had been coming in. Some of the doors to some of the booths were open, and some were closed, so there were beams of light, like stage lighting, coming from different angles and directions into the misty air above the pool. I took hold of the door to the booth, moving it slowly to watch what would happen to the patterns of light, seeing if I could change the light on the floating man and make him look different.

I never really let Kelly out of sight for more than a moment. She wasn't usually that quiet, unless she was asleep, but for a long time she didn't move, and I tiptoed around the second-floor balcony, moving the doors and playing with the light. By then the light had faded to a pale rose and wasn't strong enough to work like a spot. Right under the balcony where Kelly was sitting there was a large rock, huge, almost a whole story high. The cement was poured up to it and the tile was fitted up to it, and it looked as if the whole building had actually been constructed around that rock. That's where the hot water seemed to be coming from, bubbling into the pool. There were dressing stalls along two walls just off the side of the pool, but there were no windows like there were on the level above, and it was darker down there, more like a cave.

For just a moment, as I stood looking down into the mist, I saw a circle of light around the man in the water. It was as if he was inside a wheel, as if his arms and legs and head were spokes. As quickly as the light appeared, it was gone. It wasn't like a flash, though. It was more like a light brought smoothly up from dim to bright and back down, all in one movement. I closed my eyes to see if I could see it again, and I couldn't, but it reminded me of one of Dacia's coins, with a man in that same position, only with a five-pointed star covering him. I opened my eyes again, and I couldn't see anything but the mist with light from the sunset glowing in it. I moved quietly along the balcony rail, hoping that moving would bring the man back into sight, but if anything the mist seemed to be getting thicker and thicker. Several times as I moved, I had to pass the steps going down to the pool. I wanted to go down there and take my clothes off and get in the water, but I had an even stronger feeling to stay with Kelly. I stopped at the top of the steps and felt those two things pulling on me, one to go down there into the mist to the pool, the other to keep Kelly clearly in sight. I knew it wasn't time to go down yet.

If there was one thing that Joy and Dacia and Washington had all tried to teach me, it was never to go against myself when I had that strong feeling of knowing what to do. The only time I could remember going against it was with Joy, outside her father's farm. I stepped back along the rail, away from the stairs, feeling sick and dizzy, and I sat down for a moment and looked across at Kelly.

The only other time I could remember that feeling of being drawn to go down, but knowing I should wait, was when we had seen snake handlers in a gospel tent show, down in the South. That was the same feeling of something powerful I wanted to do, but something that was so powerful it was scary. They sang and prayed and got into a trance that felt a lot like being around Dacia sometimes, as if they couldn't see one world because they were seeing something else. These snake handlers had healed people. There hadn't been anything wrong with me, I wasn't sick or anything, or—instead of sitting, and watching other people, and being afraid of it—I would have gone up to be healed, just to feel what that power would have been like when it was doing something inside of me. Joy had said I should have gone anyway, if I wanted to, and should have told them I needed balance for walking on the high wire, but I hadn't done it.

All during the last three months, every time I had gone out to go in the water, something had stopped me, that same strong feeling saying no. Several times I had sat down by the water and closed my eyes to see if I could tell what was wrong. Every time I did, I would see Kelly floating on her back in the pool, naked and relaxed and happy. Her face would look very peaceful, as if she wasn't worried about money, or the trouble we had been in when we left Hemmings, or what was going to happen to us next. She wouldn't look worried about all the stuff she was always thinking about. In that picture in my mind, I would be sitting on one of the sets of steps going into the pool, or I would be standing in the water not far away from her, watching, being sure everything was safe, but not holding her up or touching her. I had actually tried to get her to go in, but she always had some reason for not going, and we had even had a couple of arguments about it. Finally she told me she couldn't swim, and was afraid of water over her head, and just hadn't wanted to admit it.

After a long time of quiet, I thought I heard a movement in the water, and I made my way down the steps to the edge of the pool. I don't know what had made the sound, if anything had, but the man was still floating almost motionless below the mist. I looked up, and I could see Kelly still watching him. Her arms were folded on the balcony rail, her face resting quietly on them. I sat down beside the water, took off my shoes and socks, and closed my eyes. I saw the naked man in the pool, surrounded by a wheel of light that would slowly brighten and dim and brighten, covered by a star that would brighten and dim when the rim around it did. So some moments the man would be floating alone in space, and other moments he reminded me of Dacia's coin.

The picture in my mind changed to Kelly instead of the man. Her body was smooth curves, gentle lines that didn't seem to begin and end anywhere. I looked at her slowly and carefully, without any embarrassment. It was like being stretched out in the little boat with Washington, floating on the lake, seeing big puffy clouds and feeling that I could spend the whole day looking at the curves and shapes and watching them open in one place and close in another. She was beautiful in that same way, and I felt that same kind of desire I had when I was watching a cloud, the feeling that I didn't want it to ever go away.

I had never seen Dacia's coin in my thoughts or my dreams before, but in my mind I had seen Kelly naked that way lots of times. She was always beautiful, and she was always unashamed. It was the only way I had seen her naked. Even though we were sharing the same room and even sleeping in the same bed, she was always careful to manage to dress and undress, and to slip in and out of bed, so I wouldn't see her. The longer that had gone on, the more I had noticed how strange it felt to me.

Joy and I had seen each other naked lots of times, and I had seen Dacia naked too, almost as a regular thing. So sitting there beside the pool with the man floating in the water, and Kelly watching over the railing up above, and this picture of her floating in my mind, all at once I began to remember what it had been like to have someone look me over in an admiring kind of way, just to see how I was growing and what was new. I missed us giving each other baths and missed Joy looking at me partly because she was proud and partly because she just enjoyed looking. And I missed Dacia touching my shoulders, or arms, or chest and missed her telling me how I must be a beautiful thing to see.

"If I was going to turn the lights on again," she had told me once, "it would be to get a look at you."

I could hear the sound of her voice saying that again, and I could feel how relaxed it always made me not to feel that I always had to hide myself. It was still Kelly who floated in the picture in my mind, but slowly, I began to see myself, like I was way up above watching what was happening down below. I saw myself stand up and take my clothes off, slowly, like frost melting off a window, something slow and even and natural. And when I was naked too, my arms just drifted upward and I began to float, drifting up higher and higher.

That was even better than watching the clouds. I could still see Kelly, but we were both free, not just her, and I was listening to my mind describing her dark hair and dark eyes. There was something about that voice that was different from how it had been since Hemmings. So, I just listened to it wander into saying whatever it wanted to say, and I remembered that voice a couple of years ago, seeing Joy naked, bathing or sleeping or dancing, talking about how her hair wouldn't have been red if she hadn't treated it and about how I wished I could see her with her dark, natural hair. And I was remembering when I decided she wouldn't have made her hair red if it wasn't for people teasing me because of mine. Joy was so beautiful to me, I wanted her to be perfect, and I was just sorry she didn't have dark hair. The only girl I had really cared about a lot was Veronica, and she had black hair. The first thing I noticed about her was her beautiful black hair. And seeing Kelly there in my mind, I heard my own voice, from way back, telling Joy how I wished she would let her hair grow out dark. But I couldn't remember what she had said back, if she had said anything at all.

I heard movement in the water and opened my eyes. I was looking right up into Kelly's. She was still sitting on the edge of the balcony, hanging on the rail, but while I had been watching these pictures in my mind and listening to the voices, without being aware of it I had gotten up and taken off the rest of my clothes. I was standing at the edge of the pool, at the corner where one of the sets of steps went down into the water. And when I opened my eyes, there was Kelly looking right at me. Whatever I had been feeling about hiding myself all the time was gone. It was too late. She didn't seem to mind looking at me, and I didn't mind her seeing.

I heard a movement in the pool again and looked just in time to see the man pull his arms and legs into a ball and sink out of sight. After just a moment, he stood up, the water streaming off his body. I had my eyes on him now and could just barely see Kelly. She had stood up at almost exactly the same moment the man came up out of the water, and she was leaning over the balcony rail. The man combed his hair back from his face with his fingers, brushed the water away from his eyes, and stood waist deep in the pool, looking at us, first one and then the other. His eyes were focused and deliberate.

"You're coming in?" he asked.

"Yes," I answered. "I guess I am."

I moved down the steps and into the pool. The water was warm, almost as warm as a hot bath. The pool wasn't deep, but I sat on one of the steps so the water came up to my chin.

"What about you, girl?" the man hollered, looking up toward the balcony.

"I'm going back to the room," Kelly said, "to be sure it's warm enough when you guys come out."

I heard the doors from the balcony open and close, and when I looked up she was gone.

"It's warm," I said.

"Nothing can freeze this spring," the man said. "Not even fifty below."

"Do you come from around here?" I asked.

"I was born here," he answered. "My grandfather built this place."

"You're the owner?" I asked.

The man leaned his head back, like he was opening his throat to swallow something whole, and let out a laugh that filled the whole building.

"Belongs to the Indians," he answered. "But the papers say it's mine."

"How come I haven't seen you around?" I asked.

"I come here three or four times a week," he said.

"I've never seen you," I said.

The man laughed again, but quietly this time.

"Doesn't mean I haven't been around," he said. "If we both stopped talking for ten minutes, I could probably leave without you knowing for sure whether I was here or not."

"It doesn't bother you," I asked, "that we're living here? Not paying any rent?"

"I keep the doors unlocked," he said. "People show up from time to time."

For a few moments neither of us said anything. I thought maybe he was going to prove to me that he could leave without my knowing.

"Besides," he said after a while, "I knew you'd come."

"What do you mean?" I asked.

"When I found out your momma got murdered," he answered, "I knew you'd figure out sooner or later this was the safest place for you to be."

"You know about Joy?" I asked.

He began talking, and I tried hard to stay with him and listen. He told me how he had seen Joy dance, years back, how he had wanted to come with us, but Washington and Dacia had both said no. And he told me about the others he knew, Veronica and Victor and Veronica's boyfriend, Danny. He even knew Lenny and Lenny's bother, "that moron Larry," he called him.

"How do you know all these people?" I asked.

"You and me go way back," he said. "Your old man and my old man were in the war together. In fact, they were together when my father got killed."

· 127 ·

It had gotten dark enough that the man wasn't much more than a shadow. I wanted to see his face, and I moved closer to him in the water. I was close enough to stick out my hand to shake. He took hold of it in both of his and squeezed. He told me his name was Joseph and laughed, Joseph Stalin Hardy. He said he thought he was one of the few kids in the whole U.S.A. named after Stalin. "My father loved him," he said. "Stalin said, 'Don't fight,' Daddy was against the war. Stalin said, 'Fight,' he signed right up. Always loyal to the party. Your kid's a boy? Name him Joseph, after good old Uncle Joe." But his aunt couldn't stand it and he had to live with her while his father was in the war and after he died. As soon as she found out his father was dead, she went to court and changed it to Stanley, Joseph Stanley. That was his story.

"How do you know so much about your father?" I asked. "If he died in the war?"

"From Washington and from the letters," he said. "You've read the letters, haven't you?"

"Not all of them," I answered.

"Read 'em," he said. "You'll see. Washington tells some wild stories, but you read those letters, and you'll see that everything he said about your old man was true."

"He never told me much," I said. "Even Washington. He never told me anything."

"Sure he did," Joseph said. "You just weren't understanding. But it doesn't matter."

"What do you mean?" I asked.

"According to the Indians," he said, "the water from this spring comes from deep down in the earth. When you bathe in it, you remember what's deep in you. You just have to listen and then believe what you hear."

"You're serious, aren't you?" I asked.

"I leave the place unlocked," he said, "so they can come when they want and remember what they need to."

"Do they?" I asked.

"When it's important," he said. "They don't like the pool being inside this barn. But when it's important, they come."

"I should go get a lantern," I said. "I can hear you, but I can't see you."

"Be patient," he said. "The moon's almost full. You'll see fine when it comes up."

I did as he said. I closed my eyes and laid back and waited for the moon.

Chapter

8

Joseph and I stayed in the pool that night for over an hour. The moon came out, as he had said it would, and filled the inside of the building with silver-gray light, bright enough to read by. Floating there was the best of everything. It was like sleeping and being awake. The water was easier to float in than a lake or a pond, so you didn't have to think about it, but you didn't have to completely give up thinking to do it. It was like relaxing and working at the same time, without one ruining the other. Pictures and memories and stories came to me without my having to try at all to call them, sharp pictures that were easy to see and clear voices that were easy to hear. But even though there was no real effort involved, the memories and pictures and actions all seemed important, things that needed to be recalled because they would change people's lives. It was like being logical and not feeling that you needed to give explanations, all at the same time.

One of the first pictures that came to me was Veronica's. She was wearing the white dress with the deep-cut neckline, the dress that opened all the way down to the sash around her waist. The dress seemed as if it was going to reveal everything and made me want to stare, but it hardly revealed anything and made me feel that I was rude for trying to see what I wasn't supposed to see. I remember feeling eager and excited and awkward and foolish, looking at her, but seeing her while I was floating there, I felt strong and healthy because I could tell she wanted to make herself attractive, and I felt proud and brotherly because I respected her and cared about her. Her eyes were brilliant black, black fire if there could be such a thing, and they watched me without blinking and without shame. Everything faded away until all I could see was her eyes. Then I couldn't see anything but fiery darkness everywhere, until her eyes came back, and the rest of her followed, and I was admiring her dress all over again.

Once, after Veronica faded in and faded out again and was gone, I remembered getting mad at Joy. I wanted to stop and see Veronica, instead of just passing through, but Joy had said we had to make more miles and couldn't stop. I remembered that I got mad at her and got mad at the way we lived, always traveling around so that when I met someone I liked, I couldn't get to know her. The image of Veronica faded, and I saw Joy sitting behind the wheel of the Packard in her tight blue jeans and a faded work shirt.

If it wasn't for the way we live, she was saying, *you never would have met her in the first place.*

The pictures I saw went back and forth between Veronica and Joy and then, instead of Joy sitting in the car, it was Joy kneeling on the kitchen floor of the trailer with her back against the cupboard doors. Her face looked surprised and she was holding the small wooden cross in her right hand, just the way I had found her. And while I was floating in the pool, I heard the shots ring out across the prairie and heard the whole prairie go quiet. I remembered being scared and upset, but I wasn't upset. I saw Joy clearly. She was dead, but I could still hear her voice saying, *If it wasn't for the way we live, you never would have met her.* I wanted to leave the pool, because seeing Joy like that was hard, but my arms and legs stayed spread out in the water, and something in me wouldn't move, wouldn't run away. I was awake, looking around the pool in the moonlight, but it was like a dream when you think you need to run to get away, and your legs won't move at all because they know that if you did get away, you couldn't finish the dream.

Without wanting to see it and without wanting to get away, I saw Joy kneeling on the floor of the trailer, holding the cross, looking up, and she was still alive. I looked up to see what she was looking at, and I saw her father with the gun. I was afraid that I would have to watch him make her say that she was ashamed, and I was afraid I would know whether or not she had done as he said before he killed her. I looked around the pool, wanting to remind myself that I was floating and remembering and dreaming.

Joseph was crouched in the corner, water up to his chin, watching but not floating himself. I looked into his eyes, hoping he would know what to do.

"Are you scared?" he asked.

"Maybe we should go in," I said.

"Finish the dream if you can," he said. "Washington taught you to do that. I know he did."

I closed my eyes again.

"Finish the dream," Joseph said, "if you can."

The picture of Joy's father in the trailer became very sharp. I could see the lines in his face and then the trailer and everything around him faded, and he was one of a group of men, all with guns, around a fire at night. There were three men in the group, and they had five black slaves in chains, in the shadows back away from the fire. I had had this dream many times, and I recognized it at once. They were slave catchers, and they were laughing and talking when a black man, wearing a beautiful black robe with red and green designs, stepped out of the shadows into the light of the campfire. He had a curved sword in one hand. It was Washington, and he challenged the men. One of them reached for a gun, but in two swift motions Washington split the gun's stock and cut a fine line across the back of the man's hand. The others looked frightened and did not move. Washington offered any of them who dared a chance to strike one blow, any blow he chose. But, when he had struck his blow, it would be Washington's turn.

I had seen this dream over and over again. *The magician must survive the blow.* That was the instruction Washington had always given. I remembered him saying that, and then I heard him, his voice filling the building, disturbing the water. *To dream a magician's death is a horrible thing. If he is a war-*

rior, it means slavery for his people. I looked to see if Joseph had heard it too, but he gave no sign of it, and I closed my eyes again.

The man with the cut hand came forward, took the sword in both hands, and ordered Washington to kneel. When he was on his knees beside the fire, the slave catcher pulled back the hood of Washington's robe, baring his neck. But instead of striking his neck to cut off his head, as usually happened in that dream, the slave catcher straddled Washington's back, grabbed his hair, and pulled his head back. With Washington's face turned up as high as his neck would allow, his neck stretched tight, the slave catcher raised the sword to Washington's throat as if he was going to cut it.

Don't let your head down, nigger, the slave catcher said. Slowly he let go of Washington's hair. The muscles in Washington's neck strained to hold his throat back from the sword. The slave catcher still sat on his back. The white man was smiling, obviously pleased with himself. His partners were laughing quietly at the sight of their friend riding Washington's shoulders, like he was riding a small horse. I looked back into Washington's face. He opened his mouth slowly and moistened his lips with his tongue, moving carefully so his throat would not touch the blade.

You choose cruelty rather than death, he whispered.

You gonna die, nigger, the slave catcher said. *But first, you gonna beg me for your life.*

You have struck your blow, Washington said, and he nicked his throat deliberately. A single drop of blood glistened on the blade.

The cut on the slave catcher's free hand began to bleed. It was hardly anything at first, but the bleeding came faster and faster until it looked like a serious wound, soaking his arm. The white man dropped the sword and grabbed the cut with his other hand, but the bleeding continued, getting worse and worse. Even though the sword was on the ground in front of him, no longer at his throat, Washington didn't move.

Do something! the slave catcher yelled to his friends. *I'm gonna bleed to death!*

Release your prisoners, Washington said, *and it will stop.*

Let 'em go! the slave catcher yelled. *Quick, damn it. Let 'em go!*

The white man pressed his bleeding hand against his stomach, but the blood was still pouring, soaking his shirt and pants. The others unlocked the chains, and the slave catcher fell unconscious from Washington's shoulders.

Washington rose slowly to his feet and, one by one, helped each of the captives to stand. *Freedom*, he said to each one and spoke again in a language I did not understand. *Uhuru. Uhuru.*

Washington picked up his sword and holding it in both hands, by its handle and by its point, he raised it high above his head. He faced north, then east, then south, then west. *Let no man change what we have done*, he repeated as he looked in each direction, then walked quietly into the dark.

I saw nothing at all for a while, then faces began to come. First it was Veronica, then Kelly, then Dacia, then Joy, then Washington and other men with him I didn't recognize. After the faces, I saw them all together, outdoors, in the moonlight, dancing by a fire. Last I saw Joy, inviting me to join them. *If it wasn't for the life we live*, she was saying, *you never would have known them.* Then I opened my eyes, and the face I saw was Joseph's, still sitting neck deep in the water in the corner of the pool, watching.

"Now we're ready to go in," I said.

"Don't come out until you're ready to run," he answered. "Once we're out of the water, it's going to be cold as hell until we get up to your room."

I waded all the way around the pool once to get the feeling of being back on my feet. Joseph and I looked at each other for a moment, then he hollered, "Go," and we ran up the stairs, across the balcony, through the doors, across the walkway, through the other doors, and into our room, naked. Kelly had got it warmed up, just as she had promised, and had the covers turned back over the foot of the bed.

"Into bed!" she yelled. "Both of you, quick!"

Joseph and I piled into the double bed, and Kelly threw the blankets and sheets back up over us. We shivered under the blankets for a few moments, laughing over our adventure, but were warm again before long.

"How would you have dried off," Kelly asked, "if you couldn't have come up here?"

"You're supposed to go up on the second floor," Joseph said, "and dry off in the sunlight, in one of the booths."

"But what about tonight?" she asked. "It's cold, and the sun's gone down. What about tonight?"

"I used to use the stove in the maintenance shop," he answered, "before it disappeared somewhere."

Kelly and I looked at each other, but when he laughed, we all laughed together.

"What about now?" she asked. "Now that we have the stove?"

"In the basement," he answered. "There's a warm room down there. That's where my clothes are."

"Shall we draw straws?" I asked.

"What for?" Joseph said.

"To see who has to go down to the basement for your clothes," I answered.

"I'll go," he said and looked at Kelly, "if you'll get a blanket for me, out of one of the other rooms."

Kelly left without answering, and we both watched her go.

"Nice kid," Joseph said. "How did you get her to come with you?"

"It was kind of the other way around," I said. "She helped me get away."

"Get away from what?" he asked.

"Jail," I said. "They let me go, but she helped me get out of there. I was kind of confused."

"Why?" he asked.

"Joy got killed," I answered. "It upset everything for a while."

"No," he said. "I mean, why did she help you? Kelly. Why did she come with you?"

"I don't know much about her," I said.

I heard a popping sound coming from down the hall and thought that it was probably Kelly, shaking out a blanket. She coughed and kept coughing all the way down the hall and into the room.

"This place is filthy," she said and handed the blanket to him.

"Doesn't matter," he answered.

Kelly turned away while Joseph rolled out of bed, wrapped himself in the blanket, and trotted, barefoot, out of the room. She kept looking out the window into the moonlight, even after he was gone. It wasn't all that bright in the room with just the moon and the fireplace and one lamp, but I could see well enough to tell that her jeans had gotten a little bit baggy around her bottom. I noticed it because when we had first come her jeans were so tight that I really spent a lot more time looking at the shape of her body than I should have. I guessed she must be losing weight, and I felt a moment of panic because she was pretty thin to start with. It wasn't like I was responsible for her. We were just taking care of ourselves together, but I still felt guilty thinking that she had come with me, like Joseph said, and I didn't know why, except that she had helped me. I didn't want her to get sick because of me. It was hard to think of her being sick. She slipped down into the overstuffed chair to the left of the window with all of the control I remembered Joy having when she moved and did simple things. Kelly's hair was shiny, even in the dim light, and her eyes sparkled as she stared at the moon.

"How was it?" she asked, after a long silence.

She was still staring out the window and did not look at me when she spoke.

"How was what?" I asked.

"The pool," she said. "You were out there for a long time."

"Real relaxed," I said. "It was like sleeping real solid so your dreams are real and like being awake at the same time."

"Was it scary?" she asked.

"Scary?" I said. "Why would it be scary?"

"I don't know," she said. "I just thought it would be scary."

"Whenever you want," I said, "I'll go out with you. It's good to have somebody there, but you'll see, it's not scary at all."

"That would be nice," she said. "Sometime."

"Tomorrow?" I asked.

"Tomorrow we have to go into town," she said, "with Joseph."

"With Joseph?" I asked.

"Didn't he talk to you?" she said.

Kelly turned around in her chair so she was facing me. She was looking right at me, but she looked like she was staring at something far away. I waited a moment before I answered, until I saw her look at me and look away, as if she had finally realized she was staring without really paying attention.

"No," I answered. "Should he have?"

"He told me he would," she said. "We're going to buy warm clothes and supplies and some things for fixing up around here."

"Do you really think he owns this place?" I asked.

"He knew everything that was in the letters," she answered. "How would he know all that stuff if he wasn't who he says he is?"

"He just doesn't seem like the type," I said.

"What type?" Kelly asked. "The type to have a father who died in the war? What type is that?"

"But look at this place," I said. "You said it was filthy, and all he said was that it didn't matter. People with money care about the stuff they own."

"He's gonna buy materials, tomorrow," she said, "to fix the place up. And supplies."

"Like what?" I asked.

"Like fuses to get the power back on," she said, "and get the freezer and refrigerator working. And like food and a cord of firewood."

"I don't know, Kelly," I said. "Doesn't it bother you? It's like he's Santa Claus or something."

"He's been through the winters up here," she said, "and we haven't. He understands the people better than we do, and he understands the things we have to do to make it."

"But why would he want to pay?" I asked.

"There's money in the bank," she answered, "from his father and his grandfather. He can't get it out except to do certain things, like fixing up the lodge and like hiring someone to take care of it."

Kelly got up from her chair and put more wood in the stove. Then she walked back over to the window and stared out into the valley. Her back was to me again, and I got the feeling that she thought we had finished talking about what we were talking about. It was as if she had gone far away again, in her mind, to wherever it was her eyes were staring off to before.

"And that's where the supplies come from?" I asked. "He's hiring us to take care of the lodge?"

"You, Louis," she said. "Not us. Just you."

"Why not both of us?" I asked.

"I can't explain it exactly," she said.

"You're going to leave," I asked, "aren't you?"

"Not right away," she said.

"You're tired of me," I said.

"No," she said.

"It's because my head is all screwed up," I said. "Goddamn it. I knew this would happen. It's been like a race between me getting my head squared away and you getting tired of me. I was just too slow. Damn it. I like you, Kelly. Goddamn it."

"There's more to life than whether or not I'm tired of you," she said.

"I know that," I said. "That's why I wanted . . ."

The words just stopped coming into my mind, so I couldn't say any more for a moment. It was as if I had to stop and think before I said any more, and I couldn't help myself. The words just stopped on their own. I sat in bed under the covers looking at her while she looked out the window. Both of us were quiet, but after a while she turned and sat down again and looked at me.

"That's why what?" she asked.

"That's why," I answered, slowly, "I said I would go out to the pool with you, tomorrow, if you wanted, because you've helped me a lot, and I haven't done much for you."

"What was it like?" she asked. "In the pool."

"Like dreaming," I said. "Only it's like being awake and watching yourself dreaming and seeing the dream too. It's like everything is a dream. Like talking to you now is a dream."

"Could we do it without the pool?" she asked. "Here in the room?"

"I don't know," I answered. "Maybe. I don't know."

"Can we try?" she asked.

"What about Joseph?" I said.

"I mean later," she answered, "after he's asleep. After we're all supposed to be asleep."

"We can try," I said.

Kelly got up from her chair and came around the foot of the bed and sat down beside me. She put her arms around my neck and kissed me on the cheek and then squeezed me real hard.

"I'm not tired of you," she whispered, right up against my ear. "You've helped me more than you know."

"Thanks," I said and hugged her back. "I know I've been a little bit weird."

Kelly squeezed me again and kissed my cheek again. Her cheek was wet when she pressed it against mine. I guessed that she was holding on to me as much because she knew she was going to cry as anything else. She either wanted somebody to hold her while she was crying, or she didn't want me to see her. I couldn't tell for sure which it was. But in a way it didn't matter, because it felt so good to be holding her and feeling her kind of nuzzle up against my neck. We hardly ever touched each other except by accident. I could tell sometimes that it was hard for her to stay tough and not come running for a cuddle. I could understand why she wouldn't want to let herself get used to having someone to depend on, because I felt that same way myself. But a lot of the time, it felt as if one of us, or both of us, was staying under water too long and needed to come up for air. Maybe that's why Kelly was holding on to me and crying. Maybe she had stayed under too long.

"Do you really think I can do it?" she asked.

"Do what?" I said.

"Dream and remember," she said, "like you just said."

"Sure you can," I answered.

I held her out from me at arm's length so I could look at her. Her cheeks were streaked with tears, and she kept looking down at her lap instead of at me. I tried to wipe the tears away with my hand, but she was still crying, so I dried her cheeks with the corner of the sheet.

"I don't want to go away," she said.

"Who says you have to?" I asked.

She buried her face in my neck again and began to cry, really sobbing out loud this time. I heard a noise in the hall. I thought it was probably Joseph coming back, deciding not to come in, and then going back to the room in the basement. Kelly cried and then repeated things she had already said and grabbed on to me and cried again. This happened over again three or four times, until I finally decided that she wasn't going to say anything that would help me understand, and I made her get ready for bed. Once she was in her nightgown and cuddled up to my shoulder again, I kept stroking her hair over and over and over with one rhythm and kept saying soft words in time with my hand moving in her hair, until she went to sleep. I was barely able to stay awake long enough to get her to sleep. So, when she finally rolled over and turned her back to me to get comfortable on her own pillow, I fell asleep almost at once.

I must have been right about Joseph being out in the hall and deciding not to come in, because he didn't actually come into the room in all that time. I stayed awake long enough to stretch the cramps and numb places out of my legs, long enough to wonder if it would be possible to lie very quietly in bed and experience things like those I had experienced in the pool. But I couldn't stay awake long enough to find out the answer.

When I woke up in the morning, Kelly and Joseph were both dressed and moving around. Kelly had a fire going and a pot of coffee and a pan on the stove. The thing that woke me up was the smell of cinnamon rolls heating in the pan. The two of them were being so quiet, I could have slept all day.

"He's awake," Joseph said.

His mouth was full of roll, and the words came out mumbled and muttered.

"So he is," Kelly said.

"What's in the pan?" I asked.

"Our breakfast special, sir," Kelly answered. "Roll o' Cinna Mon."

"Cinnamon rolls?" I asked. "Where'd you get cinnamon rolls?"

"Look at him," Joseph said.

He and Kelly laughed together.

"You look like you just saw a man from Mars," Kelly said.

"Where'd you get 'em?" I asked.

"They're my one weakness," Joseph said. "Don't trust me with any secrets. I'd tell everything for a couple of these babies."

Kelly held the pan with a towel so she wouldn't burn her hand. She offered the rolls to Joseph again before she passed them to me. He looked sheepish, but he took one anyway. He sat in the chair by the window with his feet up on the foot of the bed all the time he was eating and we were finishing our coffee. His white thermal underwear showed at the open neck of his shirt, and where he had his sleeves rolled up, and where his pants legs pulled up short of his boot tops. He had a wide leather band around his right wrist decorated with beautiful beadwork in an Indian design. His hair was almost long enough to touch his shoulders, just as I remembered from the night before. But even though his hair was yellow-blond, the beadwork made it seem the length it really should be. I had seen lots of farmers and ranchers, and he looked different from them. He looked like a mountain man, I decided, the kind that won't even come out of the hills for the carnivals. The rolls were hot and sticky and so sweet they made all three of us dizzy, but we ate all of them and drank the coffee before I made any moves to clean up.

"I'll go warm up the Packard," Kelly said.

It was clear outside, even though it was still dark. One thing I had already learned about being up in the Rockies was that it could be clear out, and it could look like it would have to be too warm for a coat, but actually be pretty cold, even after the sun came up. Kelly stood looking at me, but she didn't move as if she was really going to go anywhere. She was wearing jeans and a wool shirt and tennis shoes. We really did need to go into town for warm clothes. She didn't even have thermals to wear underneath. Her hair was brushed down past her shoulders and looked like she had spent a lot of time messing with it. That was usual for her, to take a lot of care with her hair, but the thing that was different was that she had put on makeup, eye shadow and red lipstick, and she was wearing that powder that smelled like lilacs. I thought she might be waiting for me to tell her she looked nice, that that was why she wasn't moving.

"The keys, Louis?" she asked.

"They're in my pants," I said.

"And your pants?" she asked.

We all laughed together.

"Down by the pool," I said.

Kelly laughed again, shook her head, and left.

"I hope they're not your only pair," Joseph said. "They'll be stiff as a board. It's about twenty-five degrees right now."

By the time Kelly got the car started and warmed up enough that it would idle on its own, I was up and dressed and cleaned up enough to go. Kelly and I sat up front, and Joseph sat in the back. The Packard was stiff from the cold and a little slow to warm up, but it was heavy and still rode well on the gravel road. We did need money for things I had put off thinking about, like snow tires and chains and antifreeze. So, whatever this arrangement was that Kelly and Joseph had discussed, it would probably work out to be a good deal because it could give us some cash to take care of things like getting the car ready for winter. I pulled out my handkerchief and wiped the dust off of the chrome on the dash. Joy was always very particular about taking care of little things on the car as soon as they came up, and she liked to keep the car clean because when it was clean it was easier to spot little things while they were little. That was the way she had put it.

About halfway between the lodge and the highway, Joseph tapped on the window with his knuckle and pointed off to the right. We were coming up on a gate in the fence that ran all along the road. It was one of those farmer gates where a couple of posts don't go down into the ground, so you can unloop a wire and just drag part of the fence back out of the way. There was an access road running under the gate, real faint, just a Jeep trail that didn't look as if it had been used very much. There was a sign on the gate that said, "No Hunting Without Permission. Trespassers Shot." Just on the other side of the fence, three or four car lengths up the trail, there was an old Jeep station wagon. It was basically dark brown, but it had so many splotches of gray and black and ox-blood primer on it that it was hard to say for sure what its main color was. They hadn't changed the styling on Jeeps since World War II, at least not as far as I could see, so I couldn't tell how old it was. The body and the paint were ugly, but even from the road I could see it had new tires all around and was probably good up in that country in the winter.

"That's the Fox," Joseph said and chuckled.

"The what?" Kelly asked.

"The Fox," Joseph said. He laughed. "You probably don't know about Jeeps, but this one's clever."

"Clever?" I asked.

"Sure," he said. "Smarter than most three or four people put together."

"Can we let this guy out?" Kelly asked, snickering.

We all laughed and drove on toward the highway.

"Is that yours?" I asked.

"My loyal friend," Joseph answered.

"Why didn't you park up at the lodge?" I asked.

"I like coming up on you without you knowing I'm there," he answered. "It's sort of my specialty."

"What a nice hobby," Kelly said.

It was still only about seven in the morning when we reached the highway and turned west toward Gunnison. Even though we hadn't gone all the way into town that often, we had gone that direction enough looking for jobs that the road was familiar. We weren't more than a mile from the road the lodge was on when we came around a curve and up behind a school bus stopped on the side of the road, lights flashing all over the back of it. I slowed up and stopped. There was a little shelter on the other side of the bar ditch. It was simple, made of plywood with no windows and a doorway but no door. The whole thing was about the size of two telephone booths side by side. One at a time, the kids came out of the shelter, crossed the bar ditch, and got on the bus. The first three were little, but the last one was a girl who looked like she was about Kelly's age, in a light tan wool coat and a stocking cap with a tassel on top, red hair streaming out from under the hat. Her dress was shorter than her coat, but she was wearing black tights, not jeans, and boots with furry-looking stuff around the top.

"I told you the buses came all the way out here," Joseph said.

"What?" I asked.

"I was talking to Kelly," he said. "I told her the school buses ran all over the valleys out here, but she didn't believe me."

We were moving again. The redhead had taken a seat at the very back, and we could see her through the bus' rear window, talking with another girl about her age.

"I want to go back to school," Kelly said.

She sounded solemn.

"What?" I asked.

"I want to go to school," she said. "Don't you miss it?"

"No," I answered. "I've never been to school."

"Never?" she asked.

"Not school like you mean," I said. "We got stuff through the mail. Joy and Dacia and Washington all helped me learn it and mail back the tests when I was finished."

"Jesus," Joseph said. "You lucky son of a bitch."

"Why?" I asked.

"Private tutoring," he said, "from Washington."

"And Joy and Dacia too," I said.

"But Washington," Joseph said. "If I could hire any person I wanted out of the whole country for a tutor . . . Jesus, you're lucky."

"Well, I want to go back to school," Kelly said. "I miss kids my own age and other girls to talk to."

"God," Joseph said. "School."

"I don't care," she said. "Sometimes you get a nice teacher, but it doesn't matter. I miss the other kids."

"They'll send a bus right to the lodge," he said, "once you get signed up."

"That's what I want," she said.

"The sons a bitches would send a bus to Siberia," he said, "if they could have one more kid to screw around with."

"I have to think about my future," Kelly said.

"Future," Joseph said and laughed out loud. "What do you want to be? A cheerleader? A prom queen?"

He laughed so loud it hurt my ears.

"Fuck you, buddy!" Kelly screamed. "I don't have no goddamn rich family leaving me hotels and money and trusses!"

"Trusts," Joseph said.

"Truss! Trust!" she yelled. "Whatever it is, it's money in the bank, and you don't have to worry, so who the hell are you to be telling me about my future?"

"All right!" Joseph yelled back. "All right."

"Give me the goddamn trust," Kelly said, "and maybe I'll worry about having the right tutor. 'The Right Private Tutor.'"

"I might do that," Joseph said. "Don't be too surprised if I do."

Joseph and Kelly quit arguing with each other almost as suddenly as they had begun. I just kept driving, watching the redhead and her friend talking in the back of the bus. She was kind of cute, even if she did have red hair. Kelly was watching them too, and once in a while she would fiddle with her hair and tug at her clothes like the other girls. If I had been able to hear her mind, I was sure she would have been hearing exactly what those girls were talking about and exactly how their voices sounded.

I could see Joseph in the rearview mirror. He was looking out the side window into the mountains. I didn't have anything to say, except that I realized that Kelly and Joseph had talked with each other a lot more than I had known. I kind of wished Kelly had talked to me about things like school and her future, but I knew I had not been in very good shape for giving her any kind of information or advice that would be helpful. If I wanted her to talk to me about that kind of stuff, I knew I was going to have to pull things together better. It seemed almost impossible that I would actually be able to help her, but it was just as hard to think of going on and on watching her stare at those girls in the bus. So I did the first thing that came to mind.

"Kelly says you want to hire me," I said, "to take care of the lodge."

"There's a trust," Joseph said, "for care of the lodge. It allows for one caretaker and a certain amount for repairs and upkeep."

"How much does it pay?" I asked.

"Two hundred," he answered, "plus room and board."

"Food too?" I asked.

"There used to be a dining area as part of the lobby," he said. "The caretaker could eat with the kitchen people, which means there's no cash for food. But we can work around that."

"If you paid me one month for the work I've already done," I said, "that would cover the winter things Kelly and I need to buy to live out there."

"Sounds fair," Joseph answered.

"Do you have that much cash?" I asked.

"I have that much credit," he answered. "I've already been telling people I was trying you out."

"Before you asked us?" Kelly said.

"Haven't you wondered," he asked, "why you've gotten away with living there and have had no problems from neighbors or from the cops? Or why you've been working under age without a work permit and you've had no hassles? People think you're working for me, trying to fix up the lodge, so they leave you alone, that's why."

"Back to the money," I said. "If we can get the things on Kelly's list and put it on your credit for the lodge, Kelly wouldn't have to spend the money she has."

"We can do that," Joseph said. "It'll be easy."

"Why are you doing this?" Kelly asked. "Why did you lie to people to protect us when we hadn't even met?"

"Because Louis and I are almost brothers," Joseph said. "Brothers in the spirit. My father and his were close in the war. We both know Washington and got from him most of what most guys get from their fathers. I've thought of Louis as my brother ever since Washington first told me what was what."

"And I'm just in the way," Kelly said.

"You're not in the way," he said. "I just don't know who you are."

"Hold it," I said. "If I'm going to stay at the lodge, Kelly stays as long as she wants."

"That's fine with me," Joseph said. "All I ever tried to say was that the trust would only pay a salary for one."

"It's the way you said it," Kelly said.

"So when we get to town," I said, "Joseph and I will go buy the winter stuff on the list, and you go get what you need for getting into school."

"Are you serious?" Kelly asked. "Are you serious?"

"It's your money anyway," I said. "If you want to go to school, you should spend it on that."

"And you won't kick me out if I do?" she asked.

"Of course not," I said.

"They won't let you wear jeans," Joseph said. "You'll have to wear dresses."

"All schools have rules you have to get around," Kelly said. "That's half the fun."

"Fun?" I asked.

"Sure," she said and kissed my cheek. "That's how you meet the neatest guys."

"It is?" I asked.

"It's how I met you," she said.

Chapter 9

We stopped on Main Street to let Kelly out. She spotted a department store with winter fashions in the window. It wasn't open yet, but the Gunnison Cafe was two doors down. I was ready for coffee, but Kelly didn't want us following her around, and Joseph knew another place we could go. He gave Kelly a phone number and told her that she could get hold of us there, or leave a message, or get directions and meet us there, whatever suited her when the time came. She didn't say when she thought she'd be finished or even ask whose phone it was. It seemed to me she was anxious to get off on her own and didn't care about those things.

Once we had let her out, Joseph got up front and gave me directions through a residential neighborhood to the edge of the college campus. We parked and he guided me along the sidewalks. I had never been around a college, not that I knew of anyway, so I had nothing to compare it to, no way to know whether it was large or small, fancy or plain, impressive or just ordinary. Joseph kept looking around and looking at me without saying anything, except to tell me the names of the buildings, as if he was waiting for me to respond in some way. It reminded me of a guy, once, who had come out to see Joy dance, several nights in a row. One night he brought a special bottle of wine. I remember watching Joy taste it and remember seeing how she looked a little puzzled, like she wasn't sure what she should do. He had even let me taste the wine, though I was only fourteen then. It was warm. That's all I remembered about it.

The main thing I noticed as Joseph and I walked along was that several of the buildings looked enough alike for it to be obvious that they went together. They all had red tile roofs, and all but one were covered on the outside with cream-colored stucco. The other one, the largest and oldest-looking, was red brick. The buildings looked Spanish to me and seemed odd up there in the mountains with the cold weather. I thought of that style of building more where it was hot, down on the desert in New Mexico and Arizona and California. But the buildings were there, so I guessed they must be all right. And they had lasted. Even the new ones looked as if they had been there quite a while, except for the student union. We hadn't been able to see it when we parked. It had large glass windows, wooden siding and shingles, and porches on three sides. It looked like the pictures I had in my mind of what a ski lodge would be like. I don't know where I got the idea because I had never seen a ski lodge, but I had a picture, anyway, of that style of building and all the skiers going in there to get warm. There weren't very many people moving around, but maybe half of the ones we saw, mostly about Joseph's age, were coming out of the student union or were going in.

"This is where the coffee is," Joseph said. "Everybody comes through here sooner or later."

"Doesn't seem like there are many people around," I said.

"It's Tuesday," he said.

I knew that was supposed to explain something to me, but it didn't. I figured that if I waited, though, I would catch on before long. Inside, it was just like a cafeteria. There was a counter where you could order food or pick up things already set out, sweet rolls and boxes of breakfast cereal, or where you could pour yourself a cup of coffee. There were three good-sized rooms on three sides of the place where you got your food. They all had lots of round tables surrounded by wooden chairs, captains' chairs. Most of the tables were empty. There was a group of four playing cards and eight or ten people sitting by themselves or in pairs. Joseph and I got coffee and a table by a window. It was kind of chilly, but we could see people coming and going.

"Is this where Kelly's going to call?" I asked.

"No," Joseph said.

He didn't say any more for a few moments, and we watched people move along the sidewalk. Most of them were dressed for warmth in wool hats and heavy sweaters and gloves and boots. They didn't seem very concerned about what they looked like, at least not judging by the way they dressed. It was too bad, I thought, that Kelly wasn't old enough for college.

"The telephone number," Joseph said, "is Veronica's."

"Who?" I asked.

"Veronica," he said.

"Rodriguez?" I asked.

"Yes," he answered.

"I don't believe it," I said.

"She's anxious to see you," Joseph answered.

"Me?" I asked.

"She knows about Joy," he said. "She's been worried about you."

"And she lives in Gunnison?" I asked.

"Since the last of September," he said.

"What about her boyfriend?" I said.

"Danny?" he asked.

"Yes," I said. "The one that got her in a car wreck."

"He's the one talked her into coming up here," Joseph said. "They have a place together."

"Wonderful," I said. "I can hardly wait to see them."

"Don't let it bug you," he said. "Your time will come. Besides, she'll be working all morning in the theater, so you don't have to see her if you don't want to."

"Is her leg still screwed up?" I asked.

"You don't notice it much," he answered.

I knew he had pointed out to me which building was the theater, but I couldn't remember. I guessed it was probably the brick one, the one that looked the oldest, because I thought that would probably be one of the first things they would build, a place to put on Shakespeare and stuff. They might even have dancers there, not like Joy of course, but way back two years ago Veronica had told me she wanted to study dance. While I was remembering that, a young woman in a green ski parka came out of the brick building and walked along the sidewalk toward us. She had no sign of a limp, and I didn't think Veronica would wear green. Besides, there were probably hundreds of girls on the campus. I wasn't going to just come there, and sit in a big window, and drink one cup of coffee, and see her first thing.

"Is she studying dance?" I asked.

It seemed like a stupid question as soon as I asked it. Even if her leg was a lot better, she couldn't be dancing on it. But usually when I thought of her, I was remembering her from when we first met, and she first saw Joy dance. If she had come with us then, she would be a dancer now, and wouldn't have a messed-up leg, and wouldn't be living with the kind of guy that did stuff like that to her. She hadn't come with us then because she wanted to finish high school, like Kelly.

Joseph didn't answer. He had been staring off across the campus too.

"What's Veronica studying?" I asked.

"She's not in school," Joseph said. "She works in the theater, but she's not a student."

"She just moved here . . . ?" I asked but didn't finish my question.

"To be with Danny," he said.

"Not to go on to school?" I asked.

"Don't worry," he said. "She asks about you every time I see her."

"How do you know everyone I know?" I asked. "It's like you know everything about my life, and I only know half."

"You've read the letters, haven't you?" he asked.

"Some of them," I said, "but not all."

"You'll see it better when you've read them all," he said. "Kelly told me you read them."

"So I haven't read these letters," I said. "Does that mean you can't answer a simple question?"

"If it was simple," he said, "I could. Washington goes way

back with my old man, just like he goes way back with yours. He used to visit my aunt when she was raising me, just like he used to spend time traveling with you and Dacia and Joy. He took me out in the mountains and taught me lots of stuff, just like he did you."

"What about your mother?" I asked. "What happened to her?"

"Big mystery," he answered. "Nobody talked about her, but Washington told me about my dad and your dad and Joy and Dacia and Dacia's brother, about how he got killed. And he also told me about how Joy wouldn't ever let him lay it all out for you."

"I just found out about Dacia's brother last summer," I said.

"Joy was a beautiful woman," Joseph said, "but she was afraid a lot."

We were both quiet for a moment. I remembered Joy telling me about how Dacia's brother had been murdered and the things that had come after that, and I realized that if she had waited one more day, she never would have told me. I missed her and was mad at her all at the same time.

"You really don't remember me," Joseph asked, "do you?"

"From when?" I asked. "Last night?"

"Two years ago," he said. "When you guys came through Colorado last time, Washington told me to come and see Joy dance because it would change my life. You know Washington, always looking for those experiences that'll change your life."

"Yes," I said, but I didn't really know for sure.

"Danny and I were both working construction for the summer on the Blue Mesa Dam," he said. "Six of us went, including the foreman. Washington was right about her, but on the way back the other guys started talking about going back the next night and then started saying ugly things about Washington and Dacia. I got hot about it, and Danny stuck up for me. We've been tight ever since."

"Danny stuck up for Washington and Dacia?" I asked.

"They kicked our butts," he said. "But we made them earn it."

"Kicked your butts?" I asked.

"There were four of them," he said, "against the two of us. Sure they did."

"Why?" I asked.

"They called Washington a nigger," he said. "But we made 'em earn it."

"And Danny helped you?" I asked.

"Got his butt kicked," Joseph said, "and lost his job, just like me."

"But he helped you?" I asked.

"Best he could," he said. "He was just a kid then, and he didn't like to fight. He didn't like to work either. Didn't mind losing the job all that much."

"How come they hired him on?" I asked. "I couldn't get on, and I don't mind work."

"His old man was supervising the explosives work out there," Joseph said. "In fact, he still does. Danny worked for him, setting fuses."

"If he was working for his father," I asked, "how come he got fired?"

"I'll tell you something," Joseph said. "Red-necks around here don't need to wear sheets, but if they did, and if they ever organized a Klan, Danny's old man would be the Grand Lizard. No doubt about it, the number 1 top asshole."

He rolled back his head, and opened his throat, and let out a big laugh like he had in the pool. The other people in the student union all looked at him, but they went on with what they were doing. Maybe they were used to him. I had never been around anyone with such an explosive laugh. While Joseph was getting himself calmed down again, I got us refills on the coffee. Before I got back to our table, the four who were playing cards also blew up, but in an argument. Someone played a card at the wrong time or something like that. Everyone looked at them and then went on with what they were doing. I was a little surprised. People didn't usually get that rowdy at the carnival, unless they came drunk, but nobody in the student union seemed to mind.

We waited in the window, drinking coffee and watching people go by, until a little before nine, when the eight o'clock classes let out. The walks weren't crowded, but there were several hundred people moving around where there had hardly been any.

The student union filled up and got way too noisy for me. In fifteen minutes or so, the rest of the people who had appeared on the walks, who hadn't come in the union, were gone. Joseph was checking the face of everyone who came through the door. He kept telling me that Danny would be along any minute, and then we could go. Finally, when the walks were almost deserted, Joseph spotted him striding quickly along, almost running. He had a black knit ski cap rolled up on top of his head, nicely trimmed dark hair, and the most perfectly shaped full beard I had ever seen. His face was tanned, and his eyes were dark brown. I looked but I couldn't see anything wrong with him at all. He was wearing a blanket-lined Levi's jacket, and snug-fitting blue jeans, and nicely shined black boots. Joseph introduced us, and we offered him coffee, but he turned it down.

"You got his license yet?" Danny asked.

"The stores are just now opening," Joseph answered.

"What license?" I asked.

"My stuff's all in the car," Danny said, still standing.

"A deer license," Joseph said.

"You mean for hunting?" I asked.

"You guys haven't talked about this?" Danny asked.

"We've had a lot to cover," Joseph said.

"Well, don't take too long," Danny said. "We should be out of town by noon. I don't want to set up camp in the dark."

"We've got plenty of time," Joseph said.

"I'm going on down to the house," Danny said. "I've got to go by Arnie's and get his ought-six for the kid here and change my boots, and I'm ready."

"I've never shot anything in my life," I said.

"You don't have to shoot it, kid," Danny said. "Me and Joseph will do the shooting. All you've got to do is carry the gun. That's the law."

"I don't know," I said.

"With or without him," Danny said, "we leave from my house by noon?"

"By noon," Joseph said.

Danny was gone, striding off down the sidewalk toward the

same parking lot where we had left the Packard. Neither of us said anything until he was out of sight.

"I've never hurt anything," I said.

"You won't have to," he said.

"But the two of you will," I said. "It's just the same."

"It's for the meat," Joseph said.

"Isn't there some other way?" I asked.

"Washington talked to you about hunting," he said, "didn't he?"

"No," I answered.

"We won't kill any animal we shouldn't kill," he said. "We won't kill anything unless you agree."

"But why should I have to go?" I asked.

"Because everybody in these mountains hunts for meat," Joseph said. "If you want them to look after you, you've got to hunt."

"Look after me?" I asked.

"You've got a lot to learn," he said.

"Why can't I learn something else?" I asked.

"I'll teach you how Washington taught me," he said, "but if you're not going, you might as well leave now, because you'll never make it here."

"I'll go," I said, "but I'm not going to kill any deer."

We took the Packard downtown to a sporting goods store and got the things on Kelly's list, along with some things for being out in the woods, like a tarp and fire starters. When we left, I had warm clothes, and a poncho to keep me dry if it rained, and a knife, and my license. From the store we went to Danny's apartment on the east side of town. Right across the street, just out of the city limits, was a fenced pasture with fifteen or twenty cattle munching on bales of hay. When I first saw them, I thought it was strange that we would be going to so much trouble to go up into the mountains after deer when the cattle were right across the road. But I stood by the car for a moment looking at them. Cattle didn't usually seem like animals to me. They were more like something people had made, like houses or cars, only alive. But for the first time they looked like creatures, too tired and too discouraged to run away. I hollered at them, and a couple of the ones closest to me looked up but didn't move, except to turn their heads, so I followed Joseph into the yard.

The apartment had been made from the second story of a family home. We went in the front door and up the stairs to a landing. When we got to the top, there were three doors facing in three directions and a window behind us, above the stairs, that let light in on the stairwell. The knobs had been taken off two of the doors, and the doors had been sealed with some kind of filler and painted shut. The third one looked as if it had been taken from somewhere else, because it didn't go with the other two. There was a design carved into the lower half, kind of like a wheel with a hub and spokes and no rim. The upper half had a large, clear glass window with little curtains on the inside. Joseph knocked and then opened the door without waiting for an answer.

As we went in, Joseph called for Danny and Veronica, but neither of them answered. I wondered what Kelly was doing if she was off somewhere trying to phone with no one at home. It wasn't even 9:30 though, and she had to pick out everything she would have to wear to school. It wasn't like just needing one thing and having to choose from three or four different kinds in the stores. It might take her all day. Nobody in the school would know her, so she could present herself however she wanted. Maybe that was part of what she liked about going, like when Joy used to make up a new dance and then the costume to go with it.

The apartment was shaped like a backward C with the living room at the bottom, just inside the door, the kitchen in the middle, and the bedroom at the top. The doorway from the living room to the kitchen was much newer than the rest of the house. They had put up paneling on the living room side, but there were V-shaped gaps between the sheets where it didn't come out right. The wall on the kitchen side was lumpy around the new woodwork. Whoever did the work knew enough about houses to get the doorway through but obviously couldn't have made a living doing it. The kitchen had a white metal sink and counter and cupboards that looked like they all came in one unit. There was a small bathroom, no bigger than you would find in a trailer, crowded into the back of the kitchen. In the middle of the linoleum floor, there was a large round table with a white oilcloth cover and three unmatched chairs, two wooden and one with a chromed metal tube frame. I glanced quickly into the bedroom. It was cluttered with clothes and the covers from an unmade double bed.

I sat on the couch in the living room to wait for Danny to come with the gun I was supposed to carry. Joseph fumbled through the records on a shelf under the record player but didn't seem to find anything he wanted to play.

"Do you know where Washington is?" I asked.

"Why?" Joseph asked.

"You talk about him all the time," I said. "Nobody would ever tell me why he didn't come with us on the last trip. I thought you might know."

"Nobody knows where he is," Joseph said. "That's what this is all about."

"What is all about?" I asked.

"They want to kill him," Joseph said. "They killed Joy, and they took Dacia to smoke him out so they can kill him."

"Took Dacia?" I asked. "Who?"

"Victor and Dacia never made it to Wichita," he said. "I don't even know if Lenny knows where they are."

"Is Lenny after Washington?" I asked.

"That's why they let you go," he said, "and followed you here."

"Followed?" I asked. "Where?"

"Lenny and his brother Larry," Joseph said, "and the three that came to the lodge are all camped in the hills 'hunting' and waiting to see if he's going to show up and save you."

"I just don't understand," I said.

"It goes back to World War II," Joseph said. "Washington fought in the Spanish Civil War, and he went back to France in 1941, when Hitler attacked the Soviet Union. He was in France, and North Africa, and in and out of the U.S. before the U.S. went into the war. I don't know the details, but he was in France when people sold out to the Nazis, and he worked with the

French Resistance and the CP in the U.S., carrying information and money and codes."

"The CP?" I asked.

"The Communist party," he said.

"Washington was a communist?" I asked.

"Oh, shit, yes," he said. "He's the one got my old man in."

"Your father was a communist?" I asked.

"Weird, isn't it?" he said. "Trust funds. Lodge in the mountains. Son of a wealthy doctor."

"And Washington too?" I asked.

"Washington worked for the Resistance," Joseph said. "It was his whole life. He knows more about who helped the Nazis and the Fascists take over than the people who write books about it. And he also knew that people they trusted sold out the Resistance. They found out most of the ones in Europe, but there were some in the U.S. too, in the party and in the government, and Washington was determined to find all of them he could. He's never stopped."

"You mean he's still a communist?" I asked.

"No," Joseph said. "But he found out that all the time that Lenny's father was in the party and was supposed to be organizing support for the Resistance in France, he was really working for the government, and they were passing names to the Fascists so they could round up the reds. Your old man was in the party, so Washington brought out those letters, to get them by the army censors. He read them, of course, to be sure, and he passed them to Lenny's old man, who was supposed to get them to Joy. The old guy never delivered the letters. Washington got them that far, but they never made it the rest of the way."

"Jesus," I said.

"I told you it wasn't simple," he said. "Other things happened, other people talked, but when Lenny got on with the government, Washington finally figured out that it was Lenny's old man who had been selling them out, because some of the people who hired him were part of the old Fascist bunch, and Washington figured they owed Lenny's old man some favors. That's when he started watching Lenny real close."

"Jesus," I said. "I don't know what to think."

"Think this," Joseph said. "Lenny's father is dead. He was poisoned. Lenny thinks Washington did it. Washington thinks it was Lenny's boss."

"Who's that?" I asked.

"Somebody in the FBI," he said. "He's a paid informer."

"You sure of that?" I asked.

"Ask Kelly sometime," he said. "She'll tell you. She knows him."

"But Joy turned everything over to him," I said. "I don't understand."

"Why she trusted him is one of the biggest mysteries of my life," Joseph said. "And we'll probably never know."

"Dacia said it was a spell," I said.

"Too bad she couldn't break it," he said.

"Do you think Washington killed Lenny's dad?" I asked.

"Of course not," he said.

"How can you be so sure?" I asked.

"I wish I knew how much he had taught you," Joseph said.

"Apparently," I said, "not very much."

"Look," he said. "Just pay attention while we go out on this trip, and you'll understand. I'm not Washington. I can't teach it to you like he can, but if you pay careful attention you'll see."

"Does Danny know all this stuff?" I asked.

"He knows Lenny is a creep," Joseph said. "And he knows Lenny did something with Veronica's old man. That's enough."

"Jesus," I said and couldn't think of anything else to say.

Joseph went back to the records, and I stared out the window at the cattle across the road. It didn't look like such a bad life. In the end they would come and put you in a truck and take you somewhere and shoot you, but until then they didn't bother you much. All you had to do was hang around and eat and not cause trouble. The only bad thing would be that nobody would look at you and just admire you for being such a great-looking cow. They would be looking at you and thinking how much they'd like to eat you, after you were dead. That could get pretty creepy.

The picture I was getting of Washington from Joseph was real different from how he had seemed to me all the time I had known him, how he seemed from what I could remember. But it did help me a lot to know that when he had disappeared, before we started the last trip east, before we got hooked up with Lenny and had all this trouble, it wasn't just because he didn't care about us any more. And another thing was that when he disappeared, it didn't mean that something bad had happened to him, that he was hurt or sick or dead or in jail. It could mean that, but it didn't have to, and I felt a lot better about that. If Joseph was right about Lenny doing things to Joy, and Dacia, and maybe to me, to try to get Washington to show himself, that meant Washington might be fine, might be doing real good, might even be about to do something big he had been working up to for a long time. That felt good too, real good. I closed my eyes and pictured him the way I had seen him in my dream, when I was floating in the pool. I saw him by the fire, holding the sword above his head, the hilt in one hand and the point in the other. Seeing that picture made me feel stronger, as if it was one of Dacia's medicinal teas.

When Danny came up the stairs, taking them two at a time, and came in with the gun I knew was for me, I was ready to go. I still had no intention of killing any deer, but I was ready for the trip. He had had a little trouble getting the rifle when it came right down to it. The stock had recently been refinished and didn't have any scratches on it, and the scope was sighted in for the guy who owned it. Danny had had to work his story around so it sounded like maybe I was interested in buying it, and all of that took time. Kelly still hadn't called, so I left a note and the keys to the Packard for her. It was real close to twelve noon when Danny got there, and it was a little after when we got everything into his car and got out of town.

Once we were in Danny's Pontiac, skidding through the curves, headed east toward the lodge at twice the legal speed limit, I realized that I was riding with the same guy who had cracked up a car and hurt Veronica. So many things had been coming at me so fast, I hadn't really thought about it until we were blasting along the road in the convertible, and it was almost impossible to forget. I was in the back seat with some of our gear, and I just held on and didn't say anything. We turned down the road to the lodge, stopped when we saw the Fox, and pulled in through the gate. It took us no more than ten minutes to move everything to the old Jeep wagon, and we were off again, but this time with Joseph driving.

Sometimes the trail disappeared altogether as we crept over a large section of flat rock or followed the bottom of a creek bed, but then it would reappear. After about an hour of that and an occasional disagreement between Joseph and Danny about which way to turn, we came out on a Forest Service road, complete with mileage markers and direction signs. We followed that until we came to a cable stretched across the road with a wooden sign hanging from it that said, "Wilderness Area. No Vehicles." Joseph pulled off the road back into the woods, far enough that the Jeep would be out of sight.

"It should be okay here," Danny said, "if the goddamn Texans don't shoot it."

I laughed out loud.

"I'm serious," he said.

"Four Texans up here last year," Joseph said, "put a blanket over their radiator to keep the ice out, and then circled around without knowing where they were, and shot the blanket full of holes."

"And the radiator," Danny chuckled.

"It was an army blanket," Joseph said. "They said the color fooled them."

"You ever see an olive drab deer?" Danny asked.

"No," I answered.

"You ever see a deer at all?" he asked.

"Yes," I answered.

"Thank God," Danny said. "I'd hate to have to pack out a Jeep."

Joseph and Danny both laughed, but I knew the joke was on me, really, and I didn't think it was that funny. We hauled our stuff out of the Jeep and arranged a camp. At least I knew what I was doing when it came to that, and I decided I would surprise them when we got closer to supper by offering to cook. Joseph passed the ammunition to me, and I took six of the heavy brass bullets for myself. They were different from the shells I had used before, the little .22s I had fired in the shooting galleries at carnivals. I rolled the bullets in my hand. Their tips were long and pointed and serious-looking and were covered with a hard copper jacket.

"What's he need ammo for?" Danny asked.

"He might get a shot," Joseph said.

"And scare everything off where we can't take it," Danny said.

"I got one my first time out," Joseph said.

"That's different," Danny answered.

"I don't need them," I said, offering the bullets to Joseph.

"Put them in your pocket," he said. "You might get a shot, and then you'll be sorry if you don't have them."

Danny pulled the rifle he had borrowed out of its leather carrying case and handed it to me.

"Don't fall down with it," he said. "If you scratch up that stock, one of us is going to have to buy it."

I took the rifle with my left hand, watching carefully to see how the others handled theirs. Joseph showed me how to load it and how to eject the bullet without firing it.

"Load one round," he said. "Don't think about a second shot. If you're not sure you can bring him down clean with one shot, don't shoot."

"Which means, just don't shoot," Danny said. "After one shot, everything on the mountain knows we're here."

"The deer already know," Joseph said.

"But the hunters don't," Danny said.

"Why do I have to carry this at all?" I asked and offered the rifle to Joseph.

"It's the law," he said. "We're not supposed to fill other people's licenses for them. So the law says there has to be a hunter for each license you fill, and that means you have to carry a loaded gun."

We still had almost two hours before dark, so Joseph suggested we hike up the mountain for a ways to get oriented. We followed a creek bed across a meadow covered with snow. The mountain on the west was already in shadow and was so steep it probably had been shadowed since shortly after noon. Joseph pointed out where he and Danny would go up the next morning. The plan was that they would set up in a particular spot, and I would follow the creek around to the other side and push the deer up over the ridge, where Danny and Joseph would be waiting. We kept on walking along the creek, the route I would take the next day. When we got to the other side of the meadow, the creek bed was in shadow too, but above us and in front of us I could see a bright, almost blinding patch of snow, reflecting the sun, and we kept moving toward that.

Once we were far enough south and high enough to be out of the mountain's shadow, we were at the edge of a nearly level plain, covered with snow that stretched from the edge of the trees, on the south side of the ridge, for about twenty-five yards to where it ended abruptly in a steep drop. Joseph pointed out where I should climb to go up the back side of the ridge. We all crossed the little plateau together and found a large rock near the edge where we could soak up the heat from the sun and look down into the valley below the cliff. From our perch up there, I could see that the creek we had followed made a horseshoe turn in the meadow, just beyond where we had picked it up, and ran south. It fed into a waterfall that fell to a pond, maybe a hundred feet down from where it went over. There were half a dozen animals, elk I guessed, feeding between the frozen pond and the base of the cliff, where the overhang protected the grass and shrubs from being covered by snow.

I had never seen elk alive before, just their heads and antlers on the walls of cafes and in the sporting goods store. They were moving so that they stayed in the warmth of the sun. On the other side of the valley there were three men leading horses down a steep trail toward a camp, where there were three other men and three other horses. Danny had raised his rifle, had it pointed toward the camp, and was focusing the scope. Joseph had a small glass that looked like half of a pair of binoculars on a cord around his neck and was looking toward the camp too. Being careful to keep my hand away from the trigger, I raised my rifle and looked through the sight, but all I could see was a moving blur, like you see when you look out a side window at something you're passing real fast in a car.

"See anything?" Joseph asked.

"Just a blur," I answered.

Looking through the scope was making me dizzy. I lowered the rifle so I wouldn't lose my balance and fall.

"You're not steady enough," Joseph said.

He showed me how to lie down on my belly in the snow, propped on my elbows so the barrel of the gun wouldn't wave around so much. I still couldn't get a really clear picture of the camp, but at least I could see the figures of the men and the horses flying back and forth in front of the circle I was looking through.

"Never rush," Joseph said. "You've always got time to get close, and you've always got time to use a sitting position or to lie down. Always get close. If you're careful, you can always get closer than you think. Get so close you can see him breathing. Take your time. There's no hurry. Count in time with his breathing. That way, you'll be sure you've got what you think you've got."

I listened as he talked and kept squinting to look through the sight. His voice seemed like it was almost hypnotizing me or something, and I started repeating the words inside my head to help me steady the gun. Finally, I got the circle to stay still around one man in a black snowmobile suit with a red and black wool plaid coat over it and a red cap with earmuffs tied up on top.

"I've got one of them now," I said. "Are they after the elk?"

"No one would shoot anything down there," Danny said. "Even the horses couldn't pack it out."

"What are they doing then?" I asked.

"Recognize anyone?" Joseph asked.

"I can't see that good," I answered.

My cheek was hurting from squinting one eye shut to look through the scope, and my arms were getting tired trying to hold the heavy gun still. I rolled carefully onto my back and lay the rifle across my chest, pointing it off away from Joseph and Danny.

"I sure as hell do," Danny said.

"They've been camped in there for four days," Joseph said.

"Who?" I asked.

"Come here and look," Joseph said.

I got up and went back to where I could sit next to Joseph. Danny had lowered his gun, but he was still looking intently in the direction of the hunters in the valley. Joseph showed me how to use the glass, and I was able to hold each of the men in the circle, one at a time, but I couldn't get a clear picture of any of them.

"I still can't see them clearly," I said.

"The three who just came down with the horses," Joseph said, "are the same three who came to the lodge the other night."

"The ones Kelly got the money from?" I asked.

"That's right," he said. "From Kansas. The one by the fire, with his back to us, is Lenny."

"Lenny," I said. "That's Lenny?"

"And that's his brother," Joseph said, "in the yellow raincoat."

"Oh, Jesus," I said. "Lenny and Larry are with those three guys?"

"They came up from Kansas together," Joseph said. "I've been watching them all week."

"And the fat one in the black pants?" Danny said, as if he was asking a question but knew the answer.

"With the red coat?" I asked, without looking.

"My old man," he said. "The son of a bitch told my mother he was going to the Gulf of Mexico to fish for two weeks."

"That's your father?" I asked. "With them?"

"Nice, isn't it?" Danny said. "The fucker."

"Let's go," Joseph said. "It's going to be dark if we don't go soon."

It was nearly dark when we got back, and got the fire going, and got something to eat, and got ready for bed. No one seemed to want to talk, so we just ate, and cleaned up, and got things arranged for the morning, and went to bed. The air was cold, but I was warm in the sleeping bag. The sky was clear, and the stars were brilliant. I started looking for constellations, trying to remember the ones that Dacia had taught me to find, but I couldn't recognize any. I thought Joseph and Danny were both asleep, and I thought Joseph was talking in his sleep, but he wasn't.

"Are you awake?" he asked.

"Yes," I answered.

"Did Washington ever tell you about the deer in Africa?" he asked. "The white deer?"

"I think so," I said.

"The ones the hunters say have magic?" he asked. "And nobody can shoot?"

"Yes," I answered. "I remember that."

"Well, tomorrow," he said, "if you see something and you know you're going to miss, you know you can't hit it, don't shoot."

"Okay," I said.

"Even if it looks like an easy shot," he said. "Don't shoot."

"Okay," I said.

"It's not necessary," Joseph said. "And it won't do any good."

It's not necessary, I repeated over and over to myself until I went to sleep. *It's not necessary.*

Chapter

10

I woke up before the others. The sun hadn't risen yet, but I could see the east side of the valley without getting out of my sleeping bag. I lay there for about half an hour, watching the blue-gray light behind the silhouetted mountains become more blue and less gray. I couldn't remember what I had dreamed, but I had that feeling of wanting to stay quiet and not talk to people or think about things I would be doing during the day until I had understood my dream. I usually had that feeling when I woke up, even if I couldn't remember the dream, and lots of times it would come to me later anyway. I felt sort of empty, as if I hadn't eaten and was hungry, but it wasn't hunger. I tried to think about people who were important to me, tried to see their faces, but I couldn't get even one to come in clear. It would have been kind of scary, I think, if it hadn't been for the fact that that empty feeling was like there was nothing inside my mind and was also real quiet, like nothing was moving around, so there was nothing that could start racing. It was when things started racing in my mind that I felt scared.

After about half an hour of watching the sky, I decided I could get up and get breakfast going. I wiggled into my clothes and was glad I had kept everything in the bag with me, because nothing was too cold or too damp to wear. When I started to get wood together, though, Joseph made faint sounds, waved me over to his bag, whispered to me that we should make as little noise as possible, and told me we wouldn't eat anything but trail mix until noon because of the noise and the smell. I rolled up my bag and found the food he was talking about in the Jeep, a bag full of a dozen small bags. Each one seemed to have the same thing, a mixture of a couple of kinds of nuts and raisins and tiny chunks of chocolate. Since I figured that my share of twelve would be four, I put one bag in each of my coat pockets and left the other two there, tucked into my sleeping bag, for later. I was eager to get moving, partly just to stay warm.

Because I knew where I was supposed to go and what I was supposed to do, I couldn't see why I needed to wait around, but Danny and Joseph, once they finally got dressed and out of their bags, wanted to go over the plan one more time. Danny especially was worried I would get "buck fever," would panic when I saw a deer and would shoot wildly, which he said happened to a lot of first-time hunters. He was afraid I would scatter the deer all over the mountain and down into the deep canyon, where there would be no point going after them. Joseph was more calm.

"If you get a shot," he said, "and you just can't pass it, don't rush. You've got nothing but time. Get close."

"I know," I said. "Get close so I can count his breathing. Use a sitting position or lie down. Load one round. See, I remember."

"If he's small," Joseph said, "don't take him. It's not necessary."

"Whatever we get," Danny said, "we have to pack out. That's why we want them on this side of the mountain."

"If you get a shot," Joseph said, "aim at his heart. If he runs don't shoot."

"Don't shoot anything running," Danny said. "The meat will be so strong you can't eat it."

"Squeeze the trigger," Joseph said. "Don't jerk it. And be sure. Don't aim for the head. Don't think about a second shot."

"All you have to do," Danny said, "is hike up the back side. They'll come right over to us. You don't have to shoot anything."

I listened carefully, then took my rifle and bullets and bags of nuts and headed out over the route we had taken the day before. Even though the sun had not yet broken over the mountains in the east and it wasn't much lighter than bright moonlight, I had very little trouble moving along. By the time I reached the little plateau and crossed it to the lookout, it was much lighter and so close to sunup that I decided to wait there and watch. I looked carefully over the valley below, finding the waterfall and the frozen pond and the bare ground where the elk had been feeding and the place where Lenny's party had been camped. They weren't there. They were gone, all six of them.

I used my scope and scanned carefully, but they really were gone. It seemed almost impossible that they could have gone out in the dark last night, the trail was so steep. But they were not there. I felt that I should do something to let Danny and Joseph know. It seemed important. I thought about shooting into the air to get their attention and even loaded a round into the rifle, but decided against it. It wouldn't tell them anything. They would just think I had gotten a shot and taken it or that I had gotten buck fever. What seemed like a better plan would be going back to the camp and then following their trail up the mountain to warn them.

I stood up to start back. At almost exactly the place where the trail I had left across the little plateau went into the woods by the creek, I saw a large male deer with big branching antlers, standing among the trees. I watched as he rocked his head back and nibbled at the lower branches, the antlers almost touching his back. He was clearly visible. I did not immediately come to the conclusion that he was a deer and I was a hunter, so, naturally, I would have to kill him. There was nothing I could see in his body or in his eyes or in the way he moved that told me I should. I had seen things that gave that message, and I remembered them—a rattlesnake once and an unhappy dog that had gone crazy from being beaten—but there was none of that in the buck.

I didn't move immediately. Nothing in the world seemed to move except that deer. It was as if everything else had stopped. It was as if I had had this idea that I needed to hurry back to the camp and had run to vault over a fence. I could see that picture in my mind. There I was vaulting over a wooden rail fence but, without intending to, I had become balanced on one hand on the upper rail, perfectly and delicately balanced, like a highwire stunt. It was like there was no limit to how long I could have stood there watching the deer, and like I had that perfect control that everybody in the circus dreams about. It was up to me to make whatever little twist would make me come down on one side or the other. It was up to me.

The thought was in front of me, like a billboard along the highway, "Drink Coke." "Kill the Deer." It wasn't everywhere, just in one of the possible directions. Balanced there in that long moment of watching, I could feel the pull of that idea in front of me. "Shoot the Deer." And I could feel something behind me too, something that had never knowingly hurt anything and that would be gone forever if I moved the wrong way. I closed my eyes, and I saw myself balanced on my hands on a rail, legs straight, back curved, toes pointed upward, and Washington was standing beside me with his hands close to my feet, as if he had helped me balance and had just let go to let me stand there on my own. *Don't rush*, he was saying. *You have nothing but time.*

I opened my eyes. The buck was still there, eating from the lower branches of the trees. I could see the steam pouring from his nostrils as he breathed. *Get close*, I thought. *If you're careful you can get closer than you think.* Slowly, I took one careful step forward, and I heard a sound. The deer heard it too and looked but not toward me. It wasn't my foot crunching the snow, as I had first thought it must be. The sound came from the valley below me. When I turned my attention that way, I realized that it was much more than a footstep. It was a large rock rolling down into the valley, hitting trees and crunching brush, and then it was the frightened screaming of a horse, up on its hind legs, fighting for balance near the top of the steep trail. The deer did not turn into the woods and hide but moved a few steps closer to the cliff's edge, as if he wanted to see for himself what had caused the noise. With each step, he also came closer to me, and I slowly lowered myself onto my stomach on the rock to watch in both directions. I raised the rifle as carefully as I could and looked through the scope. *Use a sitting position or lie down.*

When I got the rifle steadied, I could see that one man on the trail was braced against a tree, holding tight to the horse's reins, and that the horse had regained its footing. There were six men and six horses altogether, moving single file down the trail, each man leading a horse, none of them riding. I couldn't keep my one eye squinted shut all the time to look through the scope with the other, and when I let it open I could see the deer, still moving one step at a time, closer to the edge. I turned the rifle toward the deer, aware that I had loaded a round earlier and had not fired it and had not ejected it. The deer's tongue darted in and out of his mouth. A haze of warm air pulsed from his nostrils and left a visible little cloud in the cold air. *Count his breathing to be sure.* I watched the vapor puff into the air and watched his tongue flick in and out. Through the scope I could even see the stray whiskers around his chin and one big brown eye, but I couldn't keep squinting and lowered the rifle again. The deer was very near the edge of the cliff, his head tilted back a little, sniffing the wind coming from the south.

The hunter who had had problems with his horse was at the bottom of the trail, not far from their camp, but he had stopped and looked like he was going to take the horse's saddle off. Even though my cheek was sore, I turned the rifle toward him and looked through the scope again. He was drawing a rifle from the long leather scabbard on one side and was pointing toward me or the deer—I couldn't tell which—with his free hand. The other five men were all visible on the trail and had all stopped to look. The deer stood motionless at the edge of the cliff. I wondered if he felt as I did, that they would be reluctant to shoot as long as they still had horses on the trail. I wondered why the deer didn't move, but he didn't. He waited and watched. As each of the hunters reached the bottom, they tied their horses the way the first one had, and they all drew their rifles. Five of them were down and the sixth one was still a third of the way up the trail when he stopped and looked and pointed and waved his arm, as if he had just discovered for himself what the others had been watching for a long while. He was wearing a yellow raincoat. It was Lenny's brother, Larry.

Before I realized what he was doing, Larry had his rifle out of the scabbard and had fired. The deer did not jump or run but took three steps back from the cliff and then seemed satisfied.

I could hear the horses screaming again and three more shots. I didn't know for sure that it was Larry who fired them because I had flattened myself as close to the ground as I could. One of the bullets went almost directly over my head. I had never been shot at before, but it was an unmistakable experience. I couldn't tell whether or not the shot had been aimed at me, whether the hunters had seen me or the deer or what, but the sound of that one shot coming on a line straight for me was so different from the others that I could see why there was no need to panic when you could tell the shot wasn't well aimed.

The firing stopped, and I raised my rifle to look at the deer. The vapor puffed from his nostrils like before. *Don't aim for his head. Aim for his heart.* I followed the line of the deer's neck to his shoulder, and I could see his chest moving with his breathing. I was close enough that with the scope focused on the deer's chest, I couldn't see his face too, so I raised the rifle again until I could see his nose and his eye behind the cross hairs. *Aim for his heart.* The buck slowly turned his head and looked right at me. When you look a cow in the eye, it looks dumb, but the deer didn't.

Be sure.

I heard the words in my mind, but it was not the same voice that I had been hearing, remembering things. It was different. There was no sound, but it was as if the deer had spoken to me. It was as if, looking down the barrel of my gun, he knew something I was supposed to know, used to know, had been taught but had forgotten. He looked at me so I would remember way down deep. That's what it felt like. The deer was the same one I had seen in my mind when Washington told me about the ones in Africa, the ones that couldn't be shot. I looked back and stared right into his eye. He was more real to me than anything I had ever seen, but I wasn't sure that he was real, that the men down in the valley or anyone else could see him. I also knew that if I tried to shoot him, it would be impossible. I would miss. I wanted to stay there forever.

There's no hurry.

I lowered the rifle. My finger was on the trigger, but I wasn't aiming, and I swung the rifle to the side. If I did something that somehow made it possible to shoot that deer, it seemed to me it would be one of the most horrible things that ever happened.

You don't have to shoot, the voice said. *It's not necessary.*

In the distance, like a reminder of another world, two shots rang out in rapid sequence. They came from behind me, from the other side of the ridge where Danny and Joseph were. They were fired so close to one another, they seemed like two quick shots from one gun. It had seemed that a long, slow moment had passed, but it hadn't. Larry had fired from down in the valley. The horses had screamed, and I had flattened out on the rock. Then there were three more shots from below and more sounds from the horses. I had seen the deer back up and then stand still in front of me, had aimed and then decided to hold my fire. At that instant there were two shots from the other side of the mountain behind me. It all happened quickly, in spite of how it seemed for a second. The deer did not look in the direction of the shots behind us but looked, instead, toward the valley. Just as I was turning to look that way too, there was another shot from the hunters down below.

I waited to be sure the shot had not been aimed toward me before I looked. The screaming had stopped. Larry's horse lay on its back at the bottom of the trail, with two legs sticking up in the air. One of the hunters at the bottom had shot it from only a few feet away. Larry lay on his back on the trail, holding his leg, rolling back and forth. I looked through the scope, first at Larry and then at the dead horse. One front leg was badly broken. I lowered the rifle again and rolled across the big rock until I was sitting in the snow, my back to the valley but out of sight, and drew the gun up close to myself. The butt was resting on the inside of my thigh, and the barrel was pointed upward. I looked over my shoulder. The deer was still there.

It's not necessary.

The buck turned slowly and walked into the woods. The horse was dead, and I was certain one or two deer were dead on the other side of the mountain. I felt sick. *Squeeze the trigger. Don't jerk it.* This thought came to me with the idea that I was not going to hit anything, just fire the gun. It was kind of a tribute, like honoring the animals that were dead by doing something, by firing a gun at nothing. I squeezed the trigger of the rifle without thinking any more about it, just looking at where the deer had disappeared into the trees. The rifle jumped, recoiling from the shot. Its butt drove into my leg like a blow from a hammer, and the barrel struck my forehead, drawing blood and knocking me over backward. I rolled back into a sitting position and looked around, afraid I would find something else dead, but I was alone. I was bleeding from a small cut that had opened above my left eye where the barrel had struck me.

It took me nearly an hour to climb the mountain and cross the ridge. I fell several times and scratched the gunstock. Danny and Joseph were waiting near the bottom of a long, smooth rock like a slide, on the other side, that ran nearly the entire height of the mountain. Danny had been in the trees on one side of this open area, near the top, and had shot two bucks, one after the other, as they tried to run across the rock. Both deer had rolled from top to bottom, as he had hoped. He had shot them with two rapid shots from a semiautomatic. He told me the story and then laughed because he had broken the rules he and Joseph had given me.

By the time I arrived, the heads were off and the deer had been cleaned and halved, so there were four halves to be carried out to the Jeep. Danny lifted one of the halves onto my shoulders, with the legs at either side of my neck, so that by holding a hoof in each hand I kept the meat on my back, piggyback style. Joseph followed me with another, and the two of us made our way slowly to the camp. The hot blood ran down my neck and back, soaked through the hood on my sweat shirt, into my hair, through my clothes to my skin. We loaded the meat into the back of the Jeep, locked the doors, and went back for the rest. Danny stood guard over the carcass. On the second trip out, Joseph and I carried our rifles and the other two halves on our shoulders, the way we did the first two. Danny brought his rifle and the heads. Once everything was in the Jeep, we stopped to rest.

"Buck fever?" Danny asked, looking at me.

"What?" I answered.

"I tried to warn you," he said.

"Lay off," Joseph said.

"What do you mean?" I asked.

"You sounded like a machine gun out there," Danny said. "Bang, bang, bang, bang."

"It worked out fine," Joseph said. "We filled two licenses."

"The last shot was mine," I said, "but I only fired once."

"Sure," Danny said. "Who fired the others? The army?"

"Larry," I said. "Lenny's brother. He shot once, and then either he or the others fired three more shots. I couldn't tell who because I was keeping as low as I could."

"Keeping low?" Joseph asked. "You mean they were shooting at you?"

"I'm not sure," I answered. "There was a deer on the edge of the cliff near where I was. I couldn't tell whether they were aiming at him or at me, but one shot went right over my head."

"It doesn't make sense," Danny said. "Why would they try for a shot like that?"

"If they had hit both the deer and Louis," Joseph said, "they could have called it a hunting accident. But it seems pretty strange."

"They didn't hit either of us," I said, "and it wasn't something they had planned."

"How do you know that?" Danny asked.

"Because I went right from here," I answered, "to where we were yesterday, and there was nobody down there where they were camped."

"Are you sure?" Joseph asked.

"They weren't there," I said. "I watched all six of them come down the trail just before sunup. The others were at the bottom, but Larry was still partway up the trail when he fired."

"There's no telling with Larry," Joseph said. "He's so damned dumb, he could do anything."

"Let me get this straight," Danny said. "You're saying that the six of them hiked out of that valley last night, in the dark."

"I don't know when they left," I said.

"It would have had to have been after we saw them," Danny said. "It was almost dark then."

"And they had a fire going," Joseph said.

"They weren't there this morning," I said. "I watched them come down the trail. Larry fired, and there were more shots, and when I looked again, Larry's horse was down at the bottom with a broken leg. They shot it. It probably panicked and fell when the firing started. And Larry was hurt too, rolling around on the ground, holding his leg."

"You fired once?" Danny asked.

"I didn't shoot him," I said, "if that's what you mean."

"It wouldn't bother me if you had," Danny said.

"It was seeing the dead horse," I said. "I fired in the air. Just to show respect, for the horse."

"You're sure they weren't there when you first came?" Joseph asked.

"Positive," I said.

"We should have kept a watch," he said.

"We can go back up and look," Danny said. "If they really shot a horse in there, we'll be able to see it."

"I saw it," I said.

"We need to get back," Joseph said, "to check on Veronica and Kelly and to hang the meat."

"Why didn't you say something earlier?" Danny asked, looking at me.

"You were too busy giving orders," I answered.

"If they've got one guy hurt," he said, "we could get to the top of the trail before they do, if we go now."

"What for?" I asked.

"We need to get back," Joseph said.

"We could get this over with," Danny said.

"We need to get back," Joseph answered.

I didn't try to find out for sure what Danny meant. I was too tired, and so were they. I wanted to bathe and sleep. We drove down the mountain in almost complete silence, staying to the Forest Service roads and highways this time. When we got to the house that had Danny's apartment in it, he unlocked the garage, and we unloaded the meat from the Jeep into a room he had fixed up out there. It had hooks and a block and tackle so we could hang the meat, and it had little doors near the floor and ceiling to let cold air in and warm air out. The walls were just studs with insulation, covered with clear plastic stapled to the wood. Joseph left to go inside while Danny checked the temperatures inside and out and adjusted the little doors. When he had finished with the adjustments and with locking everything, Danny handed me my license.

"What's this?" I asked.

"Your license," he said. "I didn't tag 'em. So if you want to go out again . . ."

"I don't know," I said. "I don't think so."

"There's three hundred pounds of meat there," he said. "And we can always sell what we don't need."

"I don't know," I said. "I need a bath."

Danny put his arm around my shoulder. Even his breath smelled like blood.

"Don't say anything to Joseph," he said.

"About what?" I asked.

"Not tagging the deer," he said. "He's real gung ho about obeying the game laws. He was distracted by what you told him about Larry and Lenny and the others, so he didn't notice that I didn't tag them. But he's usually real gung ho."

"Let's go in," I said. "I'm cold."

The light was on in the stairwell, even though it wasn't dark outside yet. On the landing at the top of the stairs there were three large plastic bags, a bathrobe, and a pair of coveralls. Joseph had already left his clothes in one of the bags.

"The robe's mine," Danny said and began untying his laces.

We undressed quickly and put our clothes in the other two bags. It was chilly in the stairwell, and the metal buttons on the coveralls were icy cold against my skin, but I felt cleaner already. It was worth being cold for. When Danny was out of his clothes and into his robe, I followed him into the apartment. Joseph was standing in the living room in brown corduroy pants and a brown wool sweater and gray wool socks, staring out the window behind the couch. His long hair was wet, as if he had already had his shower.

"Veronica here?" Danny asked.

"In the bedroom," Joseph answered.

Danny disappeared through the kitchen doorway. I stood

next to Joseph, looking out the window across the empty pasture toward the mountains east of town. The grass was brown, but there wasn't much snow, just a few little patches in the hollows that didn't get sun. The cattle were gone. Joseph and I stood there looking into the distance. I could hear voices, Danny and Veronica, coming from behind me, but they were muffled enough by the bedroom door that I couldn't tell what they were saying. It sounded like a mild argument, and I wondered if it was as hard for Veronica to come out and talk to me with Danny there as it was for me to think of seeing them together and acting like it was no big thing. The old black Packard was parked on the street in front of the house. It was dusty and mud-spattered, and for the first time I could remember it didn't look glamorous and luxurious to me. It just looked like an old car. All the years Joy and Dacia and I had traveled, we had always stayed away from winter, and I wondered how people washed their cars when it got so cold.

"Is Kelly here?" I asked.

"Downstairs," Joseph said. "Feeding the cat."

"I wonder if she got registered for school," I said.

"See that cloud?" Joseph asked.

"Where?" I asked.

"Just past the first range of mountains," he answered. "The black haze."

"I see it," I said.

"It's the lodge," Joseph said. "They burned the lodge."

"Who?" I asked.

"Lenny and his bunch," he answered. "Danny's old man. I'm sure of it."

"I could have shot them," I said. "At least one of them. This morning. I had them in the sight, and I was steady too."

"It's all right," Joseph said. "They want us to panic. They want Washington. The harder they push, the sooner they'll screw up."

"How did you find out?" I asked.

"It's all over town," he said. "Veronica told me."

"You don't mean," I said, "that everyone knows who did it?"

"Everyone knows it burned," he said. "And there's talk it was arson. But I know it was them. That's where they went last night, then they made all kinds of racket this morning so every hunter on the mountain would swear they were in that valley when it happened."

"Shouldn't we do something?" I asked.

"Go help Kelly," Joseph said. "There's a shower down there too. You can clean up down there."

"That's all?" I said. "Feed the cat? Clean up?"

"Today," Joseph said, "that's all. Tomorrow we'll go look."

It wasn't a thick black cloud. It was just a haze. If the fire was last night while we were sleeping in the mountains, it was probably pretty much burned out by now. I didn't know how much the lodge meant to Joseph. He didn't live there, and he had let it get in pretty bad shape, but his grandfather had built it, and he had inherited it from his father, so it was hard to say. I thought back over the people I knew, to check if I was remembering right, but I couldn't think of anyone I had ever really gotten to know who had grown up in one place. I had met a lot of farmers who would come out to see Joy dance and have Dacia read their fortunes, but all the people I got to be friends with were road people, always moving. Veronica and her father traveled wherever he could work construction. The only reason they had been in the same place so long was because the big dams took so long to build. Kelly was kind of a town girl or wanted to be, but her mother was somewhere and she was somewhere else, and it hadn't taken much to get her out of Hemmings. But Joseph had always lived right around Gunnison, from what I had picked up, and might have a different feeling about having the place burn down. The only things I had, other than the Packard, were the things Kelly had brought. In a way, I guess they came and took them back.

I thought about the picture of Joy and Uncle Louis and me. It was the only picture I had seen of myself as a baby. The other thing about it was that it gave me a different feeling about Joy. I had seen her dance hundreds of times, sometimes with nothing on at all, lots of times with hardly anything, and once, I remembered, she had wanted me to go to bed with her, but the only time I had really felt a desire for her, a desire that made me not even think about being her son, was when I looked at that picture. I don't know what it was, but it didn't matter now because it was gone, with the letters and everything else. I had nothing or almost nothing. It was a little bit like when they let me out of jail in Hemmings. Not as bad, but it felt like that, and I wanted to see Kelly.

Joseph explained to me how to find the front door of the apartment below, and I went down the stairs and back along a narrow hall and under the stairs and knocked. Kelly just hollered for me to come in, so I opened the door and went in. She was curled up under a navy blue blanket on a couch that really looked like a big padded frame full of pillows. The arms and back were so high it reminded me of a booth in a cafe, but it was covered with a furry-looking kind of material. There were pillows, big ones, scattered around so four or five people could sit on the floor, it looked like, and there was a rug over maybe half of the floor that looked like fur, even though it was easy to tell that it wasn't the real thing. The couch faced a large window that stuck out from the house, so there was a place like a bench there, with a couple of pillows on it. There were two sets of curtains, white lacy ones that were drawn shut and some heavy blue ones that were open and looked as if they would block out all the light if they were shut. There wasn't much of a view, just the garage and the trunk of a big tree and a patch of dirty snow. The ceiling was covered by a large cloth that looked like it might be from India or Persia, lots of colors and tiny designs. It was fastened all around the edges and hung down in the middle, and the light from the ceiling was sort of scattered through it. The whole place reminded me a little bit of Dacia's tent.

"Where's the cat?" I asked.

"There's no cat," Kelly said.

"Joseph said you were feeding the cat," I said.

"It's just something they say," she said.

"Who lives here?" I asked.

"Nobody," she answered. "People come and go."

"Like you and me?" I asked.

"You know about the lodge?" Kelly asked.

"I just saw the smoke," I answered. "Joseph showed me."

"I'm glad you're okay," she said.

"I'm okay," I answered.

"I was scared," she said. "We heard the noise, and we could see the light from the fire, right from the living room upstairs. Didn't you hear the noise?"

"No," I answered. "What noise?"

"A loud boom," she said. "There was an explosion and then the fire. I stayed up half the night with Veronica. She seemed to know right away it was trouble, and she got me worried something had happened to you."

"What could have exploded?" I asked. "There's nothing out there to blow up."

"Sit down, Louis," Kelly said. "I have a surprise for you."

Her voice sounded happy, like she was announcing the beginning of a party, and she smiled like she was about to have her picture taken. I didn't move immediately because I wasn't really sure where to sit, but Kelly sat up straight, with the blanket still drawn up to her chin, and sort of bounced up and down on the cushion and smiled again. I picked one of the floor pillows and lowered myself onto it. I not only needed a shower, but now I was beginning to feel stiff from hiking across the mountain with the meat on my shoulders. As soon as I was settled, Kelly stood up in her blanket and kind of trotted across the room to a set of glass double doors made up of rows of windows, each one less than a foot square, separated by wood strips about an inch wide. She disappeared through the doors, but I looked into the room quickly enough to see a bed and a dresser. There were lavender curtains on the bedroom side, so I couldn't see in. She wasn't gone very long. When she came back out, she was still barefoot, but she was wearing a full black skirt that had its own wide belt and a large silver buckle, oval-shaped, with a design that reminded me a little of a clamshell. She was also wearing a red satin blouse. It had big puffy shoulders and sleeves that came down to tight cuffs just below each elbow, and it had a collar, I guess you'd call it, that made her belt buckle look like a medal hanging on a sash that went up around her neck and left a real narrow, deep neckline. She had on pearl earrings and a pearl necklace, and her black hair was down past her shoulders, on her back. I looked her up and down and stared, and she turned around a couple of times so I could see the back too.

"What do you think?" Kelly asked.

"You're a knockout," I answered. "The guys will go crazy."

"You really like it?" she asked. "You really think I'm pretty?"

"Sure I like it," I said. "I think you're pretty in jeans and a work shirt, but sure, it's great."

"It fits okay?" she asked.

"It fits fine," I said. "Expensive?"

"It's Veronica's," she said. "We're the same size in everything. She said I can stay with them and go to school, and she'll let me wear her things so I don't have to spend everything on clothes right away, just some underthings."

"That's great, Kelly," I said. "You look very nice."

"How about the jewelry?" she asked. "You like the jewelry?"

She turned her head from side to side, pulled her hair way back from her ears, and faced me and spread her neckline slightly to be sure I could see her necklace.

"Very nice," I said. "They look real."

"They are real," she said.

Kelly dropped down onto her knees in front of me so her face was just inches away from mine. I tried to look off to each side of her, but she rolled her head back and forth until she caught my eyes. Her gaze was bold and steady, and she looked into my eyes for a moment before she spoke.

"They're Joy's," she said. "Can you believe it?"

"You didn't leave them at the lodge?" I asked.

"Do you remember after you and Joseph were out in the pool?" she asked. "We were in bed, and I asked you if I could do the same thing without the water. Do you remember?"

"Sure," I said. "It's only a couple of nights ago."

"Well, I did it," Kelly said. "I had a dream. I was wearing the pearls. I was beautiful. A woman gave them to me and told me I should keep them forever."

"And you brought them yesterday?" I asked. "Because of the dream?"

"Yes," she said, "and something else. Close your eyes."

I was glad to shut my eyes. I felt like I was going to cry, and it felt better with my eyes shut. She put a thin jewelry chain around my neck and hooked the clasp in the back. The metal was cold against my neck, and the medal touched my chest with a sting that made me flinch.

"Open your eyes," she said.

I took the medal in my hand and held it out where I could see it. The chain went through a ring on the top of a round hoop made to hold a coin by putting it in the hoop and tightening a screw. The coin inside was one of Dacia's silver coins with a man on one side and a woman on the other.

"I can't believe it," I said and turned the coin over in my hand.

"I had the jeweler melt the screw," she said, "so it can't come loose."

"I can't believe it," I said.

"I brought the pearls," she said, "and that coin was with them, so I brought it too. I went shopping and couldn't make up my mind on anything. I called Veronica and met her here, not long after you guys left, and we found out I wear her size. So instead of spending everything on clothes, I just felt so happy, I went to a jeweler's and had him put the coin on a chain for you."

I knew I was going to cry if I didn't do something, so I kissed her. As soon as I did, though, she wanted to hug me real big.

"I'm filthy," I said. "I need a bath."

"You thought I was just a girl," Kelly said. "Didn't you?"

"Well, sort of," I answered.

"I had the dream," she said, "and I didn't even question it. I'm sorry about the lodge, but I've never felt better. Never."

I didn't know what to say, so I kissed her again. She pulled me closer to her and kissed me harder. I understood what she meant about not feeling like a girl because she had trusted herself and it turned out right. It sort of scared me to kiss her like that, but I did it anyway because I could feel what she was talking about. She tried to move her fingers around in my hair, but it was too matted.

"What have you got in your hair?" she asked, drawing back.

"It's filthy," I said. "I need to clean up."

"I'll wash it for you," she said.

"Do you know about the deer nobody can shoot?" I asked.

"No," she answered. "Like the big fish that always gets away?"

"This is serious," I said. "There are stories about deer in Africa that nobody can shoot, magic deer. The tribesmen aim right at them, and the arrows always miss, no matter how hard they try."

"This is real?" Kelly asked.

"Yes," I said. "I saw one this morning. I had the sight on him three or four times, but I knew I shouldn't even try to shoot him, so I didn't. Larry tried but couldn't hit him."

"Larry?" she asked. "Dumb Larry?"

"Larry and Lenny and Danny's father," I answered. "They were up in the mountains right by us, with the three men from Kansas who came to the lodge."

"Oh, Jesus," she said.

"Larry tried to shoot the deer," I said, "and almost hit me, and had some kind of accident. He hurt his leg, and I'm sure it was because he shouldn't have tried to shoot that deer. It's the same as your dream, Kelly. You knew to bring the pearls, and you're happy that you did. I knew not to shoot, and I'm happy that I didn't."

We looked at each other for a moment. We were both about to cry and about to laugh because we were about to cry.

"Let's go wash your hair," Kelly said.

"It's blood," I said. "I had to help carry out the ones Danny killed. The blood soaked right through the hood on my sweat shirt and into my hair, but I didn't kill anything."

"All the more reason to wash it," she said. "Then we'll celebrate."

"Celebrate what?" I asked.

"Trusting ourselves," she answered. "It'll be like a birthday."

Kelly drew me a tub of hot water, and while I was soaking she changed back into her own clothes, her Levi's and cotton work shirt, then came into the bathroom and scrubbed my hair with both hands. She poured pitcher after pitcher of clear water over my head, and soaped my hair again, and rinsed it again until we both laughed to hear it squeak when she drew it through her fingers. Through all of it, I never took off the chain around my neck, and even with her work shirt, she kept wearing the pearls until we went to bed.

Joseph joined the army. It was the last thing any of us expected him to do, and we all tried to talk him out of it. But he kept going back to the idea that Washington got his training in the army, and he wanted the training too. He went over a lot of stuff about Washington that I already knew and a lot that I didn't, like how important it was to him to get face to face with whatever you were afraid of so you could see for yourself that you could handle it. Washington went to Europe when Hitler was just getting going, and he was in France before the Nazis took over because he knew the French would fight, and he wasn't sure the United States would, and because the U.S. Army didn't let blacks into combat units.

Joseph also talked about how Washington was connected with the French Resistance, posing as somebody's servant, and how the letters from Uncle Louis to Joy and some from Joseph's father to his aunt had come out of Europe through the Resistance. According to Joseph, the main connection was between his father and Washington because they were both communists, and there were a lot of communists helping the Resistance. When I said it didn't sound to me as if Washington was even in the army, Joseph told me all about Spain and how Washington and a lot of others had gone there to fight, and that it was an army, and that that's where he got his training.

All this stuff came out because Joseph and I spent a lot of

time riding around together in his Jeep, and we would talk. We drove out to look at the lodge the day after we got back from the hunting trip, and we talked on the way out. Joseph and Danny had already been out there once, and he told me what to expect, so I wasn't as shocked as I would have been. It wasn't like a lot of buildings that burn and are still standing but are charred wherever the fire reached. Everything was down—all of the walls and the roofs—except for part of the stone chimney rising up from the big fireplace in what had been the main lobby. The timber and roof beams were still smoking and there were twisted pipes sticking up out of the rubble, but not in any kind of way that would have let you know where the rooms had been or what the basic shape of the building was. It was just mounds of smoking trash.

Then we went up to the cabin, on a narrow Jeep road up the mountain behind the lodge. Joseph had been living there since his aunt finally gave up looking for the right manager and closed the lodge. She moved to Chicago where the rest of her family was, but Joseph stayed behind in the cabin because he was eighteen by then and wanted to be on his own anyway. The cabin was on the lodge property, but you couldn't see the lodge from there. Joseph's grandfather had had the cabin built first, so he and his family could come out to Colorado for a vacation in the mountains and could have a place to stay while they soaked in the hot springs and took in the sunshine. Joseph's grandmother had some kind of illness that got better when they came to Colorado, and that's what gave him the idea of the lodge for his patients.

The cabin was just one large open room with a large fireplace, and high-pitched ceilings, and a sleeping loft over the half that wasn't living room, the half that was a kitchen area with a wood stove and an icebox and a sleeping area with a double bed. Joseph was a little surprised, but it didn't look as if the cabin had been disturbed at all. There were paintings on the walls, and wood carvings on the tables and shelves, and photographs of people I guessed were part of his family. On the south side, there was a glassed-in porch and a large window in the cabin wall too, so we sat on the couch, and got warm in the sunlight, and traded stories about our families and what it was like to be little boys.

One idea I did get while we were there in the cabin that first time was that it bothered Joseph that they had burned the lodge, but it would have bothered him a whole lot more if they had hurt the cabin. I got the feeling that one reason he wanted to join the army was so he would be gone from there, so they wouldn't burn the cabin too. It was just a thought I had, but one thing I did learn was that Washington was the one who was interested in the lodge, not Joseph. While he was traveling around during the war from France to North Africa to the United States and back, Washington had learned some things about how his ancestors had used different kinds of powers to help them in battle. After the war he had also begun to learn how they used those same kinds of powers for making peace when there was a feud in the tribe or for healing when people were sick. According to Joseph, Washington had said several times that the lodge could be a powerful place for healing and for helping people be strong together, so Joseph had held on to that dream that Washington would come and teach him everything, and they'd live together like family.

Joseph signed up the day after we looked at the lodge together. The next week they sent him down to Denver on the train for his physical, and a week after that he had his assignment and papers and everything. There were just a few days in there, but we got it arranged so Kelly was going to stay with Danny and Veronica, in the downstairs apartment most of the time, and I was going to stay out in Joseph's cabin. That way Kelly could go to school, and we wouldn't have to go through a big thing trying to explain to the officials why she and I were living together when we weren't really brother and sister. We decided that I would use Joseph's Jeep and leave the Packard in town with Kelly, in case she had an emergency and needed it.

I was the official caretaker of the lodge property. Joseph took me to the bank to meet the man who was in charge of the money that paid for upkeep. He had already explained to Joseph that the sheriff was saying the fire was set and that if they proved it, the insurance company wouldn't pay off without a big court battle to prove Joseph hadn't set the fire himself for the insurance money. So they decided to go ahead and hire me to watch out for the cabin by paying me just as if the lodge hadn't burned down. Joseph wanted the man at the bank to meet me because he was the one who had to sign all the checks.

The night we put Joseph on the train to go off to boot camp, it began to snow. There had been snow higher in the mountains for a long time, and we had had a couple of snows that melted during the day, but this one was different. I had never experienced anything like it, and I wanted to get back to the cabin in the Jeep while I was still sure I could make it up the little road. It was a Friday night and Kelly wanted to come with me, so that was the first of several times when she stayed over at the cabin. In the morning, everything was covered with snow, and the shapes of everything had changed. It snowed all day, and by sunset the whole valley looked like one thing. The lines between the different mountains and between the mountains and the valley bottom were all gone. The difference in the valley before and after the snow was almost as great as the difference between the mountains and the prairie.

The time in the cabin with the snow coming down was good for us. We kept the fires going, in the stove and in the fireplace, and learned how to adjust the oil lamps, and played cards, and talked. Kelly hadn't been with Danny and Veronica very long, but she had picked up a lot of information. Danny sold things. She didn't know what all he was selling, but people would come over to see him. If Veronica was home and Kelly was downstairs, she would come down until they were gone. Or if Kelly and Veronica were upstairs and somebody came, they would both go down, or else Danny would use the downstairs apartment. Some of the people who came were students. He sold the deer meat to two students who knew how to cut it up and who had a locker to freeze it and keep it in. But there were all kinds. Danny sold the rifle I had taken on the hunting trip, which was a relief to me because I had scratched it and didn't have enough money to buy it. And even though Danny talked like he hated his father, he had met with him twice, just in the time Kelly had been living there. She had the idea that Danny's father was stealing things from the construction site, and Danny was selling them, but she wasn't sure yet.

Kelly had also figured out that the telephone downstairs in the bedroom was actually an extension off of the one upstairs, and the one in the living room was a different line. But the biggest thing was, she said that Veronica got a call and that she was sure it was from Victor, Veronica's father. Kelly was there when he called. At first she thought it was a boyfriend, and Veronica was talking funny, trying not to give her any clues, but she called him Victor and said some other things that made Kelly think it wasn't a boyfriend. Then when she and I talked, up there in the cabin, and I told her that Veronica's father's name was Victor, we both agreed it was probably him who had called. I told her that Lenny had hired him to drive a truck and pull Dacia's trailer around to carnivals for a year and that that was the last I had heard of him or Dacia. We agreed that we would get together again when Kelly had found out more or for her birthday on December 7, whichever came first.

The next morning was clear and cold, so it was easy to drive Kelly into town. On the way back, I stopped where the lodge had been to see if there was anything I could do. The snow had covered up a lot of the burned wood and the stuff that wouldn't burn, so it didn't look so ugly. Except for the pipes and the chimney, it almost looked like a rocky place covered with snow. In spite of all the trash and the burned roof, the steam coming up from the pool showed places where the water would have been visible if you could have gotten straight up above it. I saw one timber that was moving just a little. I figured out that one end was in the pool, almost floating free, and I decided to try getting it out with the Jeep. After several tries, I got all four wheels chained up and got the cable from the winch on the front of the Jeep tied on to the timber. I backed up slowly until I had dragged the beam out of the pool. I made up my mind I would figure out how to use the Jeep and move at least one piece every day until I got the pool cleared out. The rest of the mess could wait, but I wanted to clean up the pool.

It was almost Kelly's birthday when we saw each other again. I went into town on the first to see the banker, and tell him what I had done, and get money for the month. He also agreed to a snow blade for the Jeep so I could plow out around the lodge to keep working, and so I might be able to get a job here and there plowing out a parking lot. By the time they got the blade on the Jeep it was time for school to get out, so I parked across from the front of the big brick building and waited for Kelly. I thought she might come out with a boyfriend and not want to see me, but she was alone and almost ran over to the Jeep as soon as she recognized it.

"Can we go to the cabin?" she asked.

"Shouldn't you go home first?" I said.

"I'll call from a pay phone," she said.

She was wearing black ski pants and fur-topped rubber boots and a maroon ski parka and a black wool knit cap, so there was no need to stop to change clothes.

"Let's call from the Sportsman," Kelly said, when we were moving. "I've got us a job there if you want it."

The Sportsman was six cabins and a restaurant and bar, all right on the edge of the river. In the winter there weren't any fishermen, but it was kind of a party place where couples would come and eat and drink and dance to jukebox music and stay overnight. Kelly introduced me to one of the cooks, and while she went off to make her call, he explained what we would have to do. When she came back, we agreed on two nights a week, and Kelly and I left.

"He's got a thing going with one of the waitresses," she said, when we were back out in the Jeep. "He comes on shift later because he's supposed to stay on later to clean. But with us coming in at closing time, he can take her off to one of the cabins. The place gets clean, and nobody knows the difference."

"It's kind of complicated," I said.

"Everything's complicated," Kelly said. "But we can earn a little money, and you have to pick me up and take me home, so I get to see you more often."

"You can see me whenever you want," I said.

"It's been almost three weeks," she said.

"I thought you'd have a boyfriend," I said, "and other friends your own age."

"My own age," she said. "I'm almost fifteen, and you won't be seventeen until summer."

"Kids in school," I said. "I guess that's what I meant. Are you sure you want to hang around with me?"

"I hate them," Kelly said.

"Why?" I asked. "They can't all be mean."

"They all know who burned the lodge," she said. "Everybody in town knows. And they all think it's funny."

"How?" I asked.

"I don't know," she answered. "They all know, though. It was Danny's old man, so he must know too. And they make jokes about Joseph leaving town. I can't stand them."

Through the rest of December and into January, Kelly and I worked Tuesday and Thursday nights at the Sportsman. If we finished up early enough to make it worth it, I'd take her home to get some sleep. But some nights it took us longer or we talked more, and we would drive to the other side of town to Jack's Diner. Jack opened at 5:00 A.M., and we'd get a nice breakfast and have coffee and Kelly would just have time to change her clothes before school. I couldn't see how she could stay awake after working all night, but she said it was just as hard on the days when she hadn't worked. Still, I think some days she went in to change and went to bed instead. She never let me wait and take her to school.

Of course, it wasn't a problem about school and sleep and work between Christmas and New Year's, and I think it was at the New Year's party at the Sportsman that the cook's wife first started to catch on. Not much more than a week later, the job was over. Kelly thought the wife was going to shoot the cook, but she didn't. She just came in one night while we were cleaning and cried and cried and cried.

By then, close to the middle of January, the snow out near the lodge was all the way over the fence posts, so not only were the lines between the mountains and the valley bottom gone, the pastures were gone. And once, for three days, until they sent in big trucks with snowblowers, the road was gone too. It was a short time, three days, but I felt completely lost, and I loved it. Then on the morning of the fourth day, I had gotten on snowshocs and come just far enough down toward the lodge that I could see the plume of steam coming up from the pool in the middle of nothing but white. If I hadn't been cold, I would have wondered if I was really there or if I was dreaming. The only signs that human beings had ever been there, except for the tracks I made every time I took a step, were the power poles sticking out of the snow where I knew the road should be and a thin white jet trail across the sky. I thought I might walk on east across the valley until I couldn't even see the power lines, but I hadn't gone much more than a hundred yards on down the Jeep trail when I began to hear the snowblowers coming.

Within another half hour I could see the two trucks, one following the other, throwing arcs of snow two or three stories into the air and leaving behind a sharply cut path. The first truck continued on up the road past the lodge and went out of sight for a little while, but the second truck pulled off, into the lodge parking lot. I guessed the driver was using it to turn around, but it looked like he thought the building was still standing and he was making access to the road, except that he blew the snow toward where the building had been. When the other truck came back down, blowing out the other side of the road, he pulled into the lot too and maneuvered until he was shooting a huge stream of snow right onto the pool. Then they both shut off their blowers and drove off down the road toward town.

Once the road was open again, I was determined to clear the Jeep trail out enough that I would be sure I could get up and down. I walked up and down several times to be sure the route would be clearly visible before I tried it in the Jeep. All that time I was marching back and forth on my snowshoes, I kept watching the lodge. The parking lot made the place look open for business, but they had piled so much snow onto the pool that it was almost noon before a chimney had melted through. I saw a small puff of steam go up, and waited, and then saw another and another until it was a little cloud again, standing straight up. I wanted to celebrate that there was something they couldn't ruin, so I stood on the side of the hill and sang as loud as I could.

"The shrimp boats are a-comin'! There's dancin' tonight!"

It seemed like a silly song in the middle of nothing but cold and snow, but it was what came to mind, so I kept singing and humming and whistling that song for the rest of the day. By sundown I had the trail open enough to get up and down easily with the Jeep. I went to bed still feeling that I needed to have a party and woke up in the morning with that song still in my head. It was Friday and I made up my mind almost the minute I was awake that I would clean up the cabin, and get cleaned up myself, and go into town. By noon I had boiled water and scrubbed the floor, and washed clothes, and washed me, and dried a set of thermal underwear over the stove, and hung a set of sheets up there so they would be dry when I got back. I put on the newest jeans I had and a black turtleneck sweater and combed back my hair. It was getting long, but I liked it.

Even though it was almost one in the afternoon, I decided to put off lunch and just head directly into town. But I only had the Jeep about halfway down to the lodge when I saw a yellow school bus coming up the road. The buses almost never came back there, especially in the middle of the day. It turned into the lodge parking lot, let Kelly out, and pulled away. She was wearing her maroon parka and black ski pants and boots. It had become her uniform for visiting me at the cabin. I honked so she would see I was coming and sang the rest of the way down.

"I was just coming into town," I said, when Kelly was on the seat next to me.

"That's good," she said, "because I came out to get you."

"Is this a holiday?" I asked. "You're out of school early."

"The wrestling team beat Montrose Junior Varsity," Kelly said. "They promised us a half day off if they won."

"And the bus?" I asked. "They don't usually come down here."

"It's up to the driver," she said. "They're all in a good mood."

"You're not going to believe the cabin," I said. "I cleaned."

"We don't have time for the cabin," she said. "You have to come into town right now."

"Why?" I asked.

"Victor called this morning," she said.

"How do you know?" I asked.

"I stayed home," she said. "I knew we wouldn't do anything in the morning classes, so I stayed home and I listened on the phone in the bedroom when he called."

"Then you went up to the school to catch the bus?" I asked.

"It was that or drive the Packard out with no snow tires and no chains," she said. "Joseph's on leave, and he did something in Denver, and they have him in jail."

"Jail," I said. "Which jail?"

"And Dacia called Washington," Kelly said. "According to Victor, Washington told Dacia a year ago some way she could always reach him and told her that anytime she said he should come, he would, because he trusts her fortunes. Anyway, she called him, and Victor thinks he's right there in Denver."

"Denver?" I asked.

"I've got the address where Victor and Dacia are and everything," she said. "Victor knows they've got a plan to kill Washington and whoever comes to help him, and he's afraid his little girl is going to get hurt. So he called and told her everything. That's how I got the address."

"Did Veronica tell you all this?" I asked.

"I told you," Kelly said, "I listened on the phone. She didn't say a word to me about it. Danny knows that Joseph is in jail, but he found that out from somebody else."

"She might have told him when you weren't there," I said.

"I was there when he told her," she said. "She already knew it from Victor, but she acted surprised when Danny told her."

"She might be worried about her father," I said.

"Danny wants you," Kelly said. "He's half nuts, wild. He wants you right away, and I think you should come."

"Of course I'll come," I said.

I drove into town as quickly as I could. We stopped at the road and I took the chains off the front, and then we stopped at the highway and I took them off the back. After that we made pretty good time, even with the snow blade making the Jeep bob up and down, making it harder to handle. I let Kelly out downtown because she said it would be better that way, and I trusted her. When I got to the apartment, the Packard was there, but Danny's car was gone. I went right upstairs and knocked, and Veronica hollered from the bedroom for me to come in.

"Danny home?" I asked, speaking loudly so she could hear me in the other room.

"Is that you, Louis?" Veronica asked.

"Yes," I answered. "Is Danny here?"

"Not yet," she said. "Maybe in an hour or two."

She was changing. I couldn't see her from the living room, of course, but the bedroom door was open, and I could hear her moving around, could hear the bed squeak when she sat on it, and her shoes rap against the wooden floor as she dropped them, and her belt buckle tinkle as she loosened it. I sat in the living room alone, listening to Veronica opening and closing drawers, pushing clothes around in the closet, moving about her bedroom. Whenever she would stand up or sit down, I could hear the bed squeak, and I could hear a thumping sound I guessed was the headboard of the bed tapping against the wall. Those little sounds were so easy to figure out, I could almost picture her going through her ritual. I looked at the records with the idea of playing some music, but I didn't find anything.

From the couch I could look out through the window in the front door onto the landing and see the sealed-up door that was now part of the bedroom wall. I heard the bed squeak as Veronica sat down, and heard the tap, and saw the sealed door move, just a little, but it moved. If there had been a window in that door too, I would have been looking into the bedroom, right over the headboard of the bed. I heard the tap again and saw the door jiggle. I looked away. I couldn't actually see anything, of course, but I felt that I was watching her dress, without her knowing it.

A kettle started whistling on the stove, so I stepped into the kitchen to move it and turn down the heat. I glanced quickly into the bedroom and then turned back so I was facing the stove again, but I had an image of her in my mind as if I had taken a picture. She was sitting on the end of the bed in a thick, chocolate brown robe. It was big on her. Maybe it was Danny's. She was brushing her hair. It was long and would have nearly covered her breasts if she had ducked her head forward, hadn't sat with her chin high and her back straight and her shoulders back. The late afternoon light was pouring into the room through a window behind her, but even that brightness didn't show any highlights of color in her hair, just a gleaming black. I went back into the living room and sat on the couch until the swishing of her hairbrush stopped, and the bed squeaked, and Veronica was standing in the kitchen doorway in the big brown robe.

She was sort of hugging herself with both arms, to keep the robe closed it looked like. I was still sitting, and she looked down at me with her sharp black eyes. I looked right back for a long moment, but I had the strangest feeling that if we kept looking at each other that way, without saying anything, she would just open the robe. It was probably just my imagination running wild. Even though I had been staying away from her, it didn't take much to think that it would really be nice to be alone with her and not be expecting Danny or maybe even Kelly, but it didn't seem smart to think about it right then, so I looked away.

"It's Danny's," Veronica said.

"What is?" I asked.

"The robe," she said. "It looks silly on me, doesn't it?"

"It looks very nice," I answered.

"I have to shower," she said, "and get ready for work. Make yourself some tea or coffee if you want."

I sat on the couch and listened to the shower and all the little noises while she got dressed again.

"Too bad I can't stay," she said. "It seems like we never see each other, but I have to help with the costumes this afternoon, maybe even tonight. The play's next week."

Before I could say anything she was out the door, clattering down the wooden stairs. I had been up early working, and I was tired enough that I dozed off on the couch and slept there until a noise on the landing woke me up. I opened my eyes and looked out through the window in the front door just in time to see Danny looking in before he came in.

"Come on," he said. "I've got a surprise."

He didn't really come in. He just opened the door and told me to come with him and closed it again. I heard his steps go down the stairs. It had gotten dark out, and I looked at my watch. It was five after six. Danny was waiting out front in his Pontiac convertible, with the motor running. I barely had my door closed when the car squealed away from the curb and jumped toward the intersection. It was like riding on the back of a springing cat.

"What's the hurry?" I asked.

"I like to go fast," Danny answered. "Why not?"

He ran the stop sign at the corner and dodged a parked truck to turn out onto the highway. There was a padded handle on the dash in front of me, and I held on with both hands. He continued to build up speed, challenging the curves.

"Too bad it's winter," I said. "We could put the top down."

"Sounds romantic," he said. "But you're not my type."

We both laughed.

We were headed east. There were several small farmhouses close to the road, with their lights on. It was right at suppertime, and there seemed to be no traffic at all, as if everyone was home, eating. I could see patches of snow on the shoulders of the road, but the pavement seemed clear, and the car wasn't slipping through the curves. Danny kept building speed until we were beginning to break loose and slide on the turns, but it wasn't from ice. You could hear the tires squealing, even over the engine. Danny had good control, but the speed still worried me. We were headed toward Monarch Pass and, it was my guess, Denver. It was less than two hundred miles from Gunnison to Denver, and the way Danny was driving we might make it in three hours, even with the mountains.

"How much do you know about the last twenty-four hours?" he asked.

"Kelly told me you wanted to see me," I said. "That's about it."

"Look under my coat," he said, "in the back seat."

I turned around so I was kneeling, leaned over the back of the seat, lifted the jacket, and peered into the dark, but I couldn't see clearly. There was a car behind us, way back there, but I couldn't help looking at its headlights, and even though they were a long way off and not very bright, it made it hard to see inside the car. But I tried.

"What is it?" I asked.

"Hang on," Danny said.

I let go of the coat and grabbed the seat back with both hands. The car leaned sharply. My reflexes were all wrong, riding backward. I glanced over my shoulder to see the road but then leaned away from the curve, instead of into it, and threw my head hard against one of the steel bows of the convertible top. We had passed the road that turned down to the lodge and were flying, almost floating, down a long straightaway. I watched out the back window until the headlights appeared again. They were even farther behind than before.

"What is it?" I asked again, when we had come out of the turn.

"Hang on," Danny said.

I clung to the seat until we were level again. I had lost my breath squeezing the seat so hard against my chest. We were climbing, not a big pass but the hills before we crossed the plateau.

"They make fire," Danny said. "Lots of fire."

"You mean we've got a firebomb in the back seat?" I asked.

I lifted the jacket again and tried to see into the dark.

"Two of 'em," he said.

"What the hell for?" I asked.

"Action," he answered. "They're gonna think we're a whole fuckin' army."

"An army?" I asked. "Why do we want to do that?"

I turned around and sat down in my seat. We were nearing the top of the grade, going close to eighty. The next thirty miles was almost all down and fairly open, through rolling hills.

"To get Joseph out," Danny said. "And Washington too."

"Washington?" I asked.

"Sure," he said. "They've got 'em both."

"I guess I had heard about Joseph being in jail," I said. "But I didn't know about Washington."

"The cops have Joseph down in county jail," he said. "It's old. It ain't nothin'. And Lenny's got Washington in a little house out on the east side."

"Of Denver?" I asked.

"That's right," he answered.

"And you know where the house is?" I asked.

"I should," he said. "It belongs to my old man."

We rode along for another couple of miles without talking. Danny had the Pontiac up to a hundred. The top was puffed with air, and I thought it might rip off at any moment.

"How do we get them out?" I asked.

"We'll leave one bomb in the county jail," Danny said, "and set the timer so we have time to get across town."

"Timer?" I asked.

"Nothing but the best," he said. "Then we call and tell 'em to let him go."

"So what if somebody finds the bomb," I asked, "and shuts it off?"

"Even my old man couldn't disarm these babies," he said. "Once the timer's set, the only thing that can happen is that it blows."

"Where'd you get something like that?" I asked.

"Connections," he said.

"What connections?" I asked.

"Let's just say," he answered, "they came from the same place as the ones that blew up the lodge."

We were close to the bottom of the grade. I could see the flashing yellow lights coming up fast. We were close to the intersection where the road that looped out in front of the lodge and up over a mountain pass came back down to the main highway again.

"Turn back," I said.

"No way, Jose," Danny answered. The car nearly lifted from the road as we crested a small hill.

"There's a lane up there," I said, "on the right, near that farmhouse." I turned around again in the seat, lifted the jacket, and rested my hand on one of the bombs. I still couldn't see it, and I was careful about taking hold of it, but I wanted to be able to pick it up if necessary and show him that I had it.

"Pull off into the field," I said. "Or I'll set the timer now."

"You're serious," Danny said.

"I'm serious," I answered.

"The word from Washington," he said, "is that the time for all this spiritual crap is over."

"Doesn't sound like him," I said.

"And he said to bring you," he said, "so you'd see for yourself."

"Just pull off like I told you," I said.

The farmhouse was dark. Danny slowed the car to a stop just beyond the house and turned off onto the little lane.

"Goddamn coward," he said.

He stomped on the gas, rammed through the wooden gate, and drove away from the highway. We followed the lane through a field until we were on the far side of a small hill and could not be seen from the road. Danny left the engine running, put the car in park, set the emergency brake, and got out. He tipped the driver's seat forward and lifted one of the bombs from the back seat.

"What a waste," he said.

He walked carefully along the lane to the edge of the car's headlights.

"I'll never understand you!" he shouted into the night air. "Lenny said you didn't have no real guts!"

He set the bomb down on the road. I took a deep breath, relieved.

"Joseph and Washington," he shouted, "all that talk . . ."

The bomb went off the instant Danny moved the timer to set it. He did not scream or jump away. There was no time for that. The flash of light in his hands expanded until it filled everything that I could see, and for a moment I could see nothing at all.

Danny, I thought. *Danny*. But I didn't make a sound.

Fire followed the light and was behind and on both sides of the car as quickly as it had appeared in front. I crouched on the floor and held my breath. I could not feel anything. I was sure that if Danny had lived for even a few moments, I would have been able to tell somehow. The first flash of fire ate oxygen from everywhere and threatened to draw it up out of my lungs. If I had parted my lips and inhaled deeply, I would have died, I know it. I would have whispered good-bye, but I couldn't feel that there was any point in it. Danny was simply gone. I was afraid to breathe, afraid to speak, afraid of moving my lips, and my mind, during the most intense part of the burning, would not form words. It was as if it would not think in words until the danger of speaking and suffocating was over.

The fire fell back to an intense column over where the bomb had been, leaving spokes of burning ground in a charred wheel on the earth, pulsing about its hub and towering axle. My lungs burned, but I had to breathe. Cautiously, I raised my head. The canvas top was burning, and the flames were near the point of falling through it. I knew I had to move.

I unlatched the door, released the hand brake, and slipped the car into gear. It began to move toward the center of the fire. I sat up, threw open the door, and ran toward the darkness. I ran until I felt the first sensations of coolness on my face. My clothes and boots felt as if they were burning, as if they might burst into flames. My skin was hot everywhere, and I began removing my clothing.

Protected from the fire by a sweeping curve of the land and naked except for my shorts, I fell to the ground and lay on my back in the snow. I stared at the stars and waited until the second explosion roared through the night. A new column of fire stood beyond the hill. Danny was gone, and so was everything that had related to him, in far less time than it took to brush my teeth or roll over in bed. Such a little moment. The bombs were gone, and the dangerous plan was gone with it. I lay on the ground, naked, looking up into the night sky, and did not move even when I began to feel the cold. I searched the sky for familiar stars until after a time I saw a set of headlights coming toward me up the lane.

Kelly pulled up beside me in the Packard and opened the passenger door.

"Get in," she yelled, "before you freeze!"

When I was in the car, Kelly asked me where Danny was, and I tried to tell her that he was dead, but all I could do was wave my arms and point. She got out of the Packard and walked up the lane far enough to see for herself. I watched her stand for a moment with her hands on her hips, staring at the fire, before she turned and came jogging back toward me, stopping just long enough to pick up the clothes I had left on the side of the hill. I almost lost sight of her because she was still wearing the black boots, and black ski pants, and maroon jacket, and black wool cap she had on that morning. She crouched a little as she came back closer to the headlights and zigzagged back and forth as if she was trying to avoid someone seeing her. When she opened her door, she handed me the clothes before she slid in behind the wheel. I still felt like wearing them might cause me to catch on fire and burn, but I took them from her and began wiggling into them.

"You're sure he didn't run off the other way?" Kelly asked.

I tried again to answer but finally had to just shake my head back and forth.

"You're sure," she said.

I nodded yes. The words had broken down in my mind. I couldn't think of words, just that flash between Danny's hands and then the fire filling the sky. I was trying to answer her, but my mind wouldn't make the words. She looked at me and I tried again, but the only thing that came out was sounds, broken-up noises. But I kept trying, and the noises kind of swirled around in my chest and throat and mouth and came out a wailing kind of song. Someone listening probably wouldn't have called it music, but as it came out I had that same feeling you do when you sing, and forget about yourself, and let it pour out.

Kelly turned the car around as quickly as she could, drove back to the highway, and pulled onto the road, headed in the same direction we had been going, not back toward Gunnison. The car was a little big for her. She had to sit up straight to see past the wheel and over the dash, but she got up speed without seeming to be afraid. We were not going nearly as fast as I had been with Danny in the Pontiac, but we were up to the speed limits, fifty-five and sixty. I could see she was working hard to keep the car moving quickly without losing control. I saw and I knew I understood what was happening—she was driving us away from the scene of the explosions as quickly as she could— but I couldn't offer to help with the driving or even answer the question she had asked, whatever it was, because all I could do was make sounds. There was a rhythm to it, though, and she picked up the rhythm and began talking to me as she drove.

"Try to talk," Kelly said. "Don't stop. Keep trying."

At first I heard what she was saying the same way I heard my own mind and my own voice. It was music, sound, a song of sounds but, right at first, not words.

"Keep trying," she said. "Don't stop. Keep trying."

Kelly kept chanting these phrases as we drove along, and I kept singing my wordless song until the words started to come out of the sound, and I heard and began to understand the words she was singing to me. We were starting up Monarch Pass.

"Denver?" I asked.

"Yes," she said. "Keep talking."

"There was fire everywhere," I said.

"Yes," Kelly said, "there was."

"He's dead," I answered. "Danny's dead."

"Yes," she said. "He's dead."

Chapter 12

We drove along for several miles, heading away from Gunnison and toward Denver. All I had been able to do was repeat the same half dozen words over and over, but I was very tired. I closed my eyes, thinking I might be able to sleep, and the words stopped. I saw Danny's hands holding the little flash of light like they were holding a star in space, and then slowly, very slowly, as if it was going to take a whole day, the flash of light grew and grew. All around the light there was a ring of fire, and it grew too and took on shapes. It was a dragon. The light was in its mouth, and it reached out with its fiery hands and pulled everything into its giant mouth. And it reached for me, but I hid under the dash while it took Danny. It took the whole car in its hand, for a moment, and let go, and then stood on its legs and reached high into the sky, dancing with some kind of evil joy. And when it looked at me again, I gave it the car and ran. The fire danced so high with so much happiness, it seemed that it would swallow the whole earth. I opened my eyes and looked at Kelly. She was still pushing the Packard along as fast as she could, intent on her driving.

"Someone killed him," I said. "He's really dead."

"Don't be afraid to remember," Kelly said.

"He went to set the timer," I said, "and the bomb went off the second he tried to set it."

"Remember," she said. "Everything."

"One minute he was cursing me," I said, "and then he was just gone. He didn't hurt, though. He was right in the middle of a sentence, and then he was gone."

"Tell me everything," she said.

"It was my fault," I said.

"No, it wasn't," she answered.

"I killed him," I said.

"No, you didn't!" Kelly yelled.

"I made him stop," I said. "I made him set the timer."

"But you didn't kill him," she said. "It was the timer."

I didn't know how to answer right away, so I waited. We were climbing Monarch Pass, going up toward the continental divide. I remembered being up there with Kelly and remembered her telling me about the lodge and about how she found out about it from Uncle Louis' letters.

"I never did read all the letters," I said. "Only two or three. And now they're gone."

"Most of them were love letters," Kelly said, "from your father to your mother."

"My father?" I asked.

"Yes," she said. "He loved her very much."

"Uncle Louis?" I asked.

"Yes," she answered. "And most of the rest were about being in the war and about Washington's philosophy. Your father and Joseph's father both knew Washington and knew each other, so they used to talk about him a lot. And that was in the letters too."

"I wish I had read them all now," I said. "I was going as fast as I could."

"It doesn't matter," Kelly said. "We're going to meet him when we get to Denver. That's even better."

"How do you know where he is?" I asked.

"I told you," she said. "I got the address where Victor's keeping Dacia. They think Washington's going to come there to help her escape."

We got to the top of Monarch Pass and crossed the continental divide in the dark, so there wasn't much to see, except highway signs giving the elevations. As we started down, Kelly leaned forward against the wheel, staring straight ahead at the road, not looking around to even see if there was something to see.

"You ever drive a mountain pass?" I asked.

"No," Kelly said. "I grew up in Kansas."

"Want me to drive?" I asked.

"No," she said. "You need to clear your head."

"What made you follow?" I asked.

"Danny liked to brag," she said. "He thought he was outsmarting everyone."

"Like who?" I asked.

"Like his father," she said. "And Lenny."

"And Lenny?" I asked. "How?"

"Lenny's a narc," Kelly said. "Danny wanted to make a fool of him. Wanted to get even with him."

"A narc?" I asked.

"An agent," she said. "He sets people up to get busted. It's his job."

"How do you know that?" I asked.

"He busted my mother," she said. "He got her a bunch of dope, and helped her cut it, and informed on her when she went to sell it."

"Your mother?" I asked. "Lenny busted your mother?"

"She's been on and off one thing or another since I was a kid," Kelly said. "But she always looked out for me."

"Where is she now?" I asked.

"A mental institution," she answered. "She tried to tell what happened. They got her declared insane, and put her away, and made me a foster child, in Hemmings. The bastards."

"Do you ever see her?" I asked.

"The last time was more than a year ago," she said. "She couldn't remember my name."

"You must hate him," I said.

"Lenny?" she asked.

"Sure," I said. "I thought he was evil the first time I met him."

"Danny hated him," Kelly said. "My mother hated him. That's how he works. Everybody tries to get even. I've been thinking about it for a long time. That's how he controls people.

Danny wanted to set a bomb and threaten to blow it up if they didn't let Joseph out of jail. He had keys to everything his father had keys to, so he could have made ten different kinds of bombs. But he wanted to get even with Lenny for the lodge. He tried to make Lenny think he had turned against Joseph and Washington and you, and he made up a story about how he needed the bombs to make it look like Washington blew himself up trying to get Joseph out. He needed the timers. Lenny gave him the two bombs, and Danny really believed he had tricked him."

"He told you all this?" I asked.

"He was mad at Veronica because she wouldn't go," Kelly said. "He wanted somebody with him. He wanted me to go. I stalled and said I wanted to think about it, and he said he'd give me twenty-four hours. The next thing I knew the two of you were coming down the stairs and pulling away in his car. You know how Danny drives. I stayed up with you the best I could."

"Lenny gave him the bombs?" I asked.

"That's how he works," she said. "If you hated him as much as Danny did, you'd probably be dead too. You wouldn't have tried to stop him."

"Then Lenny was in Gunnison today?" I asked.

"He can't be more than two or three hours ahead of us," she said.

"What are we going to do?" I asked. "Have you got a plan?"

"Think straight," she said. "Stay alive."

Neither of us talked much until we were near the bottom of the pass. The high plateau was opening up in front of us. With more space between the mountains, the sky was large and open. Most of the clouds couldn't get over from the western side of the divide, I guessed, because the sky was absolutely clear. I stared up at the stars through the windshield, but they were so bright and the sky looked so deep that it made me dizzy, and I looked away and closed my eyes. I remembered being in the Delta County Fairgrounds with Dacia on a clear night, describing the stars to her and drawing out the constellations in the palm of her hand. I also remembered after we had stayed out there for a long time, telling stories that went with the stars and thinking about the amazing things the people in those stories did, how strong we both had felt. I opened my eyes and looked up again. I couldn't pick out anything from the car that looked familiar. But I remembered the road.

"Joy and I came this way," I said. "I'm starting to remember everything."

Kelly didn't answer this time. She just kept driving, and I rode quietly for a few moments, letting the memory come.

"I could have stopped her," I said.

"Who?" Kelly asked.

"Joy," I said. "I had a chance to stop her. She had to see her father. Nobody would help her."

"I don't understand," she said.

"I'm just starting to remember," I answered.

Kelly kept driving, and gradually things came back to me, things I hadn't even dreamed much about since Joy died. I told Kelly things as I remembered them, little things like what Joy looked like riding along in the car, looking out her window, and bigger things too. I remembered telling Dacia that it would only be a few days until I saw her again, and I remembered her telling me it would be a long time. I talked to Kelly about the really big things too, because the pictures came into my mind of Joy dead in the trailer and her father dead in the loft and Danny cursing me when the bomb went off. Especially trying to tell her about finding Joy and never understanding why Lenny had encouraged her to visit her father, but remembering that he had done that, that's when I started stumbling with my words again. So, I went back to easier things before trying again, like remembering how happy Dacia had looked when she was telling us about going to see Billie Holiday, how much Uncle Louis loved to hear Billie sing. Kelly didn't seem to care as long as I kept talking and didn't stare at my hands.

"This is where I saw Dacia," I said. "The last time."

We were turning left through the intersection where the highway on the left went toward Denver and the one on the right went to Pueblo.

"I honked and waved good-bye," I said, "but she couldn't see me."

"She's blind, isn't she?" Kelly asked.

"Yes," I answered. "It was stupid to wave."

"She probably heard you honk," she said. "She was probably listening for it."

Kelly honked the horn, and we both waved toward the other road as if there were really two trucks and two trailers with Victor and Dacia and Lenny going off toward Wichita. I kept remembering more little things from when Joy and Dacia and Washington and I were all together. Like I remembered once we were eating in a park, and Dacia wanted to run. Washington walked back and forth with her until they finally broke into a trot. All the time, Dacia kept her hand resting lightly on Washington's arm, and when they had actually begun to run, the two of them laughed and laughed. I told Kelly about this, especially about how they had laughed until they fell down in the grass together.

Kelly and I laughed together in the car, but when we stopped, I remembered leaving Joy with her father on the farm and hardly driving any distance at all before I heard the shots, knowing I shouldn't have taken her there, and knowing I shouldn't have left her there, not trusting myself because I was just sixteen, and not understanding why Lenny wanted her to go there and why he wanted me to take her there when everybody else I knew would be a long way away. I tried to tell Kelly about this too, tried harder than I had a little while before.

"It's how he works," she said. "He set it up so she'd get killed, and so you'd either feel so guilty you wouldn't do anything, or you'd be so crazy with hate the cops could just kill you, and everybody would think they were heroes."

"And get on TV," I said. "One of the jailers in Hemmings said he thought they were going to get on TV for capturing me."

"Big heroes," she said. "Killing the crazy kid."

"Why?" I asked. "What did we ever do to Lenny?"

"He's crazy," she said. "And they pay him to be crazy. He thinks he's a hero. I don't know why. It doesn't matter why."

"Do you think I'm remembering all this stuff," I asked, "because we're going to die? Do you think it's like they say, your life passes in front of you when you drown or when you fall from way up?"

"You want the truth?" Kelly asked.

"Yes," I answered.

"I think Lenny plans to kill us all," she said, "Washington and Dacia and you and me too. I think he hates Washington so much, he will do anything he can think of to hurt him, and then he will try to kill him. And I think he spends most of his time trying to figure out different ways to do it. And I don't think it will stop as long as Lenny's alive, maybe not even after he's dead."

"Are you saying we should kill him?" I asked.

"I wouldn't mind," Kelly said. "But I think that's his plan. I think he knows exactly what we'll do if we hate him enough to try to kill him."

"I didn't know you thought about this so much," I said.

"I have trouble thinking about anything else," she said.

"You do have a plan for when we get to Denver," I said. "Don't you?"

"We have one big advantage, Louis," she said.

"What's that?" I asked.

"It won't last long," Kelly said, "but right now you and I are the only ones who know that Danny is dead. Which means we are the only ones who know that he is not going to show up at the county jail in Denver in his Pontiac with the bombs and a partner who is supposed to carry one of them into the jail and set it. And we also know that Lenny is expecting that to happen because he's not stupid enough to believe the story Danny gave him about wanting to go after Washington first. And we know that Lenny gave him the timer that set off the bomb as soon as he tried to set it, so we know he expects whoever takes the bomb into the jail to blow himself up trying to set it. And we know he expects Danny to either run for the hills or try to find Washington for help."

"But Danny isn't coming," I said.

"So there's a little gap in there," Kelly said. "While Lenny waits for Danny to show up, and until somebody finds out Danny's dead and gets that news to him, we've got time."

"To do what?" I asked.

"Find Washington," she said.

"That's impossible," I said.

"Not if Dacia really did call him like Victor said she did," Kelly answered. "If Dacia called him, there's a real good chance we'll drive straight to him."

"Because you think he's with Dacia?" I asked.

"1770 Locust Street," she said. "On the east side."

"Do you think Lenny knows he's there?" I asked.

"He either knows," she answered, "or he expects to know it when Washington does show up."

"Because Victor would call him," I said. "Maybe Lenny's already there. Maybe it's too late."

"Not if there's the smallest chance Danny might go there first," she said. "Lenny's not going to let himself get into the same house with Danny and one of those bombs with a short fuse."

"This is crazy," I said.

"It's all we've got," Kelly answered.

"You know, I got mad at Joy once," I said. "I wanted to call a girl I had met and see her for a half hour or so while we were passing through, and Joy said no. I got mad and told her the life we were living was crazy. And she said, 'If it wasn't for the life we live, you wouldn't have met her in the first place.' It's kind of the same thing."

"What do you mean?" Kelly asked.

"I'm glad we're friends," I said. "I'm not glad about your mother or about my mother or about Danny or all the other things that have happened, to Dacia and to Washington. It sounds sort of crazy, but I'm glad we're friends, whatever happens."

"Me too," she said. "You want to drive for a while?"

We stopped for gas in Fairplay, about seventy-five miles from Denver, and agreed to switch. Almost as soon as I took over the driving, Kelly pulled off her boots and her wool cap and loosened zippers and snaps. She was still wearing the ski clothes she had had on that morning when she came out on the school bus to get me. It seemed like a long time ago. She didn't really sleep, but she did curl up so she was slouched way down in the seat with her knees up on the dash. She seemed to nod off a couple of times, letting her head droop down on one shoulder. When she came back, she didn't start or jump, she just kind of raised her head and looked out her window. Her hair was wild and messy from being in a hat a lot of the time, but when her head rocked over and she drifted off for a moment, one of her ears peeked out, and I could see she was wearing one of the pearls.

"You're wearing the pearls," I said.

I touched my chest and felt through my clothing until I found the coin, Dacia's coin, on the chain Kelly had got for me.

"I brought everything," she said.

"Everything?" I asked.

"All the pearls," she said. "And the money left over from the jobs we've had. We can go anywhere we want when this is over."

"Where do you want to go?" I asked.

"You mean if we live through this?" Kelly asked.

"Are you scared?" I asked.

"Not really," she answered.

"Don't you think we should be?" I asked. "I don't feel scared either. But don't you think we should be?"

"I was," she said, "until I saw Danny's car burning. Before I got there, I saw the fire and heard the explosions, and I thought, 'Something's happened to Danny.' But I couldn't make myself believe that anything had happened to you. I pulled in on that little road and there you were, lying on the hillside, naked as a baby, looking half crazy, but fine. I think you know when you're going to die or something's going to happen to somebody."

"But you said you didn't know if we would live through this," I said.

"I don't," she answered. "But I don't feel scared. Whatever happens, I think we're going to be all right. Either one of us could have died in that car with Danny, but here we are. It's life. I feel it really strong, and I don't think we're going to die."

"So where do you want to go?" I asked. "If we make it through?"

"Somewhere," Kelly said, "where it's warm, where the sun shines, where you can take your clothes off, and swim, and lie on the beach, and nobody cares, and nobody is ashamed."

"Where's that?" I asked.

"We were reading in school last week about the French Riviera," she answered. "It's on the Mediterranean Sea, between Spain and Italy. Our teacher has been there and to Morocco, across from Spain on the other side of the water. He told us some stories about it, and most of the kids giggled. But it sounded wonderful to me."

"You want to marry a rich man or something?" I asked.

"Maybe," she said. "But I wasn't thinking about that. I'd like to take my mother there. Maybe she'd marry somebody rich, then we'd just work when we got bored and needed something to do."

"We?" I asked.

"Sure," Kelly said. "You and me and Washington and Dacia."

"You don't even know them," I said.

"So what?" she said. "You don't know my mother. What's the difference?"

"I guess I'm a little surprised," I said.

"I don't know about France," she said. "Maybe Morocco will be different."

"Different from what?" I asked.

"From all this," she answered. "From some people thinking they're better than everybody else, and thinking they have a right to do whatever they want if you're not like them."

"Why would it be different there?" I asked.

"Morocco's in Africa," Kelly said. "Maybe they've learned."

"We can ask Washington," I said. "He's been there."

Kelly did sleep a little after that, not long, just fifteen or twenty minutes. But when she woke up, we were just outside Denver. The highway brought us in on the south side of the city. We stopped in gas stations a couple of times so Kelly could get directions. She told me the turns to make and guided me to Colorado Boulevard. We took that north for a long way until we came to Colfax, then turned east on Colfax and followed that through a whole bunch of tree streets—Elm and Holly and Jasmine—until we got to Locust. We were just a block from the house. We had already decided that even though anyone who had ever seen the Packard could recognize it real easy, we would drive down the street past the house to see if we could tell anything about who was there and what was going on.

We were in an older part of town, so the streets were too narrow for two cars to pass if there was a car parked on each side of the street. The only thing I had ever seen Lenny drive was his pickup, and I didn't see anything of that. Victor had been pulling Dacia's trailer with a construction company pickup, and I didn't see either that pickup or the trailer. The house was covered on the outside with white plaster, and the wood trim was so dark it looked black. All the lights seemed to be turned on because there was light coming from every side of the house, even though the shades and curtains were drawn shut. The windows were covered on the outside with ironwork like you saw on fences and gates. It was kind of pretty, but I didn't think I would like living behind bars. There was even an iron gate in the archway going to the front porch, so you couldn't get to the front door without getting past the gate.

We went down to the end of the block, and turned the corner, and turned again so we could come up the alley behind the house. I had just started in when I stopped and cut the lights. There was a blue Ford, a '49 or a '50, parked in the alley under a light on a garage, just far enough down the block to be in back of the right house. There was a little cloud coming up from one exhaust pipe.

"That's Victor's Ford," I said. "I'm sure of it."

"Do you think he saw us?" Kelly asked.

"I hope not," I said. "But somebody's in there, watching the back of the house, I guess."

"Let me out," she said. "Then put your lights back on and drive up the alley. I'll walk along behind the car. When we get even with the Ford, I'll drop off and hide behind it and watch. If it's Victor in the Ford, he's sure to recognize this old Packard and do whatever he's supposed to do if he sees something. You go on around the block and come down the alley again. I'll signal you somehow if you should stop for me or go on."

"The flashlight," I said. "It's in the glove box."

Kelly dug in the glove compartment until she came up with the flashlight.

"Turn the light on if I should stop," I said. "If I don't see any light, I'll park around the corner and come on foot."

Kelly opened her door.

"Don't forget I'm back there," she said. "Drive slow."

"Don't worry," I said.

I turned the lights back on. Kelly got out and closed the door behind her. Three miles an hour was a normal walking speed. Someone had told me that once, so I kept it under that, even though that was almost too slow just for idling. I crept all the way down the alley toward the Ford. The back of the house was lit up just like the rest of it, but the curtains in back weren't heavy like the ones in front. I could see right into the kitchen, and I almost forgot about the Ford. As I came even with Victor's car and was about to look away from the house to see if I could see through the tinted windows, somebody came into the kitchen. I stopped the Packard and watched. The man stood in front of the window looking down, then tipped his head back to drink a glass of water. When he finished, he put the glass down and looked out the window right at me.

It was Washington. He looked right at me, and I looked right at him, and he moved out of the window toward the back door. I pulled the Packard in front of Victor's Ford and parked and shut off the engine. Washington was standing outside in plain sight, on the back steps, under the porch light. I opened the car door, and ran to the back fence, and fumbled with the latch on the gate, and got in, and looked up. He had crossed the yard and was right in front of me. I threw myself at him, and he lifted me clear off my feet. I cried as if nothing else in the whole world mattered more.

"Are you alone?" Washington asked when I finally let go of him.

"No," I answered. "Are you?"

"Dacia's inside," he said. "And Victor's hiding over there in his car, watching the back of the house."

"Is it safe here?" I asked.

"For a little while," Washington said. "Who's with you?"

"A friend of mine," I said. "Her name's Kelly."

"Bring her in," he said. "It's cold."

"I've got the Packard," I said. "Shouldn't we get Dacia and make a run for it?"

"Get your friend," he said. "We'll talk inside where it's warm."

I stood by the back gate and watched Washington walk across the yard to the back door. He was tall, a couple of inches over six feet, and thin, not skinny, but trim. His hair was cut close to his head, and even though he had no hat and no gloves, a turtle-neck sweater but no coat, Levi's and slip-on boots but nothing really warm, he didn't run or dance in the cold. He walked with an easy dignity so calming that I had seen him break up fights just by walking toward guys who were getting ready to go after each other.

"Washington!" I yelled.

He stopped right under the porch light and turned around toward me. He was over fifty years old, but his face was still young and gentle, dark brown, smooth, and lean. He reminded me of a racehorse I had seen once, smooth-textured, rippling power. I ran across the yard and grabbed him again and hugged him.

"You know about Joy?" I asked.

"Yes," he said. "I'm sorry you had to be alone."

Washington held me against his chest while I cried again.

"I should have stopped her," I said.

"Don't blame yourself," he said. "We all tried to warn her."

I held on until the crying stopped, and he held me without any of those little gestures people use to tell you that they're in a hurry and don't have time.

"You better get your friend before she freezes," he said, when I stepped back.

"Kelly," I said. "Her name is Kelly."

"Go get Kelly," he said, "and knock on the window of that Ford and tell Victor to come in too. He can watch from the kitchen."

I walked across the yard to the gate, hoping I had some of Washington's dignity, in spite of the crying. When I had let my-self into the alley, I started to call for Kelly in a loud whisper.

She didn't answer until I was close to the back of the Ford, and she had peeked around the fender to see if I was alone.

"What the hell are you doing?" she asked.

"Come on," I said. "Washington says to come in before you freeze."

"Are you sure it's clear?" she asked.

"Come on," I said. "You can meet Washington and Dacia too."

"What a rescue," she said and walked across the alley.

For a moment, I stood by the window on the driver's side of the Ford. The engine was still idling, and I was sure Victor was in there, even though I couldn't see through the tint. Kelly stopped by the gate and looked back at me.

"Are you coming?" she asked.

I knocked on the window.

"Washington says to come inside!" I yelled toward the window. "He says you can watch from the kitchen."

The door of the Ford popped and then swung open.

"Good idea," Victor said. "It's cold as hell in here, even with the heater on."

The three of us walked into the house together. I introduced Kelly to Victor and to Washington in the kitchen, then Kelly and I followed Washington through a swinging door into the dining room and through an archway into the living room. We were facing the front door. The hall to the bedrooms was to our left. To the right of the door was a pair of windows with a fireplace in between. At the far end of the living room, there was an entire wall covered with dark blue drapes. Dacia sat on the floor, facing the hallway, her back to the curtains. A coffee table had been set in front of her, and blue cushions from the couch and chairs had been placed on the floor all around it. Dacia's cloth, the one she used for reading the coins, was spread out on the table. Her head was covered by an orange scarf wound into a turban, and she was wearing a brilliant yellow robe with brown and gold and green designs sewn on it. I had never seen that robe before. It was beautiful, not just pretty but beautiful, the way some things are that you know you will not see very often because they are kept protected. Dacia sat on a cushion on the floor, her back straight, her eyes closed, her hands palms down on the table.

"You can talk to her," Washington said, "but don't touch her. She's not all the way in yet."

"In?" Kelly asked.

"Come on," I said.

I took Kelly's hand, and we walked across the living room to the cushions in front of the coffee table. The rest of the furniture had been pushed back against the walls, out of the way. Kelly and I both sat down on cushions directly in front of Dacia. Her hair was covered by the turban, but the lower part of her ears stuck out. She was wearing a small gold hoop in each ear. The orange head scarf, and yellow robe, and gold earrings made her skin look liquid. Her lips were moving, but I couldn't hear her saying anything. Washington came and sat on a cushion at my left, at the end of the little table.

"It's Louis," he said.

"Bless you, boy," Dacia whispered, "for coming."

"Are you all right?" I asked.

"Just fine," she whispered. "Who's with him?"

"A friend of Louis'," Washington answered. "A young dark-haired girl, very pretty. She looks a lot like Victor's daughter."

Washington looked right at Kelly as he spoke, and she didn't look away.

"My name is Kelly," she said. "He's been my best friend, ever."

"Bless you, girl," Dacia said. "It's been hard times."

A little at a time, moving slowly and carefully, we began to talk about the last year. Dacia told us how she and Victor had gone on to Wichita, and how Lenny had disappeared after several days and never had shown up. After they heard about Joy, they had traveled for a while, the two of them, until Lenny arranged for them to stay in the house in Denver where they would be warm for the winter, because they didn't have anything else lined up.

"Joseph told me you never made it to Wichita," I said.

"Joseph is a very talented young man," Washington said, "but he still has things to learn."

"Talented?" Kelly asked.

"Much of what he sees is true," Washington said. "But not everything. Sometimes he's impatient. Sometimes he tries to shape the dream himself."

"Is that why he's in jail?" Kelly asked.

"You'll have to ask Victor about that," Washington said. "Victor visited him."

I told about being in jail for a while, and about Kelly helping me get away, and about going to live in the mountains, and about meeting Joseph.

"When we're finished up here," Washington said. "That's where we're gonna go. You're gonna love that pool, Dacia."

"Washington talks and talks about that pool," Dacia said. "He thinks when you die, you gonna go off and float in hot water forever and ever."

"You'll love it," Washington said. "Then I'll be laughin' at you. 'All she ever wanna do is float in that pool.' I'll be laughin' then."

"They burned the lodge," I said.

"Oh, I know that," Washington said. "I saw 'em do it, but that won't stop no hot springs from coming up out of the earth."

"You watched them?" I asked. "You were there?"

"I didn't just watch," he said. "I showed myself, three times: once when they were coming out of the valley in the dark, and again right before they set the bombs, and the next morning when they were going back in to their camp. It was the third time, early in the morning, that got to old Larry. He couldn't control himself no more. Took a shot at me, spooked his horse, and fell, shot himself in the knee, made the horse fall."

"You were there!" I said.

"Too bad about the horse," Washington said.

"You must have been right around where I was," I said, "up above the valley."

"I saw you," he said. "I was proud of you too. Drawing down on that buck and knowing you shouldn't shoot him."

We were all quiet for several long moments. I looked up into Washington's eyes. They were steady, unblinking, sparkling black. We stared at each other and didn't say anything. While we were all sitting there, not saying a word, and while I was looking into Washington's eyes, wanting more than anything to be sure I really did understand what he had done and what had happened up on the mountain, I heard a phone ring, and heard the swinging door, and heard Victor talking from the dining room, but I couldn't make out what he was saying. Victor hung up the phone and walked into the living room. I could hear him behind me, but I didn't turn until Washington looked away and looked up at him.

"It was Danny," Victor said. "He told me to call Lenny and tell him to meet him here in an hour."

"And what did you say?" Washington asked.

"I said I'd call," Victor answered.

"Good," Washington said.

"It couldn't have been Danny," I said. "Danny's dead."

"And Veronica?" Victor asked. "My daughter?"

"She wasn't with him," I answered. "I was."

"She was fine when we left," Kelly said. "She had gone to work."

"Don't call now," Washington said. "Wait."

Victor nodded but didn't say anything and went back into the kitchen.

"You sure Danny's dead?" Washington asked.

"I saw it happen," I said. "He was holding a bomb and it went off right in his hands. I saw it."

"It was a short fuse," Kelly said. "He got it from Lenny. I think Lenny rigged it to kill him or whoever he got to set it for him."

"Who was on the phone?" I asked.

"It must have been his father," Washington said.

"It's beginning," Dacia said.

I turned back toward her. We were all quiet again for several moments. She reached into the bag in the middle of the cloth and placed the first coin in one of the quarter-sized circles in the design. Washington watched as her hand moved around the embroidered wheel, touching each of the empty circles along its rim before she selected another coin. As she put her hand back into the bag, he started to stand up.

"Washington?" I asked.

He paused and settled back down onto his cushion. Dacia placed the second coin and began moving her hand around the wheel again.

"Yes," he said. "What is it?"

"Why did you leave us last summer?" I asked.

"My teacher was dying," he answered. "I had to go, had to receive his gift. I had no choice."

"What gift?" I asked. "What teacher?"

"We met nearly twenty years ago," Washington said, "in North Africa. I agreed to bring him here if he would teach me."

"He wanted to come to America?" Kelly asked. "Was he white?"

"He didn't want to come," Washington said. "He was a warrior without a tribe. He believed it was his duty to come."

"But why?" I asked.

"Every warrior serves a master," Washington said. "For some, like Lenny, it's death. For others, it's revenge or justice. For the spiritual warrior, his duty is to freedom, for himself and for others. That is the gift."

We waited while Dacia placed another coin.

"Freedom from what?" I asked.

"From whatever enslaves," Washington answered. "Fear. The desire for justice. Whatever enslaves."

"Or darkness," Dacia said and placed another coin.

"Yes," Washington said and stood up. "In this case, darkness."

"You mean you're going to make her see again?" Kelly asked.

"Not all in one night," Dacia answered. "But this is the beginning."

"And not me alone," Washington said. "All of us."

Dacia's hand had been fumbling in the bag, but she had not come out with the fifth coin. She frowned and looked puzzled.

"Wait," I said.

I unhooked the chain around my neck, drew the coin up out of my shirt, and lowered it into the bag, into her hand. Dacia felt the coin and smiled. She placed it on the cloth. Once she had the chain arranged so that it didn't cover any of the circles, she drew and placed two more coins fairly quickly.

"That's seven," she said.

She set the bag on the floor beside her and placed her hands palms down on the table as they had been before.

"Now we wait," Washington said.

"For what?" I asked.

"Go help Victor get ready to move," he said. "Kelly and I will stay with her."

"Move?" I asked. "Where?"

"She's starting the dream," he said. "When she comes to the part where they go, we'll go."

"They?" I asked. "Who?"

"Joy and Louis and her brother, Mark," Washington answered. "Tonight she's going to finish the dream, and we're going to do whatever we can to help her."

Victor was standing in the archway to the dining room. He waved to me to come and join him. I looked at Kelly. Her eyes were on fire.

"Go ahead, Louis," she said. "It's what we came for."

Victor led me into his room to help him pack, but there wasn't much for me to do besides listen and watch. He believed there was a good chance he was about to die. He didn't seem to be afraid, or excited, or even particularly sad about it. But he did everything with care and planning, as if he didn't want to leave a mess behind. Almost everything was clothes. He folded each shirt and pair of pants carefully and placed them in his suitcase with great respect. Victor talked to his clothes as he packed them, like they were friends who could remember and would carry these messages to others after his death. Some of what he said was in English and some was in Spanish.

Being with Victor while he packed, helping him, made me think of a movie I had seen a few years back, a bullfighter film, and Victor reminded me of the matador, dressing himself in a beautiful costume so that he would look wonderful when he was killed by the bull. There had been a boy to help the matador dress, to listen to him talk about fate and the bull, and to listen as he assigned responsibilities to his cap and his sword. He had wanted to be honored, and so did Victor. He didn't tell me that he had a message for Veronica. He just said things to her picture as he took it off the dresser and put it in his suitcase, as if he trusted me to overhear and remember.

When there was nothing left in the room but a double bed and a dresser and two chairs and a writing desk, and everything that was his was packed and ready to go out to the car, he sat on the bed and spoke to me directly. He wanted me to know that the most important person in his life was Veronica, that he would do anything he could for her happiness and safety. It was one of the truly great moments of his whole life, he explained to me, when he had learned that evening that Danny had been killed but that Veronica had not been with him, that she was fine the last time Kelly saw her. Victor said that he hated violence and loved peace, but that if anyone ever harmed Veronica, he prayed he was still alive so that he could give himself to revenge. I thought about Veronica's injured leg from being in the wreck with Danny, but I didn't bring it up.

Next to Veronica, Victor told me, the person he had loved the most had been Joy. He described in detail how he and Dacia had learned about Joy being killed, and about how his heart was saddened and how something left him that would never return, and about how he had helped Dacia get through it. And he told me how after all these weeks and months of being with Dacia, he had come to care so much for her. Not as much as Joy, and not as much as if she was part of his own family, his own people, but he said it had become important to his honor that he do everything possible to keep her from being harmed, until Washington arrived.

After these messages, I thought we were ready to take things out to his car, because he stopped talking and he stood up. But when he went to the door, he wasn't carrying anything he should have been, a suitcase or his winter coat. He waved again for me to come with him, as he had when I was sitting in the living room, and led me down the hall to the bedroom next to his. It was Lenny's room, when Lenny was there, which was not very often. It was his office, his headquarters, as well as his bedroom. Victor wanted me to see the room. It had been only recently that he had gone in there, according to what he told me, and seeing it had caused him to think about things in a much different way.

The room was much like Victor's. It had a bed and dresser and desk and chairs and not much else. The walls were bare, except for one photograph which had been clipped from a magazine and stuck to the wall with a thumbtack. The picture showed a house that looked as if it might have had a fire. The porch had fallen and the windows were broken and part of the main roof was gone. It looked like the pictures you see of houses in Florida after a hurricane. There were police in white helmets holding people back from getting close. The picture was dark and I couldn't see the people very well, but it looked like most of them were black.

"It's in Nashville," Victor said.

"What happened?" I asked.

"They bombed it," he said.

"Who?" I asked.

"I will tell you something," Victor said. "I have never liked the coloreds. My family is from Spain. We do not go into the public square and tell people that we are poor, even if we must do without many things. It is not manly. But this bombing is worse, very much worse. It is a cowardly thing, to bomb a man's house when he is resting with his family. Lenny knows the man who did this. He works for the government as Lenny does. They are paid to do such things, but to me it is cowardly, and I cannot help them any more."

"This house was bombed?" I asked.

"In Tennessee," Victor said. "The home of a leader for the coloreds."

"And Lenny knows the man who did it?" I asked.

"Yes," he said.

"So what are you going to do?" I asked.

"Take care that this does not happen to Veronica," Victor said. "Many young people now are protesting too, because they feel sorry for the coloreds. Many of them have been hurt. These things must not happen to my daughter."

"Is that why you are leaving?" I asked.

"Yes," he answered.

"Won't Lenny come after you?" I asked.

"Not as long as he has Washington for his enemy," Victor said. "He has no need of me. He is like a toreador. The bull is in the ring, and he cannot let himself think of anything else. He must have his kill."

"Then why did you tell me," I asked, "that you thought you could be killed? If you're leaving, Washington's the one who is in danger, isn't he?"

"I am going to get the trailer," Victor said. "Dacia's trailer. Lenny borrowed the key and gave it back, but he was in the trailer. He told me to give the key to Washington if he came here. I am going to get the trailer, but before I bring it back I will use the key and open it and turn on the lights. If there is a bomb there intended for Washington, then I may die. But it would not be honorable to give him the key and leave."

I had no answer or question, either one. We went down the hall to Victor's room, got his few things, and carried them out to his car. The trunk opened on an electronic latch too, like the doors, and was beautifully upholstered inside, like the rest of the car. We put his suitcases in back and faced each other in the dim light from the open trunk. Victor held out his hand, and I took it to shake it, but it was limp.

"I need your keys," he said. "I have no trailer hitch on my car. We will have to trade long enough for me to bring the trailer back."

"I don't know," I said. "What if we have to leave?"

"You will not be disappointed," he said. "She goes very fast."

I traded car keys with Victor. I liked his blue Ford, but I hoped nothing would happen to him and the trailer and the Packard.

"Your mother was very beautiful," he said. "I have prayed for her."

"Thank you," I said.

"If you live," Victor said, "if Lenny does not kill us all, we will meet. Washington knows the place. Veronica and I will pray for you."

"Thank you," I said and went back into the house.

Kelly and Washington were still sitting quietly in the living room with Dacia. Kelly had moved to one of the cushions at the end of the coffee table; she was very close to Dacia and had her head tilted so that her ear was as near Dacia's mouth as possible. Dacia had begun humming, and Kelly was humming along with her. Washington was sitting on a cushion in front of the table, where I had been, and he had a long piece of blond wood across his lap. It was maybe five feet long and as big around as my wrist. He was rocking back and forth with his eyes closed, in time to the rhythm of the humming. Once in a while he would open his eyes, draw a short dagger from his belt, cut a few more strokes in the design on the pole, then return the knife to its scabbard, close his eyes, and feel the wood as he rocked and hummed. He had carved designs along about one foot of the shaft but seemed to be in no hurry to finish it.

Washington asked me whether or not Victor had gone, and I answered that he had, that he had taken the Packard and would bring it back with the trailer. I also explained that I had Victor's keys, and Washington told me to leave them on the kitchen counter where he would be sure to see them when he came back, so he could just trade keys with us and leave quietly. I did that and then came and sat on the cushion at the other end of the table from Kelly. I knew the rhythm she was humming from one of the dances Joy used to do. When I was settled, Washington began to talk to me in the rhythm of the humming, explaining what had taken place while I was with Victor and what we were expecting would happen.

The dance we were humming was one in which Joy was a wealthy, well-dressed, proper lady who took a walk one day into the forest. The deeper she went into the woods, her movements looked less and less like the women going in and out of churches and more and more like the movements of creatures. I kept my eyes closed and watched Joy dancing, while I listened to what Washington was telling me. It was the first time I had been able to see her clearly, moving and dancing, since I found her in that trailer. I knew that what Washington was telling me was important, but as I watched Joy's movements change, so I could almost see the wind that was blowing her dress also blowing the bushes and trees, I realized how much I missed her and how I did not want to open my eyes as long as she was dancing.

Washington explained that as we hummed and waited, Dacia was going deeper and deeper inside herself. This might go on for a long time, or it might happen quickly. That would depend on Dacia. They had sung this song three or four times in the last couple of days and knew the path up to a particular point. She would see her ancestors in various forms as she walked in the forest. Some of them would be animals we are familiar with, big cats, snakes, birds, and even a turtle. As I listened, I watched Joy stalk like a great she-panther and coil herself around and over trees and other creatures that became visible as she wrapped herself about them. I watched as she soared high above the earth and dove deep into the ocean where the water is absolutely calm.

Washington went on to explain that some of the ancestors would have taken on forms that were not like anything we had ever seen, that they did this because they were unhappy with things we were doing and did not want to reveal their secrets, did not want us to be more powerful if we were going to be more powerful in the destruction of our people. I remembered as he spoke that most of the times I had seen Joy do that dance, she had gone so far as to imitate the animals, and that was the end, and she would come back out of the woods a proper lady. But I also remembered a few times when she went on and danced wild and terrifying movements, as if there were demons reaching for her from every side and the only thing that would satisfy them so they would leave her alone was for her to dance with greater and greater frenzy. I saw the fire reach and dance, and Joy danced frantically so that she would not be taken by it.

Washington went on talking, but for a few moments, his voice was quiet and calm, and I lost the meanings of his words. Joy's costume was layers of scarves. When she had danced in the place where the demons were and where the fire that had taken Danny tried to take her, the scarves were like a hundred flames licking at every part of her body. But now, as I had seen her do once, only once, she touched the flames one at a time, cooled them, and dropped them at her feet. Gradually, her movements became more and more quiet, until there was almost no movement at all, just a gentle, naked swaying, like a tree in a faint breeze, like waves running back down the beach into the ocean. Joy stood almost motionless for what seemed a very long time. I remembered the moment, it seemed, more clearly than when it had happened. Joy had not moved, and no one had breathed until she did.

I missed some of what Washington was telling me, but I picked up on his words again to hear him say that beyond the resting place, she would come to the place of the master demon, the place she had not yet dared to go, where we would go tonight. Washington explained, for Kelly and me, but it also seemed to me so that Dacia would hear the instructions one more time, that Dacia would come face to face with the demon that had bargained with her for her sight. She must not run away. If she ran away then, she could become insane. Instead she was to take the staff that Washington was carving, and she was to touch the fearful thing. And as she touched it, she was to fill her thoughts completely with the words that would be spoken by the voice of the one held prisoner within her, the captive. And she was to understand that the staff represented the power of that voice inside her. And she was not to allow any thoughts to enter her mind which would limit that power. She must trust completely.

Washington repeated the instructions three times, adding that if Dacia tried to run, Kelly and I would be there to hold her. All this time, Joy stood motionless and naked in my mind.

"Open your eyes, Louis," Washington said, "and look at the staff."

"I can't," I answered.

I could feel the muscles around my eyelids quiver, but my eyes wouldn't open. It felt as if they were locked, like the catch on a suitcase.

"You're sure?" Washington asked.

"Yes," I said.

"It will pass," Dacia said softly. "After we're on the road. We should go now."

"Kelly," Washington said. "Check the back to be sure we have something to drive."

I heard movement, and we waited quietly.

"Victor must have come back," Kelly said. "The Packard is in the alley with a trailer hooked on behind it. The keys were on the counter in the kitchen."

"Help Louis into the back seat," Washington said. "I'll have to drive."

"I can drive," Kelly said.

"I want to put Dacia in between the two of you in the back," Washington said. "Louis has got ahold of something. That's why he can't open his eyes. Don't be afraid if that happens to you too."

Washington laughed.

"But we'll all be happier if you aren't driving when it happens," he said and laughed again.

There was a lot of sound and a lot of moving around. Kelly guided me out to the car, but we weren't very good at it, like a couple of kids at a dance, stepping on each other's feet. As soon as I was alone in the car, the image of Joy, slowly and quietly swaying, came back strong and clear. I felt awkward and helpless when it would have been good if I had been on top of everything, but if we were all about to die, and it was fated, and there wasn't much we could do about it, the way Victor had said, I was glad to see Joy so happy.

The car doors opened and Kelly and Washington talked back and forth to each other about what to put where and whether or not they really had gotten everything from the house. But when it was all done, I was in the back seat right behind Washington, Dacia was next to me, and Kelly was on the other side of her, and there was nobody else up front. Washington started the engine and we sat for a moment while he warmed it and while he reminded himself where all the switches and gauges were.

"Full tank of gas," he said. "Thank you, Victor Rodriguez, wherever you are."

I could hear the windshield wipers rubbing over frost on the windshield. Washington was fumbling through the glove box, looking for something to scrape the glass, I guessed. He didn't seem to find anything because he didn't get out. The radio clicked on but gave only static and some voices I couldn't understand behind the noise. Our first movement was a little jerky, and with the trailer and the three of us in the back seat, it seemed like we scraped bottom easier than we usually would have. By the time Washington had made his fourth turn, my sense of direction was gone, and the only thing I could tell for sure was that we were moving.

For a little while Washington tried to keep us informed about where we were and what way we were going, but once we were headed east toward Kansas, there wasn't much point in keeping it up. I kept thinking that at any moment I would simply be able to open my eyes and the foolishness about not being able to see would all be over. But it didn't happen, and after a while I found it was just tiring to keep struggling with it. So I began to concentrate instead on getting a sense of moving east, since I knew we were doing that.

"It's not going to be much of a high-speed chase, with us pulling this trailer," Washington said, after a long silence, "but you should know we are being followed."

"For sure?" Kelly asked. "Maybe they're just nervous about passing."

"There was a car at the end of the alley when we loaded up," he said, "and it's been behind us ever since."

"Who is it?" Kelly asked. "Can you tell?"

"Just wanted you to know they're there," he said. "The best thing, now, is to forget it. They'll make their move when they make their move."

After that we were quiet for quite a while, until Dacia started humming the dance rhythm again, and Kelly and I joined in. I would guess that we rode along humming and swaying and seeing our own private images for maybe fifteen minutes, and then Dacia began to talk. She did not say everything all at once, and sometimes there were long gaps between the words, but we were all humming the rhythm, and it was easy to follow.

"Joy and her brother, Louis," Dacia said, "and my brother, Mark, and I had all been to Denver to hear Billie Holiday. We had a wonderful time, the four of us, and we were driving back to Hemmings, at night. But the people in the town were mad because they had seen us leave together, whites and blacks together in the car. When we got close to Hemmings, they found us and they blocked the road ahead of us so we couldn't get by."

Washington waited and didn't say anything while Dacia was talking, but when it was clear that she had stopped and had gone back to chanting out the rhythm, he started talking again about walking into the woods, deeper and deeper, and seeing creatures there, lions and tigers and leopards and birds and deer and snakes that all looked like the creatures they were but that also looked back at you the way other people do when you know they have something to tell you. And without saying which animal it was, Washington suggested that we had recognized one of these creatures as wise and as one who was there to help us, and then he left a long silence when he didn't say anything except to wonder out loud what it was that creature might be wanting to say. No one talked for a long time and none of us said anything to each other about what we saw and what was said to us or what we answered back. Somewhere in the things Washington had said, he had planted the idea that we should keep quiet. It was easy for me to picture what he was talking about because I just saw myself walking out of the woods into the clearing where I saw that big male deer standing and looking at me and telling me that it wasn't necessary to shoot. And I said something back. It went over as a thought and didn't get changed into words first, but I was proud of having understood and proud that Washington had noticed that I could do it right.

For miles and miles, everything was quiet except for the road sounds and the humming. Then Dacia began again, a few words at a time, not everything at once.

"They blocked the road with their cars," she said, "and a car had us blocked in from the back. There were three cars and a motorcycle. There were more than a dozen of them with clubs and guns. Most of them had scarves over their faces so you couldn't see anything but their eyes. I remember their eyes, all of them. There was one who had a motorcycle helmet with a face mask. They surrounded the car and broke out the windows with their clubs to get the doors open. I took a piece of the broken glass that fell on my leg and held it in my hand."

When Dacia had stopped again and there was a long silence

so we could be sure that she was not going to go on right away, Washington began again. He explained to us, the way he had back in the little house, that if we went deeper and deeper into the forest we would begin to see things we had never seen before, things that were not at all familiar and things that did not even keep the same form while you were looking at them. But he encouraged us not to be afraid and to know that the creatures were not showing themselves as they really are because they were angry and unhappy with us for the way we have been living. They have great riches and important gifts to give us and power, greater strength than we thought possible, but the gifts are hidden until we know for sure ourselves that we will not do destructive things with them. Something jumped at me out of the dark. I never saw what it was. Its giant mouth was open and it swallowed me before I knew what it was. Strangely enough, once I was inside I was floating quietly over the still surface of a lake, the way Washington and I had once in a boat up in the mountains. I didn't think anything at all for a while. I had no questions and I wasn't told any answers, but I did feel strong.

This time of all of us being quiet lasted even longer than the others had. Sometimes when no one is talking, you can feel yourself wanting to say something, anything, just so someone will be talking. But I didn't feel that at all, and I didn't feel as if anyone else was either. I'm pretty sure they weren't, because the car was silent again for miles and miles. When Dacia finally did start again, it was easy because it was clear to me that she had to tell this story all the way through and that that was why we were out there instead of up in the mountains.

"They surrounded the car," she said slowly, "and broke out the windows with their clubs. I got a piece of the glass and held on to it as tight as I could. They broke the windows and got the doors open. They held their guns on us. They beat up Louis and got him down on his knees with a pistol right in his mouth. And two of them held Joy in front of him while the one in the helmet ripped her dress open and touched her everywhere."

I wasn't floating quietly on a lake any more. A giant wave of fire, like a wave of water, a tidal wave, came up over the horizon and swept over everything. I was swirling and rolling and tumbling in fire. I wasn't being burned but everything else was. There was no world left, just the fire and me. Washington was pulling the car and trailer to a stop and was easing through a right-hand turn.

"We're five miles from Hemmings," he said.

The car was rocking and bouncing, even though he was going very slow, and I could tell he was pulling off the road.

"Is that other car still following?" Kelly asked.

"He's stopped back on the highway about a quarter mile," Washington answered. "He's still got his headlights on. It'll be sunup in a half hour or forty-five minutes. Stay here. I'm going to get things ready."

Washington opened his door, got out, and closed it behind him. The motor was still running and the heater was still going. The car rocked from behind, and it was pretty easy to guess that Washington had gotten into the trailer for something. It rocked several times after that as he went up and down.

"What's he doing?" I asked.

"Rolling out a rug and setting out pillows on the east side of the trailer," Kelly said. "And he's set up the table with the cloth spread out over it."

"Can you see the other car?" I asked.

"Not from here," Kelly answered.

Washington came back to the car and waited with us as the sun came up. I could feel the warmth of it and Dacia began speaking again.

"Two men held Joy," Dacia said, "while the one in the motorcycle helmet ripped her dress and touched her all over, right in front of Louis. Then they held guns on her and on me while they chained Mark up to a highway sign. Hemmings 5, that's what it said. They used their knives to cut his clothes away until he was naked and bleeding all over. The man in the helmet came over and got behind me to make me watch while they beat on Mark. I got one arm free. I had the little piece of glass squeezed tight in my hand from when they broke out the windows of the car."

Dacia stopped again. Washington began speaking slowly and

carefully, reminding her gently that when we had gone outside and sat down on the pillows, Kelly and I would be right there with her. She was to look this master demon right in the eye, and she was to take the staff that Washington had carved for her, and she was to touch him with it. She was to take one step, at least one, toward him. That was important. And she was to touch him with the staff, trusting that that would carry all the power and wisdom she needed to free herself from the spell. Dacia did not answer, but she hummed the rhythm more and more intensely.

"They're moving the car," Washington said. "It's time to go."

I heard him open his door. He and Kelly began helping Dacia and me out of the car. I tried half a dozen times to open my eyes, but they would not. We got seated on the cushions facing the sun, at least I was. I could hear the other car pulling up. Kelly helped me move around a little, get adjusted, so I could get a good grip on Dacia's arm and shoulder and could help hold her if she started to run. Washington was right in front of us, though I couldn't tell that he had his back to us until he spoke to tell Dacia to go ahead when she was ready. She hardly hesitated at all.

"The man with the helmet," Dacia said, "tried to make me watch while they beat up on Mark, my brother."

I could hear someone walking up on us. The trailer was behind us. I could hear them coming around the trailer, and I felt a little better knowing they couldn't come up on us without Washington seeing them. Dacia either didn't hear them or didn't care, because she went on talking, just a few words at a time.

"I got my hand up inside that helmet," Dacia said, "and got hold of his ear, and tried to push that glass into his ear."

"Well, holy shit," a voice said. It was Lenny. "Now isn't this my lucky morning? The great disappearing nigger has returned."

"You're interrupting, Lenny," Washington said. "You and your friend really ought to sit down."

"I wouldn't want to offend you," Lenny said. "Is this one of your cannibal ceremonies?"

"Sit down," Washington said. "I think you'll find this interesting."

"Sure as hell is!" the other man yelled. "You'll like it, Lenny."

"Are you still drunk?" Lenny asked.

"A little," the man said. "But not too drunk to see we're being rude here, Lenny. Now sit your ass down."

"Ease off, you goddamn lush," Lenny said. "You need to sleep it off."

"Washington here is being polite," the other man said. "So sit down and listen."

I could hear some kind of scuffling around.

"What the hell is this?" Lenny asked.

"Sit," the man said, "or I'm gonna make you deaf."

I heard more scuffling, though it didn't sound like a fight, and then there was quiet.

"Now what we got comin' up?" the man asked.

"Dacia was remembering an experience she had here," Washington said.

"Well, that's fine," the man said. "Me and Lenny is real interested. Ain't we, Lenny?"

"Yes," Lenny said. "Yes."

"You can go ahead," the man said. "But when she's through I'd like to put in a request for one of them two kids over there to tell us another story, a story about how some son of a bitch sold my son some faulty hardware and blew the boy into nothing. That's the story interests Lenny, now ain't it?"

"What are you talking about?" Lenny said.

"My boy's dead," the man said.

"Danny?" Lenny asked.

"You fucker," the man said. "Don't play dumb with me. You just sit down and listen. We're gonna hear some nice stories, and hear how you killed my boy just like you planned. I want to have some fun before I kill you. That's what we come out here for. You said you wanted a little fun before we killed 'em. So you know what I'm talking about, now don't you?"

"Yes," Lenny answered faintly.

It seemed impossible, but we all got quiet for a moment. When Dacia spoke, her voice was strong and clear as if she was speaking to a large audience. She did not just continue from where she had stopped, as she did before, but went back and repeated much of the story.

"The people in the town were mad," she said, "because they had seen us leave together, whites and blacks together in the car. When we got close to Hemmings, they found us and they blocked the road ahead of us so we couldn't get by. And another car had us blocked in from the back. There were three cars and a motorcycle. There were more than a dozen of them with clubs and guns. Most of them had scarves over their faces so you couldn't see anything but their eyes. I remember their eyes, all of them. There was one who had a motorcycle helmet with a face mask. They surrounded the car and broke out the windows with their clubs to get the doors open. I took a piece of the broken glass that fell on my leg and held it in my hand as tight as I could. They broke the windows and got the doors open. They held their guns on us. They beat up Louis and got him down on his knees with a pistol right in this mouth. And two of them held Joy in front of him while the one in the helmet ripped her dress open and touched her everywhere. Right in front of Louis. Then they held guns on her and on me while they chained Mark up to a highway sign. Hemmings 5, that's what it said. They used their knives to cut his clothes away until he was naked and bleeding all over. The man in the helmet came over and got behind me to make me watch while they beat on Mark. I got one arm free. I had the little piece of glass squeezed tight in my hand from when they broke out the windows of the car. I got my hand up inside that helmet, and got hold of his ear, and tried to push that glass into his ear. He got hold of my arm and pulled and twisted and dragged my hand out. I held on to that glass," Dacia said, "and I could feel it cuttin' his face open as it went. He was furious and started ripping at my clothes. I could hear my brother screaming, 'Shoot, damn it! Shoot!' And then I heard the shots, but I didn't see it because the man in the helmet was all over me."

Lenny screamed.

Dacia had been talking about shots, and when I heard Lenny scream I thought I was hearing a shot, but Lenny just kept screaming and my eyes came open. I couldn't see right at first because of the sunlight, but when my eyes did adjust, there was Danny's father holding Lenny by the hair with his left hand, pulling his head back and to the side so he was facing us with the long scar that ran from his ear to the corner of his mouth. In his other hand the man was holding a small automatic pistol, the kind women carry in their purses, right against Lenny's head, with the barrel pointing right into his ear.

"Sounds like you," the man said. "Everybody that knows you always wonders about that scar, but now we know."

Dacia was struggling to get to her feet.

"The staff," Washington said. "Take the staff."

As he spoke, Washington turned to give the carved staff to Dacia.

"What you doing with that stick?" Danny's father yelled and fired at Washington.

The shot was just a pop. Kelly and I held on to Dacia to keep her seated, but I moved to stand up as soon as I was sure Kelly had her. Washington had fallen back a step and gone down on one knee, but he was still holding the staff in both hands.

"I'm all right," Washington said. "Go ahead and finish."

"I heard 'em shoot," Dacia said, "and I heard Mark scream, and I heard Joy scream, but I couldn't see anything except that man all over me. And then he raised the visor so I could see his face, and that's the last thing I saw, that face with that cut from his ear to his mouth."

Kelly and I let her stand up this time. She stood straight and dignified. I scooted up behind Washington so he could lean back against me, and took the staff and raised it up to Dacia. She took it in both hands and felt carefully from one end to the next, going over the designs slowly. She turned it and adjusted her hands, and stepped forward, and reached out with the staff and touched something none of us could see.

"Oh, God!" Dacia yelled. "It's starting. It's starting."

She dropped the staff at her feet and covered her eyes with her hands.

"Help her back to the car," Washington said. "I'm fine."

I stepped up to take Dacia's arm, but Danny's father waved

the gun, so I just stood there with her rather than trying to move off toward the car.

"Come on, Lenny," Danny's father said. "On your feet."

He pressed the gun into Lenny's ear as he had before and pulled him to his feet by his hair.

"I thought these niggers might want a chance to help educate you," Danny's father said. "But I can see I'm gonna have to do it myself."

Lenny didn't answer. The man started pushing him toward his car.

"I got to teach you about these timers, Lenny," Danny's father said. "Got one right over here in the car. Come on, boy. Let's go wake up your little town."

The man pushed and dragged Lenny to his car and drove off toward Hemmings without looking back even once.

"Warriors for justice," Washington said.

"What?" I asked.

"Every warrior's got a master," he said. "I told you that. It's the cruel hearts that serve justice."

Kelly and I got Dacia into the back seat of the car and then got Washington into the seat beside her. It hurt him to move, but he wasn't bleeding much at all. We got the pillows and the cloth and rug and table back in the trailer and got the trailer closed up. I slid in behind the wheel, and Kelly got in the front seat on the passenger side, and I started the engine.

"I lied to Joy," Dacia said. "I couldn't make myself tell her that he ripped her clothes, and that he raped me, and that she saw 'em shoot Mark and I didn't. She was crazy out of it. Finally, the only way Louis got her calmed down was in bed. But even then she was suffering all the time he wasn't with her, until you, Louis. It started things over for her. It was like you healed her from the inside."

Dacia leaned forward and hugged my neck from behind.

"You gotta dream about it," Washington said, "and reach out and touch it till it ain't nothing. That's how you do it."

Dacia leaned back in her seat and hugged him, but he flinched.

"I forgot how much you love to be bossy," she said.

"Go ahead, Louis," Washington said. "Let's move this thing."

I was careful not to scrape bottom going back out onto the highway.

"Do you want a doctor?" I asked.

"I want that hot pool," Washington said.

"We'll try to make Gunnison," I said.

"Does it hurt?" Kelly asked.

"It feels like I ate too much," Washington said.

"Don't joke," I said.

"I'm not," he answered. "It's a little thing."

We rode almost all the way back to Denver without talking. Once we were quiet, we all seemed to get real serious. Finally, when we were just half an hour out of the city, it was Kelly who spoke.

"Have you ever been to Morocco?" she asked.

"Lots of times," Washington answered. "Why?"

"Is it different there?" she asked.

"Different how?" Washington asked.

"All this fighting," Kelly said.

"Nothing wrong with fighting," Washington said. "Until you're strong enough to change, it's about all you got."

"But people here are after other people all the time," Kelly said. "Louis and I were thinking of going somewhere else."

"It doesn't matter where you go," Washington said. "Whatever you're supposed to do will find you. Evil is everywhere, doggin' you, wantin' you to come out and fight. And the people you love won't leave you alone neither. You can't find freedom by running away."

Kelly didn't ask any more. Washington pulled Dacia up closer to him, and even though you could tell he was hurting, he fell asleep and slept almost all the way to Gunnison, even while we were stopped for gas. When I went into the station to pay, they had a news story on the TV about a guy who had driven into a little Kansas town with a hostage and blown the two of them up in his car right in front of everybody. They showed the burning car and a local cop who said there was nothing he could do to stop it. I remembered his smile.

When I got back out to the Packard, Washington was still asleep, and Dacia was cuddled up on his shoulder. Kelly stayed up front, but she didn't say anything and went off to sleep almost as soon as we were moving again. I wanted to tell her I'd take her to Morocco, if she wanted to see for herself, but I didn't want to wake her. I was glad to be driving. I couldn't have slept anyway. I couldn't wait to find out what Washington meant about fighting until you were strong enough to change. After all, I was almost seventeen, and I knew it couldn't all happen in one night, but I knew he had the secret to my freedom.